IN SHELLY'S LEG

In Shelly's Leg

A NOVEL BY

Sara Vogan

ALFRED A. KNOPF   NEW YORK   1981

THIS IS A BORZOI BOOK
PUBLISHED BY ALFRED A. KNOPF, INC.

The author wishes to thank the National Endowment for the
Arts, the Iowa Writer's Workshop, and the Wallace Stegner
Award Foundation for their support and encouragement.

A portion of this novel appeared in a slightly different form
in the *Iowa Review* under the title "Silent Movies."

The song "Shelly's Winter Love," from which lyrics are
quoted, was written by Merle Haggard. Copyright © 1970,
1973 by Blue Book Music, Bakersfield, California.
Used by Permission.

Library of Congress Cataloging in Publication Data
Vogan, Sara.
In Shelly's leg.
I. Title.
PS3572.O2915   1981   813'.54   80-20390
ISBN 0-394-51451-3

Manufactured in the United States of America
First Edition

TO EVERYONE

FROM THE EASTGATE

TO THE TRAIL'S END

1976–1979

IN SHELLY'S LEG

Sit in the bleachers and watch the women practice. It is a round-house practice, the women fanned out in a rough star pattern. The man pacing the foul line wonders idly about the woman playing third. She has been with the team five years now and has always worn gold loops hanging through her earlobes. He has never seen her without them. He wonders if she wore those loops as a child, solid gold stuck through slits in her ears. Maybe she has hundreds of pairs of those same earrings. Sometimes they glint in the sun.

He looks out past third to the dark green firs covering the mountainsides, snow lingering around their tops, and over to the newly green leaves of the Lombardy poplars lining the left-field fence. This ballfield was once a homestead, the poplars imported as seedlings from France and carefully packed in wagons with tools and food and scrap quilts, essentials for a new life in these flat northern valleys of the West. Poplars were the first settlers' only lasting mark upon the land, tall plumes against the sky planted in rows fifty to one hundred years ago as a design to break the wind.

The man notices the wind stirring the leaves and looks back to his pitcher. She is working on her knuckleball, throwing it without a spin so the seams look parallel. The pitch dips and weaves through the air before it crosses the plate. It lands in the catcher's mitt lightly, not enough force to overcome the breeze. The catcher flips one of her black braids back over her shoulder before returning the pitch and signals for another knuckleball. The batter swings and misses. The ball sounds more solid in the catcher's glove and she nods her approval to the pitcher.

The batter steps back from the box and flexes her ringed fingers against the handle of the bat. She readjusts her stance. Once both hands are on the bat, the pitcher fires off another knuckleball. It passes the batter so quickly she merely turns her head to watch it go by. "Give me a break," the batter yells.

The pitch is another knuckleball and the batter connects, lining the ball out near second. The man waits for the shortstop to move, but hears her laugh instead. She is not in position to make the catch, standing too close to second and talking to a woman with her hair in rollers, bound by a scarf.

"Look alive out there, ladies," comes a call from first base. "We're all supposed to be practicing. This ain't no hen session." The woman at first does a cartwheel, her gray sweatsuit flopping loosely around her body. "See!" she calls again. "I'm freezing my tits off 'cause I can't get no action from you broads." At second, the woman with her hair in rollers pounds her glove while the shortstop moves out to where the ball is lying in the grass. She fires it off to first and straightens the hem on her sweatshirt, making it even across her hips. It reads: A WOMAN'S PLACE IS IN THE HOUSE AND THE SENATE.

The next hit is a pop-up to the shortstop, who takes it easily and tosses it to first. "I don't need to practice this shit," the shortstop says.

"You need all you can get," the catcher calls. She turns to the batter. "Keep your head down and your ass in."

"Let me do the slider," the pitcher says.

"No," answers the catcher, flipping her braids back again. "Five Valleys pitches a lot of knuckles. Somebody on this team better be able to hit one."

The man on the foul line lets them go through six more knuckleballs before he blows his whistle and the star pattern begins to change. The pitcher and the catcher remain in the center while the other women move around them. He sees this game as dance; the women keep time to the positions they play and the whole field becomes a song.

The batter hands the bat to the woman with the gold loops and then moves out to replace the woman in the gray sweatsuit at first. The man watches as each woman swings one position to the left. He pays particular attention to the woman in curlers while she runs a windsprint out to center field. She is new this year and he studies her run, arms to the side, pumping.

"Let me do the slider," the pitcher asks and the catcher signals okay. The pitch comes across like a fastball but breaks and slides left underneath the swing of the bat.

"Crap," the woman with the gold loops says and the man notices her auburn hair is coming loose from her ponytails.

"That's a good one," the catcher calls. The next slider is too low and bounces on the plate. It is returned without comment. The batter rests the bat on her shoulder and touches at her earrings.

The pitcher runs a finger along the elastic line of her bra encircling her ribcage. She stamps at the mound with her toe for a moment before replacing her glove and winding up again. The slider comes across fast, drops to the right.

"Crap," the batter says as she swings and misses.

The next ten pitches are sliders; three bounce and the batter gets one hit, a dribbler that is picked up by the stocky woman with glasses now playing third. She throws it to first, hard. While the ball is returned to the pitcher, the woman at third looks around for the cigarette she has dropped and crushes it out with her foot.

The man at the sidelines blows his whistle again and the star pattern flows once more to the left. The stocky woman from third takes one of the lead donuts and limbers up with a few hard swings of the weighted bat. She sloughs off the donut and calls to the pitcher: "Let me work on the curve."

"No," says the catcher. "You can hit a curve clear to the trees. Try something new."

"Risers," calls the man from the sidelines.

The pitcher walks around the mound for a moment, playing with the straps on her bra again. Finally she sends off a wild pitch, the release coming too close to her ankle. It sails upward so high that the catcher jumps but cannot field it. The ball bounces off the top of the cyclone fenced backstop.

"Curves is easier," the stocky woman says as she takes a few more practice swings.

The catcher pulls the ball out of the mud and returns it without comment. The pitcher kicks at the mound a few more times and sends off another riser that passes the batter just below the waist and beneath the hard cut of the bat.

The stocky woman stamps in the box and pushes her glasses up her nose. "As soon as I hit one of these mothers I'm leaving," she says. She swings past two more pitches. For the third pitch she shifts, bending more at the knees, leaning left, her ass out behind her at a greater angle.

"You're so easy," the catcher says. "If this was a real game I'd signal up for your curve, just like you wanted."

"If this was a real game," the batter answers, "I wouldn't have to listen to your yapping."

The pitch is another riser. The batter swings hard and the metal bat rings as she connects solidly with the ball, lofting it over the head of the skinny left fielder and almost to the line of Lombardy poplars. She gets another hit to the same hole on the next pitch. The catcher stands and yells out to left field: "Look alive out there. Play her deep. Save you all that running."

"It's good for my figure," the left fielder calls as she moves back. "I can't get all my exercise in bed."

The batter swings hard on the next pitch, so hard the momentum of the swing spins her around until she ends up sitting on the plate, tailor fashion, with the bat lying behind her. The catcher laughs before sticking out her hand and helping the stocky woman up. "Don't bust your buns before the games," she says.

The batter lights another cigarette and begins to move off toward the parking lot. "I got to go get my kids," she says.

"Come on, Sullivan," the woman with her hair in rollers yells. "All this fresh air ain't good for my hairdo."

"I'm getting cramps," the catcher complains as she stretches and loosens the chest protector.

The pattern in the field begins to break, some of the women lighting cigarettes or unwrapping pieces of gum, scattering the burnt matches and shiny pieces of foil across the muddy grass.

Sullivan says nothing as he watches the women walk off. They look fat and sluggish but that will wear off them by June. "Go home," Sullivan says, although it is not necessary. "Maggie and Rita. You stay and work on those sliders."

There are shouts of 'Goodbye' and the slammings of car doors as Maggie, the pitcher, and Rita, the catcher, come over to Sullivan to complain.

"Don't you want me to go to work?" Rita asks as she unhooks the last strap of the chest protector and lets it slip to the ground. "Think of all the money you're going to lose if you make me stand out here to catch those dustballs of hers."

"Ten minutes," Sullivan says. He turns to Maggie. "They're coming off your wrist wrong." He demonstrates with his own hand how the ball should roll. Taking her hand in his, he turns it a few times, showing her the feel of the angle. Maggie goes back to the mound and Rita squats behind the plate, leaving the mask and chest protector lying near the backstop.

"Make no mistakes," Rita calls out to Maggie. "I've already had my nose busted once. A second time won't improve my looks."

"Trust me," Maggie says. "I never make mistakes."

Sullivan leaves the base line and goes to stand on the top tier of the bleachers. Overhead, three mallards are flying north, their silhouettes sharp against the snow on the mountaintops. Sullivan believes there is always snow on the mountaintops, except in August, just before the women's fastpitch softball state championship.

one

When Margaret was a child her father told her no man goes to war thinking he is fighting for the wrong side. He made it sound as if confusion and indecision were reserved especially for women. Many years later in a book about dolphins Margaret discovered a statement her father might have liked: what the mind believes to be true is either true or becomes true in the mind of the believer.

A man's got to do what a man's got to do. That was another thing she had learned.

The day Sullivan shot the dog Margaret wondered what her father would have done in Sullivan's place, whether he would have agreed with Margaret and waited or simply shot it. Sullivan did not even seem to think about it, either before or after he fired that single bullet. He walked out behind second base and set one of those big logger boots on the dog's head, read the tag on the collar and said he would call the owner, John Portis. He said nothing during the ride back to town in his three-quarter-ton GMC pickup that always showed the dust. He was just quiet, and maybe thoughtful.

When Margaret got home Woody was working on his Morris chair. The big red chair, just about the largest piece of furniture they owned, sprawled upside down in the middle of the living-room floor. Copper banding and lint balls drifted around, mixed in with the diagonal cutters, magnetic tack hammer and upholstery tacks. In her own house, the house Mike bought her so she could raise his kids up decent, it seemed nothing here belonged to her. Woody's pedal steel guitar, Woody's reel-to-reel, Woody's sheet music, his mandolin, rhythm guitar. His chair. Even the picture above the mantel was of Woody's grandparents, the ones who owned the ranch out in Oregon.

"Sullivan killed a dog this morning," Margaret said. "It belonged to the Portises." She put her mitt down and began taking off her sweat jacket.

Woody carefully poured epoxy into one of the frame joints. "You should ride with Rita or someone when Sullivan's drunk." He put the glue down and pressed with his palms on either side of the joint.

"He wasn't drunk. He killed it with one shot."

"Sullivan taking up target practice?"

Margaret eased past Woody and his chair and went into the kitchen for a cup of coffee. He doted on that damn chair, a chair about as pretty as a fire hydrant. It had been his grandfather's, the one in the picture. When he moved in with Margaret three years ago he took it apart. He sanded and varnished, tightened springs, repacked stuffing under holes in the upholstery. He tried patching the coarse red fabric to contain the feathers of wadded cotton that escaped from the arms and seat. But every patch seemed to spawn new leaks of gray-white fluff that floated throughout the house and always ended up stuck to new Jell-O in the refrigerator or on the hand soap in the bathroom. Last night Woody stepped on a tack on his way to the bathroom. And today he was taking the damn thing apart again, trying to make the old piece perfect. She couldn't understand why all this couldn't be done in the garage where she wouldn't have to see it or trip over it or end up eating it in their meatloaf.

Margaret called to him from the kitchen. "Sullivan said it had rabies. But I'm not so sure."

Woody hammered on the old oak frame while Linda Ronstadt's voice soared over his tapping and banging. "That dog only had two legs," Margaret yelled. "One in front and one in back. It walked on its ears!" She stepped quickly into the living room and snapped off the tape. Putting the hammer down slowly, Woody rubbed the palms of his hands on his jeans.

"Okay," he said. "I get it. Open me a beer while I go to the john." He reached around her and flipped the reel-to-reel back on, keeping the volume low this time, and walked off toward the bathroom.

In the kitchen again, Margaret could barely hear the music. That was good. She knew those songs as well as Woody; she could sing any one of them by heart. Yet each time she heard Woody and his band do those numbers she was surprised how the song changed. Margaret liked the country-swing recorded versions better than the skip-a-beat jazz renditions that Woody's band, A Little Left of Center, played each night at Heart of the West. The key changes, the way they manipulated the beat, made the songs sound sarcastic to her.

"No beer?" Woody pulled an Oly from the refrigerator.

"Sullivan said it had rabies," Margaret said again. "But you couldn't really tell." Margaret had watched the fluffy border collie, loping with its body at a diagonal, as it wandered through the outfield, following the line of chokecherry bushes out by the fence and heading toward the poplars back of left field. She and Rita had been standing by Rita's baby blue Edsel when they heard Sullivan shout from the top of the bleachers: 'Get yourself to work!' Rita left to go open Shelly's Leg for Sullivan's regular daytime drinkers.

"Anybody hurt?" Woody asked.

"Everyone was gone by then. Sullivan had me and Rita working on my sliders. But then he made Rita go to work so it was just me and Sullivan. And the dog. It came out over the top of the hill behind right field."

"You should have gotten your buns out of there," Woody said. He looked at her with those flat glittery eyes, eyes that seemed to have been painted under his lids, pale blue and white. The color of a winter sky on a sunny day.

"I didn't want him to shoot it." She saw the dog panting heavily in the cold morning air as it raced in crazy circles around the deserted softball field.

"You should know better than to cross Sullivan."

"I didn't cross Sullivan," Margaret said, wondering if in some way she had. If in some way she had not understood the signs. "I just didn't want him to shoot it."

"Why the hell not? If it had rabies."

"Well, what if it didn't? What if it just needed a vet or something?"

"Then what was it doing out there? There's no Portis out that way."

"How the hell should I know? It was a pet. It had a collar on."

"You don't go near it, collar or not!" Woody drained his beer and gave a snort through his nose, a sign to Margaret he was angry or upset.

"Look, it's okay," she said.

"Listen Maggie. Ever have rabies shots? Twenty-four of them in the stomach. You get your tail out of there."

"Nothing happened. I said it's okay."

"You're the one wanted to talk about this."

Margaret stared at her empty cup. She wanted to tell Woody about the professional, almost mechanical way Sullivan had shot that dog. He aimed down the rifle barrel like someone in a movie. One shot. Linda Ronstadt sang "Heart Like a Wheel." Soul like a spoke, Margaret thought. The depth of a teaspoon.

Woody traced the florid gold of the beer label with his finger. "We got a gig for May fifteenth," he said in the silence between cuts. "Play breaks and a late dance at the basketball playoffs."

"Playoffs?" The long white hair of the border collie's ruff flashed as the small dog turned, flipped in the air to bite at something behind its back, something only the dog could see hovering near its tail.

"The high school basketball tournament."

"What?" Margaret was surprised to see Woody, a beer bottle in his hand, sitting across the table from her.

"A job. We're going to play for the high school basketball playoffs."

"Well, good. How much?"

"Good bucks. That okay with you?"

"Sure, why not?" Margaret reached for a spoon to stir her coffee. Not until the metal spoon clanged against the ceramic cup did she remember it was empty.

"It's May fifteenth." Woody stared at his beer bottle.

"That's the dinner. You didn't accept did you?"

"Yeah I accepted." He pulled another beer from the refrigerator.

In the sixteen years Sullivan has run Shelly's Leg there are only two nights of the year when the bar is closed. May fifteenth, the official opening dinner for the women's fastpitch softball season, and August fifteenth, the official closing dinner. Those nights, and the three days back in 1974 when Shelly died and was buried. The women on the team bring their favorite recipes on their best china and silver for these dinners, arranging the food over the plywood covering for the pooltable. Food for broken-legged horsebreakers, deep-eyed barmaids, summertime cowboys, autobody men, hairdressers, realtors, schoolteachers, and some who work the Unemployment Act. The regulars at Shelly's eat, drink, connive, dance, and bullshit one another about new jobs and might-be lovers and sometimes about the women's chances to take the state softball championship again. If they win this year, it will be seven in a row.

"You can go without me," Woody said.

"But it's your elk."

"You don't need me to do the elk. Just like I don't need you to go get it. Anyhow I don't play softball."

"That's never stopped you before. You're just being stubborn. Or selfish. I can never figure which. I want you to come."

"And I want *you* to start taking what *I* do seriously." Woody mimicked her voice. He paced in the kitchen. "This band ain't going to take off if we don't get any exposure."

"Exposure? You call a high school basketball game exposure?"

Woody slammed his fresh beer down on the kitchen counter. Foam billowed out of the top of the bottle and dripped off the counter onto the floor. "I'm tired of running with a dinky band that plays a hotel bar in the boonies of Montana. I'd like to make some real music. Play other towns. Those kids come from all over the state. They have proms and stuff. I want to follow up that deal with the Warner scout. Cut a record, for Christ sakes!" He mopped at the spilled beer absently.

"I saw Charley Pride once," he said, "and he started his set with a bang-up number. I mean not just a kicker, a bang-up number. Put his whole self into it. And then he said: 'I always try to sing my best when I'm in Montana. 'Cause I don't want to work for the Anaconda Company no more!' Shit! Charley Pride didn't get to be more than half famous by turning down gigs. He busted his ass. He sang for free. Just so he could get some practice. So he wouldn't have to work for the Anaconda Company no more."

"I know," Margaret said. "He's from Great Falls."

"Don't you laugh. It's true."

Woody's tempers were like rain showers on a sunny day: unexpected and short-lived. They could talk about Sullivan now, but Margaret waited, watching Woody's back.

"What's with you?" she asked.

Woody left the kitchen, turned Linda Ronstadt up loud, and began hammering on his chair again.

"Stop that!" Margaret followed him into the living room and shouted over the music. "What's eating you?" Maybe, like this morning with Sullivan, she had missed some of the signs.

Woody held one of the steel springs in his hands, working it back and forth from one hand to the other, trying to recoil the sprung wire back into a tight cylinder. Pressing the spring into the bowels of the chair with his foot, Woody stretched the copper band over the bottom and began hammering it to the dusty frame.

"Do you have to do that now?" Margaret asked.

"What?"

"Stop that. Talk to me."

Woody straightened and looked steadily into Margaret's face. Sometimes he looked at her as if she were something unexpected in his daily life, a strange animal or bird he was discovering for the first time and trying to name. His flat eyes looked at her nose, her mouth, looked past her face and into her bones.

"What's the matter?" she asked as she turned down the volume on the tape. Woody's eyes flicked back and forth across the planes of her face. "You can get out of it, can't you?"

"Why should I want to get out of it?" He sat down behind his pedal steel and began chording, syncopating the beat. "Good bucks. Might get us some real gigs."

"We've looked forward to this party all winter."

"You have. I have more fun at the rodeo."

"Stop. Just stop," Margaret said. "Quit being so damn nasty."

"Maybe you'll go with me for a change. Forget the softball."

"Sullivan would be disappointed."

"Fuck Sullivan." He threw a jazzy riff into the middle of the second verse of "Silver Threads and Golden Needles." He played it louder and louder, bending the notes and slowing the tune down until Linda Ronstadt sounded like a fast whisper underneath the mournful music of the pedal steel.

Margaret turned off the tape and stood looking at Woody. He ignored her, developing the riff but playing softer now. She said, "I only play softball for a couple of months."

"Smoke me a cigarette." Woody worked his hands over the metal strings of his steel. This was a pantomime he went through once or twice a year, asking people to smoke so he could smell it, or borrowing cigarettes so he could burn them in ashtrays. He claimed smoking would hurt his voice.

"You say I make you nervous when you play."

Woody reached for a Marlboro, lit it and left it lying in an ashtray. He looked Margaret dead in the eye. "You don't make me nervous. You get drunk."

"Once!" Margaret hissed. "Once I got drunk down at the West. You were playing grab-ass with the barmaid!"

Without thinking, Woody took a drag on the cigarette. "Damn. Here. You smoke it."

Margaret stubbed it out.

"Anyhow," his voice was more conversational, "I want you to come hear us at that tournament." He smiled, but only his mouth moved.

She was going to keep her voice low, calm and rational. "That's the night of the dinner." She had explained it as if she were speaking to her children. Pulling a few strands of hair from behind her ear, she began shredding them with her fingernails.

"You'll go bald like that. Bald women are supposed to be very sexy."

"Who played this gig last year?"

"Nobody. This is the first time. Lloyd drummed it up." He looked at her and smiled. Margaret realized she was staring at his face as if it were alive on its own, the corners of his mouth breaking through his full red beard. He began speaking slowly, like people on television explaining how to operate a simple machine. "It's like the tour. You don't want me to do it because it would change all your little systems around."

"I can't quit my job and pull my kids out of school for your band. We've been through this before."

Suddenly he stopped chording and came to stand behind her with his arms around her waist. "Ah, Maggie. When you were a little girl, didn't you dream of being cast away somewhere, away from everything you knew? Didn't you dream of someone like me to be there? Didn't you make up all the fun in your mind?"

"No. I didn't."

"Sometimes I don't think you ever were a little girl at all. All little girls are supposed to have dreams like that."

"Now how would you know what little girls dream about?" Margaret relaxed in the circle of his arms.

"I cheated. I asked Allison."

"Allison dreams of being cast away?"

"Well, no. I just think she should dream stuff like that. That you should have dreams about leaving all your cares behind." He kissed her gently on the ear. "I want you to dream of me."

"You don't understand." She began to tense, getting ready for this argument that had been running through their lives for the last six weeks.

Woody took her hand, leading her to the couch. "Come here."

"Now wait a minute."

He set her on the couch, reached down and jerked her sweater over her head. He unzipped her jeans.

"The kids," Margaret said. Woody silenced her with a kiss, pushing her back on the couch, his hands cupping her breasts. Margaret began to rock against him. Her arms circled his shoulders and stroked his back.

"Let's remember what's important," Woody whispered in her ear as he unbuttoned his Levi's and settled himself on top of her.

Margaret was moving with him, felt the ball of her belly tightening, the muscles tense as she began to sweat. Woody's tongue flicked against her nipples while his hands opened her. His hands were cool on her skin and she felt the little calluses on his fingertips. Taking her breast in his mouth, Woody placed himself on her, holding very still while Margaret moved up against him. She arched her back, locked her legs around his knees.

Opening slowly as a flower, Margaret held Woody as he crept up inside her. His hair rubbed rhythmically against her cheek. Such fine hair, Margaret thought, and then did not think as the color behind her eyes disappeared.

When they finished, Woody turned his head toward her face and looked at her for a long moment. Sometimes Margaret felt sorry for men; sex could not possibly be as pleasurable for them. She wondered where they went in their minds when they came. She wondered where she went, what that space was.

Holding his hand behind her neck, Woody brought her face to his and kissed her slowly.

Then he was up, rebuttoning his Levi's, tucking in his shirt. He walked quickly to the front closet and grabbed his jacket. "I'm not going to your dinner." He turned to face her as he stuffed his arms in the sleeves. "I have to work. If we are going to have cares and worries, one of them must be about money. That's the American way."

Margaret felt cold and embarrassed. Her bones ached. She searched his face for something to say. "I do dream of you."

"Fine. See you."

"Where are you going?" Margaret tried to sit up on the couch.

"You know the answer to that, Margaret." He drew the whole word out, pronouncing each syllable, her proper name sounding foreign on his tongue. When they had first met three years ago, he said he always wanted to know a girl named Maggie, like the girl in the Rod Stewart song. He had called her Maggie ever since.

"Timbuktu." He stepped through the front door.

Margaret stood slowly and struggled into her sweater. She stood alone in the middle of the living room with the red Morris chair still upside down. Timbuktu. Always Timbuktu. He might as well say 'Guatemala' or 'Istanbul.' "You are acting like a child. Adam is more mature than you are." She leveled a kick at the oak frame. "You are so dumb you don't know the difference between sit and shit!" There was nothing for a moment, then her toes began to throb, a distant humming at the end of her foot. She stared at her pitching shoe, unable to see the pain. Margaret sighed and stretched her arms behind her back.

Perhaps she was missing all the signs. She would not drag Adam and Allison around the country on a band tour. Not for the summer. Not for the fall. She would not send them up to Mike in some god-damn pipeline camp in Alaska. Mike, their father. He left them years ago. She would not go humping around the country in the wake of a two-bit band that was lucky to have a job at all.

That was sensible. Charley Pride be damned. But there was something she could not quite get hold of. She was sure Sullivan would understand Woody's pipedream band tour as easily as he understood to shoot that dog. While she dickered and fussed, Woody and Sullivan would steamroll everything in their path. The Portis children went to school with Adam; how would they feel if they knew Sullivan had shot their dog?

She could still hear the rusted engine of Rita's Edsel pulling away from the field, the coughing and choking as Rita coaxed the cold motor. Sullivan stood on the top bleacher with the bill of his baseball cap pulled low over his eyes and his hands stuffed tightly into the pockets of his jacket. He stared off into right field, toward the line of chokecherry shrubs hiding the back fence, beyond that to the flat valley floor, lime green of new aspen and poplar against the black green of the firs. A dark raven wheeled across an empty gray sky, flapping off toward the south. The border collie yapped and barked in a cracked voice. The dog leaped, chasing at something that was not pursuing it, nosing forward to stagger and fall. Margaret watched Sullivan sizing up the dog's condition.

"You should have left with Rita," Sullivan had said when he saw her climbing the bleachers to stand by him. With a glance he indicated she should get up on the top tier.

Margaret had asked: "What's wrong."

"Rabies."

"Don't shoot it," Margaret said, watching Sullivan load the gun. "Please. Don't," she said, cutting her eyes back to the collie, its body listing like a ship. She heard the report of the .22 as the collie jumped. In the bushes, sparrows and swallows fluttered away. The collie lay still on the grass behind second base.

two

The bungalow Rita rented by the side of the Clark Fork fascinated Margaret. As a house it seemed like an afterthought, yet if it had been an outbuilding it was impossible to figure what type. Too rambling for a shed, maybe it had been a small corral, sided and roofed with walls thrown in at odd places. The other puzzling thing was the house's smell. Like perfumes and air-fresheners, the seasons in Rita's house were a concentration of the smells outside, stronger than real roses and pines.

Rita's thick black hair hung combed down over her eyes and she sorted it left to right, searching for gray hairs she plucked out. She was surprised Margaret would criticize Sullivan. "What else would he do? What would you do?"

Margaret sat on the couch stroking Bruegel, Rita's big Belgian hare. His long ears were the color of little girl's ballet slippers and his soft fur made Margaret think of pelts, trappers and mountain men. She imagined men who could live by what they could pack on a mule, their days filled with soft fur, shining gold in leather pouches, coffee that smelled of metal and wood smoke. She knew these were images from television and movies. When she and Adam talked about mountain men she tried to stress the maggots and blood-filled ticks in the animal's skin, the loneliness, rain and wind sweeping over the high plains. Adam was as romantic as his mother about the West and said he would explore Antarctica when he grew up if the West was all tamed. He badgered Woody, asking when they would have enough money for a pony. Adam, at nine, believed he must get in training to be an explorer.

"Sullivan once told me about the time his dad lost sixteen head to rabid wolves," Rita said. "A whole pack of them, mouth-foaming mad. He and Old Ernie heard them in one of their northwest fields and they got their guns and rode out there horseback. The wolves had a bunch of their steers boxed in a coulee, cut off by some cliffs and a big tangle of willow. Those wolves hit on anything, the steers, each other. Weren't frightened of the gunshots either. They held the horses and shot down into that coulee, the horses all skittery with so much blood on the air. They had to kill them all twice. Once from up the hill to get them quiet. And then one by one they reshot each wolf and steer just to make sure. Then Old Ernie rode back for the tractor and Sullivan had to stand guard. Shot everything that came by so the rabies wouldn't spread. Eagles, rabbits. It got on his nerves, said he got to thinking about shooting insects. Then they plowed a big hole and buried them all. Seven god-damn wolves and sixteen steers."

Rita picked up a box of fish food and walked over to her aquarium, the gray-blue twenty-gallon tank that took up most of one wall. She sprinkled the dried food on top of the water, watching the veiled angels, silver gouramis, pale whitish kissing fish, dart to the surface and slice back into the bottom of the tank, avoiding each other with swift, angling turns.

"When was this?" Margaret asked. She could still see him standing on the bleachers, the baseball cap barely covering his graying hair cropped close to his head. She tried to imagine him wearing a Stetson. Maybe he rode bareheaded, down off his horse shooting wolves.

"He was a kid."

Margaret tried to picture Sullivan as a kid, a gray-headed kid in those flowered Hawaiian shirts with the little drawings of bare-breasted brown girls dancing on the cloth. Sullivan smelled of grease, motor oil, and Old Spice. She could never really see men as children; she always thought of Woody as a Little Leaguer with a full red beard, scampering around the bases, short-legged but with powerful arms and shoulders. She saw Sullivan as a gray-headed child shooting wolves. In her mind the wolves looked like German shepherds.

Bruegel hopped off Margaret's lap and nosed Rita's ankle as she stood teasing her fish with a glass rod. "I thought he lived in Seattle as a kid," Margaret said.

"Later. In boarding school." Rita rapped her rod against the glass, trying to dislodge Dempster Dumpster, the procostimus.

"That's when he met Shelly," Margaret said. It wasn't that Sullivan was the quiet type. He told jokes about the news, talked about his cars or the softball team. But he never said much about himself. Even when his father, Old Ernie, sat in the bar, they rarely spoke. Sullivan would buy him a beer like anybody else. You had to be told they were related.

Shelly died before Margaret met Woody and began hanging around the bar, before Margaret joined the softball team Shelly had organized and managed. Sullivan always keeps a rose in a cut crystal vase on the back bar in memory of her. As day bartender, Rita takes care of the rose Deadeye delivers each morning. On Saturdays Deadeye sometimes brings several roses, roses that will not be salable on Monday. Rita sticks them in vase-shaped Michelob bottles all along the back bar, saving one in the cooler for Sunday.

In the team scrapbook there are pictures of Shelly in her maroon and white striped uniform, the long skirt reaching almost to her ankle to hide the loss of her right leg. Some pictures show her crutches, some show her leaning on Sullivan's arm. In all the pictures she is smiling or laughing, holding trophies or kissing one of the women on the team. Above the jukebox is a large stylized photograph of her in grainy black and white. She was a serious looking woman, thin nosed with wide set eyes. There is a bullet hole in her throat. Rita told Margaret that Sullivan shot the portrait drunk one night with the handgun he keeps under the bar.

"Sullivan loved her even then," Rita said.

"Romantic horseshit. Woody said she married some architect."

"That's what Sullivan told me. Said he went into the Navy to wait for her to grow up. And when he got back it was too late. She was married. So they had their affair. Right up to the end."

"Men do the damnedest things."

"Oh, I think it was Shelly's idea. Sullivan would have married her anytime. Sometimes he's even wished they had kids." Rita turned the heater on the fish tank down a notch and the little orange light went out.

Ever since Anthony left Rita last fall, Margaret has had a fantasy about Rita and Sullivan. She knows Rita fixes roasts and cakes that she brings to the bar to share with Sullivan. Rita takes his oil-stained clothes to the laundry. Margaret would like to see Rita move into Sullivan's little apartment above the bar, or see Sullivan here, in Rita's odd house. It would make them both happy, Margaret knows that. "You ever think of taking up with Sullivan?" Margaret asked, smiling so she wouldn't feel so uneasy. She wasn't sure she could ask Rita a question like that.

Rita stared at her, hard. "Didn't your mother teach you manners?"

"Curious. I'm sorry. I just asked."

"What do you want to know? Who I sleep with? Or Sullivan?" Rita's expression softened a bit. She raised an eyebrow. "You thinking of trading Woody in?"

"Just forget it. It's none of my business."

"I gave up men when Anthony left. It just didn't seem worth it. Sometimes if I'm real horny I go see Birdheart." Rita laughed. "Sullivan's got a woman out by Lolo Creek he calls 'Hand Job.' When she calls he says: 'Is that Hand Job? Tell her I'm not here.' "

"That's terrible. You and Sullivan should get together."

"We tried it," Rita said. "But it was like two cripples thrashing around in *her* bed. So I went out and met Anthony."

They were quiet, Margaret watching Rita, who stared out the window at the ice-laced edges of the Clark Fork. The four of them, Rita and Anthony, Margaret and Woody, had drifted through drunken holidays as a group, spent winter evenings cooking up fancy dinners for each other before playing marathon games of Scrabble or Charades. They pooled their camping and fishing gear for weekends tramping through the Bob Marshall Wilderness to sleep under fir trees and the starry blackness of a natural sky. During softball games Woody and Anthony sat together to watch Margaret pitch, Rita catch, saying the girls were as good at boxing off a batter as any. Woody had told Margaret that Anthony would not be back, and for a long time Margaret wanted Rita to talk to her about it. But Rita never mentioned Anthony's disappearance, only an occasional vague plan about things they would do 'when Anthony gets back.'

"Woody says he's not going to the dinner. And I don't know what he's up to. I look at him sometimes and it's like there's no-body in there. Blue skies and nobody home."

Rita turned to face Margaret. "Do you know what I remember about Anthony? His eyes. In my mind he's in black and white, like photographs. Still pictures. But his eyes are always blue. Real hard and glossy, like an agate, shiny like marble. Sometimes I dream about them, that they are drifting. Spying on me."

"All I ever see are parts. Bones. Teeth. Eyes. They never come to-gether to anything. Like paper doll clothes, you can change them around. I think you should have had Anthony's teeth; they would have looked good on you. Every day I expect to see something in Woody's eyes. And they never open up."

"You think I should have had Anthony's teeth?" Rita laughed, her own big teeth setting off her strong Gros Ventre features. "Anthony had baby teeth. I wouldn't want his teeth."

Margaret wondered if other people noticed their teeth, felt pains inside their bones, could not see into the human eye. "I should get me one of those big old *Gray's Anatomy* books," she said at last. "Study up on it. Memorize how it's all held together."

"What you better get," Rita said, "is a one-way ticket back to the real world. Indians don't count eyes and teeth. They count souls. So many souls in this lodge, so many souls in that. A very service-able unit. Takes care of everything." She walked into the kitchen, Bruegel at her heels.

"The *Joy of Cooking* says this is supposed to soak thirty to thirty-six hours." Rita peered into her kitchen sink. "Think I can get that off without using the yellow soap?"

Margaret looked at the short quarter of a country-cured ham soaking in cold tapwater. She sniffed; it smelled like water, almost neutral. The wet blue and yellow mold glistened under the fluores-cent light.

"Had my brother James ship it from Vermont."

"I'm not going to eat that," Margaret said. "Not on your life."

"Sure you are, Maggie. Anyhow, it was Woody's idea. If you don't like it, blame it on him." Rita took a wire brush, the metal shiny and new, and began tentatively scrubbing at the mold, the mudlike casing sloughing off into the sink.

Margaret poured herself a glass of wine from one of the Mason jars under the counter. "Where would Woody get an idea like that?"

"His mother used to make them." Rita continued scrubbing at the ham, a little harder this time. "I thought it would be fun. A surprise for you guys."

Margaret didn't believe Woody knew about a ham like this, a ham covered with bright mold. It must be some Indian cookery of Rita's; if it didn't go right, she could blame it on Woody. She watched Rita put a kettle of water and vinegar on to steam. Rita checked the cookbook again.

"Woody doesn't want to go to the dinner," Margaret said at last.

"My brother James thought this was for the dinner and he wanted to send me blintzes and lox. He said this was a crazy idea when I called him. Blintzes and lox. Wanted to mail me a Freezer-Crate of them." Rita scrubbed harder at the ham.

"I think he's right. I'd rather have blintzes and lox for dinner than whatever this is going to be. What are you doing for the party?"

"Chocolate mousse," Rita said. "But blintzes and lox?" She turned, the wire brush in her hand. "I wanted to send James some pemmican like our grandmother used to make. They're all fish-eaters up there, you know. And he said 'No,' he was getting into crepes!" She went back to scrubbing at the ham. "Getting into crepes. Christ!"

"Woody doesn't want to go to the party," Margaret said again. She wanted Rita to tell her everything would be all right. She trusted Rita to know these things. "Said he has a gig at that basketball tournament."

Rita laughed. "Before Anthony left he used to pull stunts like that. Anthony would say he had these jobs. And while he was gone the people would call up and want to know why he wasn't there."

Margaret stroked Bruegel, sipped her wine. None of this was making sense. Woody had Rita cooking a rotten ham. James, the most militant Indian Margaret had ever met, was in New England working for AIM and getting into blintzes and lox, crepes. Sullivan shot a dog on their softball field less than a week ago. Anthony had cheated on Rita. She was drifting. There was a logic here, but not one natural to her.

"Woody didn't ask you to do that ham," she said.

"Sure," Rita said. "He said his mama used to make them. With green beans and hot applesauce."

"I didn't know his mother could cook. That stuff would poison a normal person. And I bet you we'll have to feed Allison a peanut butter sandwich."

"According to the *Joy of Cooking,* this will be a culinary treat, straight from the rurals of Eastern America." She lowered the scrubbed ham into the steaming kettle and poured a glass of wine before seating herself next to Margaret. "You got some reason to mistrust Woody?"

"We've always gone to the dinner together. Last year he got off work for it."

"If you don't believe him, why don't you go down to the Field-house and see."

"No."

"Why not? Get the drop on him."

"Get the drop on him," Margaret repeated. "If he's there, there's nothing to worry about." She frowned as she tried to puzzle out the logic of this. "If he's not, then I'll just get worried. He'll have an excuse. There's nothing to worry about, right?"

"Woody got a reason to excuse himself to you?"

"I'm getting paranoid," Margaret said with a laugh. "I'm making up things to worry about."

"Go on his tour," Rita said. "It'll be fun."

"You think I should go on that stupid tour?"

"Suit yourself. He'll do it without you."

"He's even got you into the act now! Next thing I know he'll give Adam a suitcase for his birthday. Listen: I am not going. I can't go. I don't want to be stuck in some podunk town with two kids, no money, and a band that's out of work."

"You got it all figured, don't you?" Rita said. "It's dead before it hits the ground. It could be fun. And it would be good for the band. They are getting too big for this town. They can do things. And think of the kids, you know, a change of scene."

"There won't be no softball on the road, Sweetstuff. You going to pitch and catch yourself? Coker can't throw a decent curve, and that's her best pitch."

"Oh come on. Your life can't revolve around that. You listen. You play that game as long as I have and a lot of the thrill wears off. It's just a game. Keeps us out of the bars for a couple of hours. It's a lot more fun to see some new country than to stare at the same piece of earth forever."

"I know all about new country. New country is not the answer to every problem. I pulled up stakes once for new country. And I ended up the mother of two children," Margaret held up two fingers to emphasize her point, "alone and broke. I ain't doing that again."

"Live and learn. Be smart this time."

"I am being smart. I'm staying home."

"Suit yourself," Rita said. "You could leave the kids here and fuck Woody under the stars from here to the coast, clear down to Mexico and back."

"Terrific idea, just great! Let them think they have been deserted by both their father *and* mother. Thank god you are no child psychologist."

"Send them up to Mike in Alaska."

"Has Woody been coaching you? You seem to know all the lines."

They sat silently at the kitchen table, sipping wine, looking out the window at the late Montana spring. A bird sang in the cherry tree down by the Clark Fork. A few blocks away someone choked a lawnmower. The kettle sighed with the boiling ham.

"How'd you let Woody talk you into this ham?" Margaret asked. "Mail it all the way from Vermont."

"Bar talk. I thought it would be fun. Never heard of the damn thing before. But James knew about it. He says the taste is too strong for him."

"Well," Margaret said, "let's hope Woody likes it."

three

Nine year old Adam patiently explained to his mother and sister that there were over two million possible poker hands. There might be two million blades of grass on their lawn, he said, or maybe two million stars in the sky. Seated at the kitchen table, the gray early May rain spilling outside, the three of them studied their cards, the backs decorated with paintings of pheasants in flight. Margaret had promised Adam a set of honest-to-god Bicycle cards, regulation cards for real poker games, if he could learn all his multiplication tables. "Poker is a mathematical science," she had told him. "It's not like the tooth fairy."

"Hit me," Allison said. Allison was six, just finishing first grade. Although she knew her numbers and all the face cards, Allison preferred to draw a card, no matter what.

With his best grown-up sneer Adam said: "I bet you don't need a card. I'm not going to give you one." He folded his hands over the deck.

This was one of her children's rituals and Margaret watched Allison's face swell with anger, puffing out around the eyes, slackening into folds at the corners of her mouth. She was always surprised how ugly her children looked when they thought it useful. Adam stared at the top of Allison's head, a trick Woody taught him. A trick he had not quite mastered yet. They sat like that until Margaret reached over and took a card off the top of the deck and handed it to her daughter. Allison smiled, the kind of smile children wear in framed photographs. She withdrew a card from her hand and slapped it on the table with studied precision.

"You threw away a jack, you dummy!" Adam toyed with the pile of rejected cards, arranging them so that nothing showed but pheasants' heads. "You're too dumb to play with."

"She might be going for a straight," Margaret said. "Finish the hand."

Adam kicked the legs of the table. He studied his knees and the way his feet seemed to swing from them.

"Finish the hand," Margaret repeated. "I'll give you three to one I beat you." In Margaret's hand were two aces, stark white with bright spots of color in the center.

"That's dumb. You don't give odds like that." His small hands stirred the pile of cards, scooting them round and round on the wooden table.

He was right, of course, and Margaret felt somewhat uneasy because Adam was catching on to so many of her tricks these days. She lit another cigarette and waited, worrying that this poker thing might be getting out of hand. Adam just wanted to gamble. Woody was no help, always telling Adam about famous cardsharps and poolshooters. Amarillo Slim and Minnesota Fats. When Adam couldn't get Woody to shoot pool with him down at Shelly's he would spend the afternoons in the garage with his friends betting nickels, dimes, and quarters. The change jar Margaret kept lost money by handfuls so that she had been forced to move the jar to the top shelf of the kitchen cabinet. Allison didn't like the jar out of reach. She would sometimes spend the afternoons counting their collection of loose change, separating the dimes and quarters, making special piles for the Canadian coins, saving out buffalo nickels. As Margaret used to do with her own mother, Allison looked forward to the day when she and Margaret could roll the pennies, dimes, nickels, and quarters into brown paper changeholders and take them down to the bank.

"Three to one," Adam said. "Dimes." He pushed his dime into the pot and began studying his cards as though he had never seen them before.

Margaret put her cards down one at a time: a five of diamonds, a six of spades, a nine of diamonds, and then the two plain aces, hearts and clubs.

"Shit," Adam said. "You bet to lose. You owe me thirty cents." He picked up the cards, shuffling them rapidly, showing off postures he imitated from Woody. Margaret took three dimes and placed them on Adam's queens.

Carefully stacking the dimes to the right of the rest of his money, Adam said: "I'll have to lose that. It's unfair." He continued shuffling the cards, trying to arch his small hands around the deck the way Woody did.

"Let me deal," Allison said.

"No."

This was the time Margaret hated, late afternoon before Woody came home. Sometimes Margaret wondered if her children loved Woody more than they loved her. Each night they waited for him, fussy and sullen if he did not show up, which was happening more and more frequently since this band tour idea had been hatched. It wasn't as if she didn't know where he was: he was down at Shelly's Leg. Adam knew that and if Woody didn't show soon he would want to ride his bike down to Shelly's in the rain. Then they would both be gone, shooting pool or playing the pinball machines while Allison fussed that she never got to have any fun. Margaret did not believe children should hang around bars, but Woody encouraged it, said it added some excitement to their lives. Try as she might, Margaret was never comfortable watching Allison perched on a high-backed stool, her fat hands pushing the flippers while loose dimes rattled over the glass cover of the pinball machine.

Margaret tuned out her children squabbling over the cards as she rose from the table. She let them fight; it kept them busy. From the refrigerator she pulled out a head of lettuce, some black olives, carrots, and a winter tomato.

"Mom, tell her there's only one dealer."

"It's my turn!"

Waiting for Woody was as if her life were prepared to stand still until sunset or the sound of his step on the porch, whichever came first. Her whole body waited for that moment when the streetlights came on, making itself ready for something that could not be guessed beforehand, could only be recognized after the waiting was over when her muscles seemed to shift and sag into something like rest.

"Mom!"

"Put that away," Margaret said. "Help me make this salad."

The simplicity of her children delighted her. She heard their chairs scraping on the linoleum, felt them standing beside her, watching her hands remove the cellophane from the lettuce head. Giving them each a big china bowl, she put Adam to work grating the cheese while Allison tore up the lettuce. They were quiet now, intent on their work, when they heard the front door open and close.

"If we had a dog," Adam said, "no one could come in like that. We would know."

"We already know," Allison said. "It's Woody."

Woody leaned against the kitchen door frame, a wooden match stuck back in his teeth. "Sure, it's me. Who'd you expect?"

"We need a dog," Adam said. "Then if someone strange came in, not you, we'd know it."

"Oh yeah?" Woody grinned. "Since when are we expecting strange men around here?" He laughed at Adam's seriousness, the long face Adam pulled when he felt slighted. "Put a dog on your 'Wish List' and we'll see what we can do."

Adam frowned. "I already got a dog on my 'Wish List.' Two of them. A bluetick hound like you had when you were little, so we can go hunting and stuff. And a German shepherd for everyday, to guard the house."

"Two dogs?" Woody shook his head. "Two dogs," he repeated. "Two dogs is a lot of dogs to wish for when a fella doesn't even have one yet."

"I might as well wish for seven," Adam said. "And a pony too. None of them have come true. When do the wishes start coming true? My 'Wish List' is getting pretty long."

"Mine too," Allison said.

"Wishes start coming true," Woody said, "when you make the right wish."

"How do I know?"

Woody winked. "You'll know. You just get a feeling that what you want is a real good thing, not just for you, but for everyone."

"I don't want a dog," Allison said. "I want a cat. Cats are nicer."

Woody smiled at them. "I got a wish that will be just the right wish for tonight." He sidled up to Margaret and slipped his arms around her waist. Cocking his head on her shoulder, he said: "I wish we went out to eat and to a movie after that."

"Oh boy!" Allison said. *"Snow White* and pizza. Kentucky Fried Chicken!"

"Rollerball! Woody Allen!"

Margaret smiled, ran the bone of her jaw along Woody's cheek, pleased Woody had avoided the dog topic again. She remembered the Portis children; they told Adam their collie ran away.

Lying in the hot tub, Margaret felt better than she had in days. She swirled the water gently with her toes, feeling the warmth lapping around her breasts, her nipples hard as acorn caps. If anything could spoil her mood it might be the bathroom itself, nothing more important than a small room in her house. When she and Mike had bought this house shortly before Adam was born she spent all her pregnant energy filling it. Something about the clean, broad lines of the house frightened her then, something about the emptiness of the new rooms and the heaviness of her swelling belly. She believed she could control that fear by filling the walls with color and pictures, the floorspace with furniture and plants. Seven months pregnant she moved slowly through the new house, painting walls, framing pictures, making curtains, repotting plants. She sanded and varnished used furniture, covered empty walls with bright swatches of cloth. Lying on her back in the night, Mike asleep by her side, a baby kicking in her belly, Margaret thought her house seemed frightfully empty.

Mike called it Neo-Gypsy Storefront, a phrase brought from Philadelphia that his mother used to describe the hippies in their colorful clothes who reminded her of beggars camped in empty buildings during the Depression. And now, all these years later,

Margaret was beginning to agree with Mike about the house. It was gaudy, fussy. Filled with color that never let the eye rest, that demanded you look to the next pattern or picture. She wanted a starker, cleaner look. All white. White walls, white curtains, white furniture, with only an occasional bit of chrome or black. She would keep the plants in their red clay pots, take the faded Oriental and rag rugs up from the floor.

In the next room Woody was tucking Allison and Adam into bed. They were laughing and Margaret realized how long it had been since Woody told them a bedtime story. Something had been lost this winter. Adam had turned surly. Woody wanted to travel away from Montana. Even Allison had developed secrets she would not share. It seemed traitorous of Allison not to share with Margaret. Adam was the baby she and Mike had conceived. Adam was the baby they seemed to have carried together. But Allison was Margaret's own child, a secret from Mike hidden high in her womb for nearly five months. Allison left her mark on Margaret, the rivered maps that covered her breasts, the stretch marks Woody would run his tongue along ever so gently, leaving little cool trails across her chest.

After such a fine evening Margaret wanted to be smooth, warm and silky when she crawled into bed. She had almost forgotten they could have sex in the evenings. It had been such a long time now since she and Woody went to bed right after dinner, the kids watching TV until it was time for Woody to go to work.

Margaret rubbed the soap slowly around her breasts, down her belly. In Yellowstone last summer they lay in hot pools together under Milky Way stars, holding each other in the water, listening to crickets and night warblers, scaring each other like children with stories of grizzly bears and mountain lions. Woody taught Adam to fly-fish while she and Allison gathered wild flowers and watched the Whistling Swans. They saw moose, bison, coyotes, elk. They canoed down the sun-sparkled Firehole, cooked on the stone hearth in their cabin, named the constellations when the sun finally set. One night as she and Woody were putting Allison to bed Allison asked, "Do you hear that noise?" They listened to a bullfrog in some nearby pond, a few crickets in the underbrush. "That," Allison said, "is the stars talking. We can't hear them at home because they are farther away. Out here we can hear them. We just don't know what they say."

Part of that memory seemed unreal to Margaret now. Woody's carefully phrased dinner table talk, Margaret's back to him as she broiled fish on the fire, when Woody would ask Adam if he would like a brother, or what Allison would do if they had a live doll. And the awkward conversations in bed, whispered so as not to wake the children when Woody would say: 'Why not? You've done it before. And I've never had a kid, at least as far as I know.' It would give them a reason to get married, he said. A reason for him to finally get divorced.

That was another continent, a trip to another land, now that Woody wanted to haul $6,000 worth of equipment, five men, a woman and two children through Oregon, California, Arizona, New Mexico, to play in bars and at college dances where no one knew them, much less wanted to pay to hear them play. It meant giving up her job and pulling the kids out of school. Maybe selling the house or subletting. The house angered Margaret the most, Woody selling Mike's house.

Her bath seemed cold, the evening not so pleasant. Margaret wished she had never heard of this tour.

"Do you know," Woody said, standing in the open door of the bathroom, "that you have a perfect 1950's body?" He smiled as he crossed the tiled floor to sit on the toilet next to the tub.

"Terrific. I love being twenty years behind the times."

"The Age of Nostalgia." Woody's eyes ran along her body stretched out beneath the clear water. "Sometimes I want to dress you up. Put you in pointy-toed shoes, real nylons with seams down the back. A pullover sweater that shows your breasts. And a flared skirt with a wide black belt for your tiny waist."

Margaret laughed. "And my big ass."

"Someday I'm going to take you down to that used clothing store and buy you a complete Fifties outfit. Blue. All blue. I'd make you wear it too."

"If that outfit turns you on as much as you say, I won't be wearing it long." Margaret huddled her shoulders deeper in the bath-water. "I'd rather have a feather boa. You can wear that in bed."

"If I got you a feather boa, next thing you know you'd start drinking martinis and wanting a baby grand to stretch out on."

"That only happens in movies. Skip the piano. I'd settle for a feather boa and a bed. Maybe some satin sheets."

"How about the pointy-toed shoes? And some black stockings with seams?"

They laughed for a moment then fell silent. Woody pulled a pack of cardboard matches from his breast pocket and began snapping off the round red heads and dropping them into the soap dish. He pulled a cigarette from Margaret's pack, lit it solemnly and began touching off the match heads one at a time. Each one went off in a little burst of blue fire, sizzling slightly in the leftover soap.

"I asked the kids if they wanted to go on a vacation," Woody said at last. "They thought it would be great. Adam said he'd rather do that than have a dog."

"You mean the tour, don't you?"

"Yes." Woody touched off another match head that sizzled and sparkled in the air. The bathroom smelled of burning sulfur, rotten eggs. "I talked to Lloyd this afternoon and he said he can set it up for a little over three months beginning August or September." He did not look at her. "Whichever you'd like."

"Will you go without me?"

"Yes."

"Then why ask the kids?"

"Because I want you to go with me. I said 'vacation.' It doesn't mean we'll have to take them on the tour."

"There's my job."

"Quit. Get another later."

"The kids have to go to school."

"Send them up to Mike."

"Mike abandoned those kids! Allison doesn't even remember him. No visits, no birthday presents, no Christmas presents. Four years. And Alaska, for God's sake! Send them up to some pipeline camp in Alaska!"

"Be a great experience for them. I wouldn't mind going to Alaska myself."

"Well, then go to Alaska. I've got kids. And a house. And a job."

"We could sell, sublet, store the stuff. I know all the arguments, Maggie."

Margaret got out of the tub, the water now gone cold. She grabbed a towel and quickly covered herself, patting at her body behind the screen of terrycloth, her back to Woody. "I have to think about the kids."

"Not my kids, you don't." Woody's tone was very even. "You wouldn't have my kid."

"You are impossible. You want a divorced mother of two to get pregnant by a married man who's too damn lazy to get divorced from some woman he left back East."

"Phyllis."

"Yes. Phyllis."

"I told you I'd get divorced if you got pregnant. I said we'd get married and all that."

"So kind of you."

He crushed out the cigarette in the soap dish. "I don't think I want a kid."

"Christ! It's not like buying a new car."

"Maggie." Woody spoke slowly, softly. "We have to start making some plans, setting up those dates. I want you to come with me."

Margaret turned to face him and Woody met her stare. "I never told you about why Allison was born." Woody lowered his eyes, listening as he stared at the toes of his boots. "Mike seemed to be drifting away from me." She tugged on the towel, hiding herself. "And he seemed to be taking Adam with him. He was around three then and Mike hadn't really been too interested in him before. But kids get to be a lot of fun around that age and Mike started playing with him, taking him everywhere he went. It was like Adam had become Mike's toy. Exclusively. Like I had nothing to do with them anymore except keep them fed and dressed. So I got pregnant.

I love being pregnant; my body always feels so good. No sickness, backache. And you have a little piece of your man inside you. I did it so I wouldn't be lonely. I did it to try and keep Mike, just like I came out here with him ten years ago." She wound a towel over her hair. "But I just couldn't tell Mike. And when he found out he was furious. And we never did patch that up."

She looked at Woody for a sign he understood. "What I am trying to say is that at one point in my life I would have done just about anything to keep a man, a man who finally left me. I won't do that anymore. I won't do just anything to keep a man around."

"That's a disgusting story," Woody said, meeting her eyes for the first time.

"I'm not going to change my life around for anybody. It just doesn't work."

"Jesus Christ!" Woody stood up. "I'm asking you to have some fun, not to dismember yourself or destroy your life."

"I don't think it would be fun." Margaret walked out of the bathroom.

In a moment Woody followed her into the bedroom and sprawled across the bed, his boots just over the edge, watching Margaret work the blow dryer through her wet hair. He watched her hair turn from a dark wet color to the fine air-blown blond. Margaret continued running the electric brush through her hair until Woody got off the bed and pulled the plug at the wall socket.

"I'll even forgive you," he said as he came up to her and ran the palm of his hand along the crown of her head, working his fingers under her hair and caressing the back of her neck, "for turning a very nice evening to shit. But before I forgive you, I want to tell you a story." He dropped his hand and went back to stretch out on the bed. "When I was a kid I traveled a lot. In the summers my mother would send me up to live with my dad. He did the jazz circuit out of New York, but a couple of summers he had full gigs at some resort and we'd hang around there. Always something new, though. Newport, we did the first one in '54. I loved it. Got to see a lot. In the summer was the only time I was really close to music. And I got to know my dad. I liked him. Summers were the big times of my life." He shifted on the bed, arranging himself more comfortably. He smiled at Margaret and she thought he looked quite happy. "But you, you had one bad experience and you are letting it bulldog the rest of your life. The lives of your kids. You are so determined that the only way you can keep your head above water is to get a stranglehold around the neck of the guy who is trying to save you. Stand on his shoulders if you can. You got to keep everything locked up tight. It don't work that way."

"It's worked fine so far."

"Has it now?" He smiled again. "Well, it's not going to work with me, Sweetheart. I'm not going to drown while you stand on my shoulders and holler for help. I'm going on that tour. You don't like it, stuff it."

Margaret felt her ears ringing, her hands becoming numb. "Are you trying to tell me you're leaving us?"

"Not exactly. I might come back."

"But only if it doesn't work out, right?"

"Something like that. But maybe that's not the point. I see it this way: I'm asking you to have a little fun with me. Like Yellowstone. A big camping trip. We'd make some money, follow up on that Warner guy that wanted us to do a little studio work, maybe a demo. I'm asking you to go on a vacation, look around at the rest of the world for a while. But you don't want to, and to my mind it seems you've become a person who just doesn't like to have any fun. I'm just a fun-loving boy. Maybe we just ain't compatible no more."

Woody collected his long legs under him and pushed himself off the bed. He smiled again and walked too casually toward the hall. "I'm going to go have a drink and think on this," he said. "I suggest while I'm gone you do the same."

Margaret listened to the heels of his cowboy boots clipping softly through the house. She heard the front door open and close, the two steps it took him to cross the porch. In the remaining silence Margaret felt naked and cold huddled under the wet bath towel. In the back of a bureau drawer was an old flannel nightgown her mother had given her years ago, the nightgown she wore only when she was sick, as if to remind herself she must take care. Pulling the nightgown over her head, Margaret wished it were more complicated, wished the old nightgown had buttons or snaps or strings or bolts, so she could concentrate on putting some type of armor together. She wondered if she should cry, but did not feel like it, crying being the next scene in any movie after the boyfriend walks out.

four

In 1956 Shelly and Sullivan used to meet on the beach at Dry Lagoon and once Shelly saw a godwit. "Isn't that a wonderful name?" she said. "Marbled Godwit. It's a type of curlew." They walked closer and watched the big sandpiper startle, run a few steps then rise on its long cinnamon wings to fly over the marsh and behind a covering of scrub willow.

"All the things I ever wanted to see are gone." She let the water foam over her toes as a wave died at her feet.

"Gone?" Sullivan asked. "Gone," he said again and his voice implied he did not believe her.

"I want to see Paris in the Twenties. Flocks of Passenger Pigeons. The game preserves of Africa before the War."

Sullivan sat on a rock and pulled her onto his lap. His hands stroked her bare legs. "I'm glad your wants are simple. Most women want complicated stuff. Money. Houses. Rich husbands."

"That I got," Shelly said.

"That," Sullivan said, "is why you can afford to want to see Paris in the Twenties."

Shelly circled her arms around his neck. She touched her forehead to his and her hair made a coppery tent around their faces letting the sunlight shine through. "I think we should take a trip," she said.

"To Paris in a time machine?"

"Let's go to Texas and see the last Whooping Cranes. Go to Alaska and look for curlew."

Gently, Sullivan removed her from his lap, sliding her onto his place on the rock before walking a few paces up the beach. He could feel her eyes upon his back. He searched the beach for a present, a sand dollar, a bird's egg, some small delicate thing to give Shelly before he answered. As he walked he saw nothing but sand, handfuls of it that would slip between his fingers if he tried to give it to her. He turned, his hands empty. "How do you plan to do that?"

"Same way we do this."

"Get a divorce," Sullivan said. "We can go anywhere then."

Shelly stood and walked over to him, looping her arms around his neck and nestling her body close to his. "Someday," she said, "we will meet like this and that word will never come up. You know that? We'll just forget to talk about whether I'll get a divorce."

"Not until you do it."

Shelly laughed. Sullivan still thinks of her laugh as a musical instrument, the sounds as varied as an orchestra with the mystery and passion of fine music. "Never," Shelly said. "We'll get old. We'll struggle through the sand to meet on deserted beaches, clutching at our canes. Then we'll rub each other with mentholatum in motel rooms after geriatric sex."

Sullivan unbuttoned her blouse and cupped his palms to catch the rise of her nipples in the centers of his hands. He looked at her eyes, the long lashes and clear whites that ringed the steady blue of her stare. Looking at her eyes, his hands upon her breasts, and knowing that she was looking back at him, into him, Sullivan wanted to speak. He wanted to make a demand. But he knew that between them there was no space for words.

In these years since Shelly's death, Sullivan has prided himself on the truth of his memories. He is glad he is not an imaginative man, that his memories are as clear and true as the moments were in time. He remembers colors and smells, whispers of sound fill his mind as he sits behind her bar and stares at her picture above the jukebox. It is a good portrait and was taken just a year before she died. He regrets the bullet hole in her throat, the star pattern fanning out across the glass over her face when he fired that shot. He regrets his anger at her death and wants only to remember the good years, twenty good years in his life. He remembers the beauty of her body, even after she lost her leg, and the color of her hair. He regrets not cutting it and thinks of it growing in her grave. He wonders if the copper color has lasted, if it would keep the smell of her body. Sometimes he wonders what will happen to her bar if he should die. Once he talked it over with his father, Old Ernie. "What if," Sullivan had said, "what if some drunked-up Indian down off the Res. comes in here and blows my guts across the back bar for the money in the cashbox? What then, huh?" Or what if, Sullivan thinks to himself, he dies a natural death, dies with a pain in his heart and a ringing in his ears? Old Ernie laughed at him and said not to worry; Old Ernie could take over if anything happened to his son. At almost eighty, Ernie believes he will live forever, plagued with nothing more serious than gout or rheumatism, depending on the season.

"That woman turned you all around," Ernie would say. "Made you afraid of the wrong things. You got to fear something else, something you can fasten your mind to. For me it's fishes," Ernie said. "Big ocean-type fishes. I can deal with fearing fishes. I can't deal with fearing death."

When the shifts are slow Sullivan will talk about it over order sheets for potato chips and cases of booze. Rita is the most optimistic about death. Rita believes in fires; says she dreams about them all the time. Fires and eyes, strong Gros Ventre symbols reserved for the men of her tribe. Some night when they are all drunked up and having fun, Shelly's Leg will just explode with fire. It will take them all: Sullivan, Ernie, Birdheart, Amos and Randa, the ladies on the softball team and their men. There will be nothing left to worry about after that.

But Birdheart, who has seen more death firsthand than a mortician can imagine, Birdheart laughs at Sullivan. "Give yourself ulcers thinking stuff like that. Shelly wouldn't care for that a bit."

*   *   *

In about an hour Sullivan can turn off the blue neon sign that flashes a high-heeled shoe above the front door. The women will arrive for the Kick-Off dinner, their ninth of these dinners that signal the official beginning of the women's fastpitch softball season. While the women cook up some dearly loved recipe, bathe, curl their hair, apply makeup to their faces and perfume to their thighs, Rita has half a dozen men stuffing flowers into empty liquor bottles. Sullivan was pleased Rita remembered to ask Deadeye to bring all the leftover flowers from Garden City Floral. Every flower that would not be salable on Monday was at this moment strewn across the bar at Shelly's Leg. Blue asters, yellow chrysanthemums, golden lilies, pink carnations, bright orange black-eyed daisies. The men sat at the bar, a drink in front of each of them, with piles of flowers and lines of empty green liquor bottles. Rita thought clear bottles would look tacky and magnify the stems. For over a week she had collected dark bottles in a corner of the cooler.

"Too bad you couldn't get some ferns," Amos Espinosa said. He selected a giant rust-colored mum and seven black-eyed daisies and arranged them in a Cinzano bottle, the daisies flanking the base of the mum.

Deadeye took a sip of his red beer. "I'm no thief," he said.

"Of course you are," Amos said. He looked down the bar to Rita. "Hand me some straws. I got a bunch of carnations here with busted stems."

Rita gave him a box of Sweetheart straws and began mixing him another Cutty ditch, tall. A ditch was any drink mixed with water, as in irrigation ditch, in a tall or short glass.

"Golf," Amos said to Rita. "You ladies should take up golf." He sipped his new drink and straightened the daisies in the Cinzano bottle. "It's all in the wrist," he said. His meaty hands assumed a grip in the air above the flowers. "Same grip," he said. He flexed his clenched hands, turning the left wrist in, the right wrist out, taking a few practice swings through the air.

"Same grip, right Sullivan?" Amos offered this advice to the Shelly's Leg team every year. He claimed as a young man he had gone golfing on the regional circuit, had made some money every summer. At almost three hundred pounds, it was hard to imagine

Amos as a slender man walking the course in double-knits and swinging a club. He claimed he still played. "Taft was a golfer," he always said. "Taft weighted three seventy-five."

"Would ruin their arms," Sullivan said. "Like swimming. Builds up the wrong muscles."

"Christ," Rita said. "It ain't like we're trying out for the Olympics." She took two more bottles of flowers out to the tables in front of the bar.

"Swimming," Amos said with a short laugh. "Just cause *you* can't swim doesn't mean it's bad for someone else." He laughed again, lifting his face into an almost normal expression. The older Amos got and the more he drank, the more Sullivan thought Amos's face slid. It looked like the flesh of his face was slipping down his facial bones to pile up around his neck like chilled honey. The eyes, forehead, and nose were still firm. But the cheeks and jowls seemed to run together. Sullivan touched Amos's face once two winters ago. The giant fat man had fallen off his bar stool and knocked himself out. Sullivan tried listening through the layers of thermal clothing to hear if the heart was still beating. He could not tell if Amos was breathing. In the panic of that moment Sullivan tried to remember his First Aid training in mouth-to-mouth resuscitation. Cupping his hands around the sagging mouth, Sullivan was surprised at the softness of Amos's skin.

"Ever been to Kansas City?" Woody asked, speaking to no one in particular.

"Went through Kansas City in the Navy," Sullivan said. "Terrible place. They have fat grass out there. They cement their creeks."

"Bullshit," Woody said. He picked up a few asters and looked at them absently before stuffing them into a bottle. He played with them, scooting the stems up and down the bottle neck, trying to arrange them by height, line them up by color.

"You betcha," Sullivan said. "One of the mayors had a brother in construction. Had him cement all the bottoms of all the creeks. Just to keep things neat. Nobody'd want to go to Kansas City. Terrible place."

Woody took it as a question. "Wouldn't mind going there with the band. Might hear some good jazz."

"No jazz in Kansas City," Sullivan said. "Never heard a word."

Amos asked: "Maggie want to go to Kansas City?"

Woody stared at his flowers, poked a few of them around then pushed the bottle across the bar. "She's got to work," he said at last.

"You seen the official Kansas bumper sticker?" Sullivan asked. He wiped up the bar with a gray rag, looking alternately at Woody and Amos. "SUICIDE IN KANSAS IS REDUNDANT."

Sullivan laughed and polished the counter in little circles. "SUICIDE IN KANSAS IS REDUNDANT," he said again, chuckling and smiling.

"You go crazy out there," Amos said. "They say people who live without mountains or oceans go crazy. Stone cold crazy."

"Those sumbitches think the earth is flat."

Rita returned to her place behind the bar. "Where?" she asked.

"Kansas," Woody said.

"They got fat grass out there," Sullivan said. He put away the bar rag and pulled out the heavy metal calculator to check Rita's register. "Everything out there is a fat, calf-scour green. Even the people." He began punching numbers, watching the narrow white paper with little purple figures come spitting out of the top of the machine.

"I don't know," Rita said. "I always thought of places like that as jails. You got to want something pretty bad to take the trouble to go through. Only time I was in the Midwest was on my way to Baltimore."

"I never minded it," Woody said. "You got the sky on top, the ground on the bottom." Rita rearranged the flowers in his bottle, setting a golden lily in the center. "Out here," Woody said, "you only got the sky on top most of the time. Sometimes you got the ground off each shoulder, like up in the mountains."

"I knew a guy from Sedalia, Missouri, once," Rita said. "He hated it out here. Said the mountains hemmed him in. No place to breathe. That's near Kansas City, I guess. They have tornadoes out there."

"They got a good art museum in Kansas City," Amos said. "Chinese I think."

"Me," Rita said, "I'd like to go to the desert, and to the ocean. My brother James wants me to go to New England but he's so weird I don't care to see him right now. I'd like to travel some, though."

"Wish Maggie had that idea," Woody said. "Can't get her out of the god-damned house. She wouldn't go see a circus."

"Give her time," Amos said. "She's just scared."

"I'd go," Rita said. "Be fun. I'd go down and visit those Pueblos. They have their shit together down there. That's where my brother James should be, not off with some bunch of Yankee bluebloods."

"You're about as Indian as I am," Deadeye said. "You'd be real white if you'd get me another beer and quit yapping."

"Watch your mouth, Ugly," Woody said. "She'll get you a beer when you get your flowers in them bottles."

"I'll get him a beer when I god-damn feel like it," Rita said. "And nobody tells me when." She reached into the baseboard cooler and pulled out two Buds, Eastern beer, cracked off the caps with one smooth motion of each hand and set one in front of Deadeye and one in front of Woody. She took no money from either pile of change. "That suit you?" She began mixing Amos another Cutty ditch.

"You giving away my booze?" Sullivan shoved the calculator back on the shelf underneath the bar.

"Yeah," Rita said. "And with the money I'm saving you I'll run off with Woody here on his god-damned tour."

Sullivan smiled at her. "Your logic."

The last door along the far wall opened and Birdheart walked sleepily into the bar, trying to tuck the too-short ends of flannel pajama tops into a pair of jeans. When Shelly bought this building back in 1963 it had been a family grocery, a laundromat built into the side, an apartment above the first floor, and three small storage rooms along the back. Over the years Shelly had those rooms turned into sleeping units, asking anyone with a bar tab over an unspecified amount to work off his bill by paneling, plumbing, carpentering, or painting. She was going to make it a motel, the Rio Montana Motel. But soon after the storage rooms were remodeled Birdheart, Deadeye, and Valgaardson moved in and although there is a Motel sign above the old laundromat, there have never been any other tenants.

"How many times I told you to get dressed before you come into this bar?" Rita began mixing a bourbon ditch for Birdheart. He came across the room in that slow, sloppy way tall men sometimes have. His long trap-jaw was unshaven and the stubble of beard heavy for a man so blond. When clean-shaven he looked much younger. Birdheart puzzled Sullivan: a man blond enough to be Scandinavian with a one-word name like an Indian. When Sullivan once asked Birdheart if his name meant 'small-hearted' or 'fragile,' Birdheart replied: 'It means I'm the meanest son of a bitch this side of Laos.' Sullivan often wishes Birdheart would get mail. He would like to see an envelope addressed to Birdheart c/o Shelly's Leg.

"Will you look at that," Rita said, reaching across the bar as she slid him his drink. She rubbed the flannel of the pajama top between her fingers. "Little horses," she said.

"Found these outside the Salvation Army," Birdheart said. "And here I thought they were supposed to give stuff like this to the poor."

"Bottoms too?" Deadeye asked.

"And little red buttons," Rita said, taking one between her fingers and pulling it across the bar, toward her eye.

"Let go." Rita let go. Birdheart took his drink down neat.

"Did you find that this morning?" Deadeye's interest in what Birdheart found was professional. After tending bar for Sullivan most evenings, Birdheart would go out to the dump on the far side of town and drive a city garbage truck two nights a week. He finished up around ten, just as Rita was opening the bar and Deadeye delivered the rose in memory of Shelly. Over breakfast beer Deadeye and Birdheart discussed what they could fence from the garbage route. They split the profits fifty-fifty.

"They have a rip in the back," Birdheart said and swiveled on his stool to show them a long tear from neckline to tail. Very even, straight down the backbone.

"Looks like some poor bastard got shucked right out of those," Sullivan said.

Deadeye asked: "Did you find them this morning?"

"I found something this morning you can't fence."

Amos said: "Deadeye could fence his mother."

Deadeye ignored Amos. "What did you find?"

"A finger. A human finger."

"Ah, bull," Woody said. "Nobody's going to throw a finger in the trash."

Rita said: "The hospital, right?"

Birdheart smiled at them and pushed his glass across the bar for a refill. "I found it back of the AmVets."

Deadeye said: "Let's see."

"Nope."

"Is it in your room?"

"Nope."

"What'd you do with it, bury it?" Deadeye asked. "Which finger?"

"I'd say right index, by the shape of the nail and the wrinkles on the knuckle. Woman's. It had nail polish on it."

"Christ!" Woody said. "A woman's. Shouldn't you tell someone?"

"I just did," Birdheart said. "I told all of you." Then he laughed, his head thrown back flashing his large, even teeth.

"You're nothing but trouble," Sullivan said. "Go get dressed. Rita here has to go home and get ready. We're going to have us a party here and you are not coming in your bedclothes."

"Sour owl shit." Birdheart slid off his stool and moved around to the cooler behind the bar. He stood next to Sullivan, smiling down from his entire six feet six inches. The top of Sullivan's head was even with his nose. "You sound like an old mess sergeant," Birdheart said. "And you don't want to sound like that."

Birdheart reached into the cooler and grabbed a Rainier, cracked off the cap and walked back to his room. On his door was a black and red sign that said: WE REFUSE THE RIGHT TO REFUSE SERVICE TO ANYONE.

From the shelf under the cash register Sullivan pulled a paperback edition of *One Hundred Years of Solitude* and climbed the short step to the restroom. Inside the second stall he looked for his mark on the right hand wall. 223. A series of numbers ran around the stall at just about eye level. 223 is the page where Remedios the Beauty ascends to Heaven. During the months of Shelly's dying in the apartment above the bar, Sullivan would read in the men's john. He marked the page number on the wall in case he got drunk or forgot. This was his third reading of the book and he could never remember where he was. He didn't really care about that so much, but hated to dog-ear his books. He wanted them to look new, the spine uncracked each time he picked one up.

On the door of the stall the numbers ran in six columns, the six times he had read *Moby Dick*. The lefthand side contained five columns, the recorded pages of *Two Years Before the Mast*. Sullivan had read these books in the Navy, borrowing them from his buddy, Otis Tooley, when they were on duty in the Aleutian Islands. Unimpressed with them at the time, Sullivan now reads them over and over again. He remembers the salt smell he only noticed ashore and the rocking motion of the boat that made landing on volcanic islands seem so unsteady and unsure.

There were other marks on the stall walls, looking more like scribbles or scratches, not set up prominently like Sullivan's favorites. GBTAR was for *Good-Bye to a River,* a book by John Graves about a canoe trip down the Brazos. Graves was an old Texas man who talked about the Comanches as the greatest horsemen of the Americas. Sullivan liked that idea and thought he would probably like Graves if he ever got down that way again.

He read to page 242 in *One Hundred Years,* where Amaranta weaves her shroud. 'It might have been said that she wove during the day and unwove during the night, and not with any hope of defeating solitude in that way, but, quite the contrary, in order to nurture it.' Sullivan liked that line, nurturing solitude. He wondered if Márquez had ever been to Mexico, if they would meet and he could talk about Shelly. Marking 242 on the wall next to 223, Sullivan went back into the bar.

Birdheart, dressed in clean Levi's and a pearl-buttoned embroidered cowboy shirt, stood behind the bar talking to Rita and

Woody. Rita was ready to go, her purse lying next to her drink.

"I thought you wanted off early," Sullivan said. "To go get ready."

"I did," Rita said. "And I am." She raised her glass and toasted Sullivan. "Old Woody here claims he's not coming."

"Fine," Sullivan said. "More for the rest of us."

"Now don't you want this to be a good party? Not much fun if half the folks are off watching little kids play basketball." Rita pulled a pout. She held her profile to Woody with her chin thrust out as she sometimes did. Sullivan knew that pose. If Woody didn't know what that pose meant, her chin and chest slightly forward, the line of her backbone straight and true, Sullivan sure did.

"Basketball?"

"We're going to do breaks at those high school playoffs," Woody said.

"Maggie going with you?" Sullivan asked.

"She'll be here. She's home cooking up right now."

"Elk again?"

"Sure. Elk. A spiked buck."

"I hate elk," Sullivan said. "Reminds me too much of dog."

Rita said: "Woody's trying to talk me into giving him a ride down to the Fieldhouse. And I'm trying to talk him into bagging that gig and having some fun with us."

"I'll bet you are," Sullivan said.

"Maggie's got the truck," Woody said.

"I'll bet she does." Sullivan walked behind the bar and made himself a drink. He believed he'd been in this business long enough to know the signs of a train wreck coming when he saw it. In a way, Sullivan was relieved. Since Anthony left last fall Sullivan had been watching Rita, waiting for her to make her move. He expected her to hook up with someone long before now and had some fantasies about what Rita had been up to all this time. Sometimes she stayed with Birdheart, but that was nothing serious. Maybe Indian bucks or a black dude. Sullivan could not imagine her masturbating. But he could imagine a woman. Which one he couldn't decide.

"Buy me a drink," Rita said, "and I'll give you a ride."

Birdheart said, "If *I* buy you a drink, will you stay?" Rita wrinkled her nose at him.

Sullivan leaned across the bar with a shot glass full of Chivas. "You know," he said to no one in particular, "when I was in the Navy I had a buddy, maybe I told you about him, Old Otis. Otis Tooley. And he was a smart son of a bitch. Used to watch me and give me advice. I was young then, didn't know dip shit. Otis once said you could tell what kind of man you were dealing with by the look of the woman with him."

"Maybe that's why they call women 'dogs,'" Rita said. "Same thing goes for dogs. Any bruiser with a poodle on his chain, well, you just know what he's looking for."

"Otis said if a man looked like his woman," Sullivan nodded at Rita, "then he is a narcissist. That is, if both parties look alike, then they are in love with themselves, not with each other."

"Oh," Rita said. "Serious talk. This apply to women too?"

"Sure does."

"That's crap," Birdheart said. "Doesn't work that way for lots of folks."

"Now this is Old Otis speaking, remember that," Sullivan said. "I don't know I believe it myself. But Otis said if a man looks exactly opposite his woman, then he hates himself." Sullivan drained his glass smoothly.

He turned to Woody. "Otis would say: 'Sullivan, you watch yourself. You're in trouble. That fancy blond you was with, why, she don't look nothing like you.'"

"He got you both ways," Woody said.

Rita said: "Some people just take a natural shine to someone. They don't analyze physiology."

"Otis had preferences," Sullivan said. "His woman looked just like him." He turned again to Woody. "Like you and Maggie. You two look like you could be related. Her hair's a little blonder, yours has some red. But you guys are about the same height, build. Got the same nose. Otis said a man's got his head on straight if he is his own best friend."

Sullivan turned to Birdheart. "Now you take Rita here," he said.

"Little dark thing that she is. Ain't she a dandy? But none of us could get mixed up with her."

"Sullivan," Rita said, "you out to ruin my social life?"

"Not a bit, Sweetheart. But think about it. You get mixed up with old Birdheart here, or Woody, and Otis would be all over your fancy ass. He would say: 'Just look at them boys. They must just hate themselves. That woman's exact opposite of them.'"

"That's just a man's view. A woman might see it differently. Maybe she'd like a nice blond man to set off her looks. Like a real white scarf on a black dress."

"Oh boy," Birdheart said. "A fashion accessory. What happens when she takes off that black dress?"

Sullivan poured himself another shot. "According to Otis, both parties be in big trouble."

"According to Otis," Rita said, "I got no choices in this joint but you."

"That's the way I always wanted it," Sullivan said with a smile.

Rita's smile looked as if she were baring her teeth.

Woody said: "I don't see what all this proves."

"Oh nothing," replied Sullivan. "Just a story I thought you'd like."

"What ever happened to Otis?"

"Died," Sullivan said. "Otis had another theory ended up killing him. He believed you have germs in your body. He was right. They digest your food and stuff. But Otis hated that notion. Said it cluttered his thinking to have good germs in your body since most germs are bad for you. So he drank a quart of Scotch a day to kill them, every one of those suckers. And he died, five, six years ago. Bad liver."

"All this is real nice," Rita said, "but I've got a chocolate mousse to make." She drained her glass and pushed it across the bar.

"Yeah," Woody said. "We'd better go. I got to get set up."

Rita slid off her bar stool and grabbed her purse. "Anyhow," she said, "a person shouldn't waste a bunch of time and talk on a man whose own ideas killed him. Sullivan, that's the dumbest collection of crap I ever heard."

Sullivan smiled at her, then at Woody. "So glad you liked it."

"You're drinking too much, Sullivan," Woody said. "Your stories have all gone to hell. Maybe I'll stop by later."

"You do that," Sullivan said, cocking his glass at them. "You do that. And don't worry. Old Maggie will have a good time."

Sullivan finished his drink as he watched Woody and Rita moving toward the door, Rita's walk a little too loose in the hips and legs for his taste. He watched their timing as Woody got far enough ahead of Rita to open the door for her so she wouldn't break stride.

Sullivan and Birdheart smiled at each other and Sullivan said: "I have seen this tawdry shit all my life."

"Ain't it the truth," Birdheart said as he took a shot of Sullivan's Chivas.

five

Margaret took the rag curler from Allison's hair and watched the fine blond mass fall of its own weight into a fat, even ringlet. Her mother had called them Shirley Temple curls twenty years ago and Margaret remembered how her mother's long fingers had wound through her hair, soaked the hair in thick green setting gel before binding the curl with a rag. Margaret unwound another curler and felt Allison's body tense with excitement beneath her hands.

Once certain things get started, Margaret thought, they become a bitch to stop. She simply remembered things too well and dealt with them the same way, time after time. She still missed, almost mourned, the loss of an onyx ring her mother had given her for her sixteenth birthday, a ring she believed she had left in a restroom on the Pennsylvania Turnpike when she and Mike first came West. Mike said that was a good sign; they were leaving things behind. But Margaret preferred to have things stolen than simply lost. For weeks afterward she believed she could go back to that restroom and the ring would still be sitting on the edge of the porcelain sink. Or that it would mysteriously turn up in one of their suitcases or boxes. She still regrets throwing away a gold-plated safety razor her grandmother gave her and can remember how she hesitated before dropping the glittering razor in the wastebasket after her grandmother gave her a Lady Remington one Christmas. She wishes she had that razor now, and the ring, hidden in a drawer somewhere. If she had them she would save them for Allison.

The one time Margaret consciously tried to change her patterns it backfired. She decided to learn to play a musical instrument, study calculus, and understand competitive chess. Music would teach her a non-verbal response. Calculus could show her abstract relationships. Chess could teach her the mechanics of aggression, the devious strategy of competition. She reasoned all this would give her different ways of relating to the small problems that filled her days. She bought an expensive six-string Martin guitar, a book called *Introduction to Calculus,* and an ivory chess set before telling Mike about her plans. She was excited about the possibilities before her and hoped Mike would want to share them with her. Mike laughed at her, teasing her for days about the new person she would become, a combination Leonard Cohen, Werner von Braun, and Bobby Fischer. He called it 'Margaret's Personality Playoff' until he discovered the price of the Martin guitar. Angry, he demanded she return it. They couldn't afford it, he told her. There were better things to spend his money on than guitars his wife couldn't play and games she didn't understand. Margaret returned the guitar and the ivory chess set and spent part of the money on a blue gingham maternity dress. Five weeks later, after an autumn weekend biking and camping up the Blackfoot, Margaret was pregnant again. She believed she could feel it, the exact moment.

Her plan for tonight was simple: show Woody she didn't need him to go to the party. Perhaps it would make him jealous when he realized she was not all dressed up for him. Woody would have to show soon; it was almost seven o'clock and if he really wanted to impress those high school kids he would change into one of his flashy shirts. If he didn't show by seven Margaret would have to leave without seeing him. Rather, him seeing her. He would come down to Shelly's if the kids weren't home whenever he was done. Margaret was sure of that.

Under the camper shell of Woody's pickup Allison tucked in Billie Jean King, her Barbie doll dressed in a pair of jeans and a tiny red flannel shirt. Allison informed Margaret she wanted Billie Jean King to grow up and become Champion Lady Barrel Racer someday. Maybe she would race on the pony Woody kept promising

Adam. Tonight she had left Phyllis Schlafly and Gloria Steinem at home and agreed to let Billie Jean King sleep in Woody's pickup during the dinner. The kids promised Margaret that when they got tired they would join Billie Jean King while Margaret stayed on at the party. They would be their own babysitters; it would be an adventure.

Margaret fluffed her hair with her fingers and pulled back her shoulders. She pinched her nipples so they would stand erect under the thin gauzy shirt she wore over her flared velvet slacks. She thought she looked quite nice, almost sexy, as she and the children came through the back door of Shelly's. Margaret carried the roasted elk haunch on a Doulton china platter that had been her mother's. Adam and Allison each carried a bowl of gravy, Adam holding the elk drippings thickened with flour in an old china bowl decorated with hand-painted birds and Allison carrying the Hot Cumberland Sauce in the little tureen that matched the platter. Roasting an elk haunch was simple enough, but Margaret got real pleasure in preparing the Cumberland Sauce, mixing in the cayenne and cloves, brown sugar, raisins and almonds. Most of the sauce went home with them, too strongly seasoned for the folks at Shelly's Leg. That was just fine with Margaret; she would reheat it in the morning and serve it on open-faced elk sandwiches.

They were making a nice entrance when Margaret sensed a familiar ringing in her ears, a premonition she had developed when Adam was just a baby. She turned as Allison's tureen hit the floor.

"Dummy!" Adam kicked Allison, almost dropping his own bowl of gravy. Allison began to cry.

The little round tureen lay in scattered fragments across the linoleum, small chips of blue and white china floating in the oily sauce. The beautiful bowl had been reduced to bits smaller than Allison's fingernails. Allison was still crying, not as a schoolchild would, but in that long, loud, babyish bawling that always tempted Margaret to slap at the sound. Adam scolded, harping at Allison about how she'd broken Mom's bowl, that everyone was looking at her.

"Stop that!" Margaret said. "Both of you, go sit down." She took the bird bowl from Adam and set it with the food on the plywood slab covering the pool table. Deadeye appeared beside her, his half-empty red beer angled so that some of it dripped into the Cumberland Sauce and china. He winked at her with his good eye.

"Hey kids," he said. "Want to play some shuffleboard?" He patted Allison's hair heavily and herded them toward the other end of the room. Margaret watched them, thinking it might be best to just go home.

Birdheart knelt beside her with several rags and a dustpan. "You'll just ruin your outfit," he said as Margaret began to kneel next to the mess.

Margaret watched the oily sauce soaking into his stiff jeans. "I'll do it," she said but remained standing, watching Birdheart. There was no way to reconstruct the bowl, yet she kept searching for pieces big enough to save.

"That's a good girl," Birdheart said. He slopped more of the sauce onto his dustpan, wiped a few more aimless patterns across the linoleum and dropped a handful of sawdust over the slick stain. "Now I'll take you up to the bar and buy you a double. You're behind here. Have to catch up." He rose and took her arm, guiding her to the bar and Margaret could see his long eyelashes sweeping up and down, studying her body. She breathed deeply, pulling in the muscles of her stomach.

Deadeye was getting a refill on his red beer, long on the beer and short on the tomato juice. "Coming in on the arm of another man?" he said. "You should take care of your own man. That's what a woman's supposed to do."

Birdheart said: "Lay off."

"Want to see what happens when a woman don't take proper care of her man?" Deadeye set down his beer and began fumbling with his right eyelid.

"Oh don't," Margaret said.

"For Christ sakes." Birdheart sounded disgusted.

Deadeye reached for his beer. "I must be getting old. Back in my youth women would beg me to take it out. Now they just say: 'Don't do it for Christ sakes.'" He poked the glass eye with his index finger, setting it back in the socket properly and running his fingertip over the contoured sphere of the iris.

"You look like one of them Alaskan dogs," Birdheart said. "You should get that thing to match instead of a blue one and a brown one."

"I'm going to get me a lavender one," Deadeye said. "Then I'll go down to the playground and see if I can get a lot of little girls to do just anything for me. Like that Charlie Manson fellow."

Margaret said: "I think it's going to take more than a lavender eye."

Deadeye tried to grin and wink at the same time and managed only to screw half his face into a leer. "I got that," he said, patting his crotch.

As Deadeye wandered back to the shuffleboard game, Margaret looked around the bar. Coker, her relief pitcher, was talking to Edithanne, the third-base person, the only member of the team who preferred 'base person' to 'base man.' Edithanne, their token militant. Diane, the new girl, stood in a corner and flirted with Valgaardson. Irene, Miriam, and Lolie were playing Keno with Shirley. But Rita wasn't around. Margaret looked again and realized she was searching for Woody. She turned to smile at Sullivan, who stood across the bar.

"What'll it be, Maggie?" Sullivan stood under a hand-lettered sign that read: ABSOLUTELY NO ONE BEHIND THE BAR FOR ANY REASON.

"Make this lady a double," Birdheart said. "In a fancy glass."

Margaret noted the beer kegs lined up beneath the shuffleboard game like so many silver dwarfs and watched Amos Espinosa pass by the kegs with a wave at her and go behind Sullivan to grab a bottle of Tanqueray.

"Somebody's stealing your liquor," Margaret said.

"Somebody's always stealing my liquor," Sullivan replied. "If I didn't let them steal from me they wouldn't come drink with me."

Birdheart said: "You make a lousy bartender. I want you to get us some drinks here. Fancy drinks for the lady."

"She's big enough to order her own," Sullivan said, and leaned across the bar between them, his back to Birdheart.

"Where's Rita?" Margaret asked.

"I got just the drink for you," Sullivan said. He pulled out a dusty bottle of Wild Turkey, washed the sides of the bottle with a rag and set up two shot glasses. He poured them full.

Birdheart poked Margaret in the ribs. "He gives a broad hint, don't he?" Birdheart raised himself and reached a long arm across the bar to grab a bottle of tequila. "If he gets to boring you, just whistle."

"For you," Sullivan said as he pulled a golden lily from an assortment of flowers next to the cash register. He slipped the lily down the front of Margaret's gauzy shirt.

The lily stem jammed in her bra. Margaret shifted the flower, hooked a finger under the elastic and straightened her back. "I look like I got three breasts," she said. "A big inverted nipple in the center of my chest."

Sullivan laughed. "You are a Wild Turkey indeed."

"Me? I'm just a Sage Hen, Sullivan. Have been all my life."

"Oh Maggie." He smiled at her broadly. "You're just dreaming. You are more like," he seemed to be searching for a name, waving his hand in the air as if calling to it. "An English Sparrow," he said at last. "A city bird imported from another country."

"I'm catching on," Margaret said. "Lived here almost ten years now."

"That don't got nothing to do with it," Sullivan said.

"What?" Margaret said. "I don't even know what you are talking about." She wondered if he was trying to tell her more about shooting the Portises' dog.

"You and Woody."

Margaret's ears seemed to ring again but she looked into Sullivan's eyes to see what all this meant.

If this was a staring contest, Sullivan wasn't playing. He touched up both shot glasses and looked out over the crowd, not evasively, more like a store clerk searching for shoplifters. There were things about men Margaret knew she didn't understand. Maybe she had been with Woody too long, his pale glittery eyes that gave away no secrets. When Margaret looked into a man's eyes all she ever saw were the mechanics of vision. Eyeball, iris, pupil, lens. Not the truth and lies, the deep-seated feelings a woman was supposed to see in a man's stare.

"It strikes me this way," Sullivan said, cutting his eyes back to her with the same wary glance. "Between two people, one always feels more than the other. With me and Shelly, I know I loved her more. And even then there was this contest to see if we could get a rise out of the other. You and Woody are not fighting about a band tour."

Margaret gave a short snort, the type of noise her mother would have called 'unladylike.'

"You want to be the power," Sullivan said. "And so does Woody. So you guys have set up this little contest to see who is going to push the other around."

"Sullivan, I don't know where you get off." She was quiet for a moment and then said: "When I was a kid my mother told me I would grow up and find a good man who would take care of me. She made him sound like a fairy prince or something, even when I was old enough to date. She thought of Mike that way. Magically, this man would walk into my life, take it in hand and I would live happily ever after. Well," she said, looking Sullivan right in the eye, "that might have been the case for my mother. My dad took good care of her until he died. But I've learned something since the divorce. There ain't no magical man. Not just anybody's going to save your life. At some point you've got to start doing it on your own."

"You make divorce sound as final as death," Sullivan said. "Let me tell you a story about experience. A sad story." He shook his head and laughed. "Now a shark is nothing but experience. Centuries of experience. Got a brain about the size of a dime. I was in Rhode Island out of Narragansett Bay and I saw this little sand shark half in the water, half out on the rocks. Experience tells a shark to keep swimming, pulling the water in and out of its mouth. This little shark was lying on the rocks with its mouth going like when it swims." Sullivan illustrated with his hands, opening and closing the palms hinged together at the wrist. "All that shark was doing was grinding little grooves in the rocks with its teeth. Experience can only do so much. If that shark had a brain as big as the bottom of this shot glass, he would have realized his ass was still in the water. He would have given a big swoosh with his tail," again, the hand flipping on the oaken bar, "and he would have jacked himself back in the water. He would have lived."

"What happened?"

"I crushed his head with my heel. I hate the buggers."

"I got a story for you," Margaret said. "About instincts." She played with her shot glass, rolling it on its bottom rim so the bourbon swirled in the center. "When Mike and I were married we knew these rich people from Boston and they had a summer place down in Wisdom. One summer they showed up with a raven they bought in some pet store. Its tongue was split so it could talk and its wings were clipped so it wouldn't fly away. It never talked and spent all its time hopping around on the ground collecting shiny things, like foil from cigarette packs. It was a terrible thief and would peck your ankles. I hated it."

Margaret held the shot glass still. "Then one night we were sitting out watching the sun set. Across the fields, birds were settling into the trees, making lacy patterns against the sky." She waved her fingers through the air as if playing chords on a piano. "They were calling to each other as they chose their treetops for the night. The raven looked up and stayed quite still for a moment. Then it went over to a yellow pine that grew next to the house and it hopped, and climbed, and fluttered its broken wings, working its way up from branch to branch. Climbing up the pine so it could sleep in the top like any other bird." She smiled. "When its wings healed, by fall, it flew away. South."

"Christ," Sullivan said. "The things a person ends up learning."

The air in the room changed with the serving of the food. Margaret picked out the smells of baked trout and sage as the covers came off more than two dozen different dishes, reminding her of the warm, friendly smell of people and food at the Pedersen Pretzel and Potato Chip Company her father had owned when she was small. Margaret could imagine the gentle rustling sound the potato chips made as they poured down the long tin chute to cool before falling into the holding barrels atop the bagging machines. She remembered the sounds of cellophane being separated by blown air, the clatter of the chips as they fell into the bags, the hum of the heat sealer.

"Damn," Sullivan said. "There's one hell of a choice." He and Margaret decided not to duplicate anything, Margaret making selections from the right side of the table while Sullivan worked the left. Margaret chose German potato salad, mushroom caps stuffed with clams and blue cheese, smoked rainbow trout, lasagna, and a sour cream quiche covered with thin slices of Canadian bacon. Sullivan helped himself to Margaret's elk roast and gravy, enchiladas, vegetable tempura, roast duck, smoked turkey, and mocha almond chocolate cake. They moved over to the corner where Amos Espinosa and Randa had pulled two little bar tables together. Randa was lighting the long wax tapers in Amos's pewter candlesticks.

"Swap you some duck for one of them mushroom caps," Sullivan said. He cut cleanly through the slice of meat and speared it with his fork, holding it out to Margaret across the table. She took the bite neatly into her mouth, just the tip of her tongue running along the underside of the fork. In turn, she spooned up one of the fat baked mushroom caps and offered it across the table to Sullivan.

"Champagne?" asked Amos.

"This is the life," Sullivan said as he fed Margaret tempuraed cauliflower. She reached carefully across the table with a forkful of cheesy lasagna.

Randa was arguing with Birdheart while Amos filled their glasses. Randa's small body, frail as a bird's, reminded Margaret of her father's bookkeeper, an equally small woman who had talked about numbers with an intensity usually reserved for religious causes. Randa, her square, wire-rimmed glasses perched halfway down her nose, rooted through her oversized red handbag.

"You should care about *something,* you know," she was saying to Birdheart.

Birdheart laughed. "I do, Randa. I care about getting in your pants. Haven't had any ass over fifty since I left Da Nang."

"You're foul," Randa said. She pulled out a frayed clipping and handed it to Birdheart. "Read this," she said. "I cut it out because I knew no one would believe me."

"We believe you," Amos said. "Drink your champagne."

Dear Abby,

My boyfriend and I love each other very much and have been going together for three years. About two years ago I found out he was seeing another woman and I locked myself in a closet to protest. He visits me almost every day, sometimes bringing me food, or candy, or flowers. However, I am getting very tired of this. I want to learn to shoot pool. I would come out if he would quit seeing this woman.

What Should I Do

Birdheart handed the clipping to Margaret. "This can't be a genuine 'Dear Abby,'" Margaret said. "There's no answer."

Behind her glasses, Randa's eyes curled in on themselves. She brandished her long-stemmed glass at Margaret and Sullivan. "It just said: 'Everyone has a problem. Send your problems to Abby.' That's all. But let me tell you this. I don't blame Abby one bit for not answering. It's tricky."

"Don't be disappointed," Amos said. "We'll find a way to help that girl."

"Sure," Birdheart said. "Just what that girl needs. Help from us."

"I'd like to write her," Randa said. "It's not good for her in that closet. Not enough fresh air, exercise."

"Don't forget she wants to shoot pool," Sullivan said, stretching a forkful of elk over to Margaret.

"I'd write her," Randa said. "I'd write her and say: 'Honey, you just come out of that closet. Old Randa will take care of you. Forget that mean old boy.'" Randa was smiling now, pleased with herself.

"You better not," Birdheart said. "We do not allow weirdos in this bar."

Sullivan offered Margaret another large bite of elk, soaked in gravy. "It's okay," he said. "A bar never has its full quota of weirdos. That's why we're here."

"You make us sound like we're living in Ekalaka," Amos said.

"Ekalaka?" Margaret asked as she gave Sullivan a spoonful of quiche. She decided to take a plate of food home to Woody. Poached steelhead, lemon meringue pie.

Sullivan asked for another bite. "Sure Ekalaka," he said. "It's got a dead-end road into it. Got to turn around if you want to get out."

"The problem there," Birdheart said, "is that you got to have someplace to go."

"It's better than living in a closet," Randa said.

"I don't know," Amos said. "It's safe. Secure. And he visits her every day."

"I like closets," Birdheart said. "You could call my room a closet. I like to imagine they kept brooms and flea soap in that very room I call my home."

Margaret said: "Still, you can't learn to shoot pool in a closet."

Sullivan paused, a forkful of smoked turkey suspended in front of him. He looked at Margaret, studying her, and then smiled. "That's right. There's a whole lot you can't learn in a closet. Got to get out and do it."

Margaret looked back at him evenly. "I know what you're getting at Sullivan, but it's not the same."

He shrugged his shoulders and offered her the turkey.

"How old do you think that girl is?" Randa asked.

Across the room Margaret could see Adam and Allison playing cards with Silent Sam, Valgaardson, and Shirley, their center fielder, a blond, green-eyed whore who worked the Keno table for steady income. Margaret watched Adam kneeling on his chair, looking boldly down the front of Shirley's dress, ignoring his cards and the hand signals Silent Sam used for betting. Shirley caught Margaret's eye and winked. Adam did not realize the women were watching him as he stared down the front of the black dress, expecting to find something new between the soft folds of skin. The stakes were roasted almonds and Margaret watched Allison eat a handful of her chips.

It was time for the dancing, the serious drinking. Most of the paper plates and napkins had been thrown in the big trash can, the left-over food covered and stored with purses and coats to be taken home later. Birdheart, Deadeye, and Margaret listened to Sullivan recount Birdheart's CIA tour as a cargo kicker in Cambodia.

"Laos," Birdheart said. He did not look up as he continued paring his nails with a pocket knife.

"Laos," Sullivan corrected as he went on to tell them how Birdheart had machine-gunned his commanding officer when he was ordered to torch a village.

Margaret had heard this story before, or several similar to it. It was a love story about Birdheart's romance with a Saigon whore and the order to burn her family's village. Sometimes when Sullivan told the story, the little dark-eyed whore was giving birth to a child there, maybe Birdheart's although Margaret couldn't remember Sullivan saying that specifically. Other times the whore had pleaded with Birdheart in Saigon to spare her family. But the story always ended with Birdheart turning his M-16 on the officer and his aides, mowing them down like a reaper through wheat, Sullivan often said.

Sometimes Margaret thought Birdheart had buried himself in this little Western town to hide from those Marine days. He never told the stories himself, just sat listening to Sullivan, changing the details now and then as if afraid to hear the same story more than once. She wondered how Sullivan knew these stories. Occasionally she suspected the whole ritual was a fabric of lies.

"That's a bunch of romantic horseshit," Margaret said. "You're too pretty to be a killer. Maybe I don't believe you were in the war at all."

Closing his knife with a snap, Birdheart grinned at her. "Want to see my scars?"

Cold air swept them as the back door opened and Rita stood in the doorway, her straight black hair pulled back in a severe braid encircling the crown of her head. She was all in black, tall black leather boots, a black velvet skirt that clung to her hips and swirled about her legs at mid-calf, a black high-necked cashmere sweater lying quietly over her breasts and shoulders underneath the hammered silver of a squash blossom. The only spot of color came from a handful of bright yellow flowers she carried like an offering. Margaret thought it must be a cold night to go picking flowers without a jacket.

Rita walked unsteadily toward them, the movement in her hips exaggerated to make her skirt swing wildly about her legs. "I made a chocolate mousse," she said to Sullivan, "but now it's all gone. So I brought you this. For you." She handed him the wilted body of a small buttercup crocus, yanked from the ground, drops of mud splattering the table as the roots swung through the air.

"You shouldn't have," Sullivan said, taking the crocus daintily from her and holding the muddy stem away from his clothes. He looked closely at Rita, studying her face.

Laughing, Rita sang in a loud, imitation Southern twang. People on the dance floor turned to look at her.

"I really had a ball last night.
Held all the pretty boys tight.
I was playing double, swinging singles. . . ."

"That's enough," Sullivan said. "You always sing when you're drunk?"

Rita laughed at him again and turned to Birdheart. "I made a chocolate mousse," she said. "But now it's all gone. I brought you this." She handed Birdheart another of the wilted crocuses from the bunch in her hand, great globs of dirt clinging to the roots.

"What the hell," Birdheart said. "Keep this filth outside." He tossed the flower at the trash can, but missed, the crocus too light to carry across the room. It landed near the pool table, sliding a bit on the floor.

"Parties are such fun," Rita said.

"You missed the party," Sullivan said. "But I do believe you are in time for the fun."

"I might just be the fun."

"Don't you have anything for the lady?" Birdheart asked.

Rita sat down heavily on a chair, stretching her legs out so Margaret could see the mud clinging to the high wooden heels. The flowers slipped down the velvet lap of her skirt and fell one by one to the floor near her feet. Margaret couldn't keep her eyes off the bright yellow flowers and watched each of them dropping in turn. She was embarrassed for Rita. Rita who was usually so careful, so prompt.

"For the lady," Rita said. "For Maggie, my best friend Maggie."

She reached into the hidden pockets of her skirt, sending the remaining flowers tumbling to the floor. "Maggie and I have been best friends for years. We share all each other's troubles. We always will." It sounded like a formal toast to signify some great occasion.

Margaret watched Rita's face, the hard bones just under the skin. Rita looked like she was posed for a photograph, head set at a delicate angle, eyes unblinking, gathering in all the pale bar light falling on her face.

Slowly, Rita's hand came out of the pocket, her face never changing. She reached across the small space between them. "For you," she said.

Margaret placed her hand under Rita's extended fist and felt the nails of Rita's fingers brushing her own flat palm. In Margaret's hand lay a small, white stone, smooth oval, shaped like a perfect bird's egg.

"A stone," Deadeye said. "Just a rock."

Rita said: "Eskimo women place them under their tongues when they sing."

"We've had enough singing for one night," Sullivan said.

Suddenly Rita turned her full attention to Sullivan. "I did real good, Sullivan. You should have heard me. They loved it."

Margaret sat with the stone in her palm and felt her body tightening, her ears ringing. There was a pinching near her nose and her eyelids seemed to be stretched over a dry, sandy surface.

"Save your singing for the shower," Sullivan said. "I want to dance." He took Margaret by the arm, not asking or demanding. Holding her lightly, he led her off toward the dance floor.

When Shelly died Sullivan quit hiring live music and let Rita pick the tunes for the jukebox. He did not enjoy what he called 'Modern Dances.' He wanted to know his partner was dancing with him, not with the next dude over. "Orange Blossom Special" gained speed while Sullivan two-stepped Margaret around the dance floor, waltzing in quarter time, his hand pressed a little too firmly against her back, his chin buried in her hair. Margaret stared at the green and yellow palm trees etched on his blue shirt. This was the scene she had been waiting for: Woody walking in and seeing her in another man's arms. She didn't care who, Sullivan, Birdheart, anyone else. There was a jealous streak in Woody, which might be why he wanted her to go on that band tour so damn much. In her mind Margaret had been rehearsing this moment all evening—the cut of her clothes, the way her hair looked. But it didn't feel right and Margaret knew it wouldn't come off as she had imagined. It was high school strategy.

"What's this about Rita singing?" she asked.

"Probably took a shower," Sullivan said. "You know, this song reminds me of when I was a kid. Old Ernie used to be a pretty fair fiddler."

Margaret found herself staring at the clock. She watched Diane, the shortstop, new this year, as she coaxed Birdheart onto the dance floor. While the other women seemed to know where they stood in this bar, among these people, Diane had not yet found her place. She wore too much makeup and her clothes looked as if they belonged on a mannequin, not on a woman who played softball and drank beer. Margaret had watched her sidling up to one man after another all evening. Two weeks ago Diane made a pass at Coker's husband. Coker was good-natured about things like that. She had said: "Take him if you want him. Recycle him. I'm afraid I've had his best years."

Margaret relaxed and drifted in Sullivan's arms. Halfway through "Satin Sheets" he said: "Let's have a drink." He kept his hand on her elbow as he detoured behind the bar for a bottle and walked Margaret around the dancing couples to their table. Woody squatted with his back to them and his elbow on Rita's thigh. The heels of his cowboy boots were caked with mud.

"What do you think of people who bring mud into a bar?" Sullivan asked, still holding Margaret by the arm.

Deadeye said: "Shoot them in the elbows and knees."

Woody looked up. "Hello, Sweetheart." He flashed Margaret a warm grin. "You going to shoot me in the elbows and knees?"

"Any reason why she should?" Sullivan asked.

"Tracking mud on a rainy evening become a crime?"

"Ain't raining."

Woody rose and took the unopened bottle. "Drink?" He cocked the bottle toward Sullivan, who gave no sign. Woody uncapped it and took a long drink, then wiped the lip of the bottle across his sleeve and handed it to Rita. She slowly poured her shot into an empty glass and offered the bottle to Deadeye, who said: "Never touch the stuff," before taking a long pull and giving the bottle to Margaret.

"We'll have to get you a glass," Sullivan said.

"You treat her like a proper lady," Woody said.

"Any reason why he shouldn't?" Margaret stepped forward until she felt Sullivan's hand, holding her to his side. The backs of her ears began to ache.

Woody laughed. To Margaret's mind, the voice and the laugh were not his own. It sounded like Woody trying to imitate Sullivan's laugh, a wry chuckle that stuck like broken gears.

"Maybe we could sit down," Margaret said. The three of them standing in a ring around Rita made Margaret feel unsteadily balanced among them, aware of Sullivan's hand on her arm and the puzzling fact that Rita would not look at her, had not looked at her since they returned from the dance floor.

"Look at the regular gentleman," Woody said as Sullivan pulled out a chair for Margaret.

"He's got manners," Rita said to Woody. "Dandy manners."

"Manners!" Woody snorted. "This is a party. We're supposed to be having fun, not manners. Dancing and farting around like a big happy family. Not all long-faced and formal and seated."

Deadeye stood with his beer in his hand. "I had a rotten childhood," he said. "I think I'll go find me some grownups, all formal and seated." He moved off toward the beer kegs lined up beneath the shuffleboard table.

Rita spoke up in her bright bar talk, the thin patter she served with her drinks all day. "Seems like we've been sitting here for years," she said. "Just years and years, all of us together."

"Good party?" Woody asked.

"Real good. Lots of fun," Sullivan said.

Behind them the music still played and Margaret could hear the tapping and scraping of feet on the dance floor, the talking and laughing blending into the music as if part of the song. Except for the noise from the dance floor, this party seemed silent to Margaret, the people becoming background noises like traffic in a city heard from an apartment ten floors up. Only Woody's voice seemed to cut through the smoky air. Perhaps he was talking too loudly; Margaret couldn't pin it down. Even Rita was quiet, watching the movement of the conversation between the men. Margaret stared at her, hoping to catch her eye.

Woody reached over and patted Rita on the arm. "Rita here made her debut tonight," he said.

"Debut?" Margaret couldn't think of a single talent or skill Rita possessed that would require a debut. She had stood behind Sullivan's bar for six years, keeping the men and women entertained with her talk and the drinks she mixed. She needed no debut for that.

"Singing," Woody said. "She sang like a little bird for those kids. Hell, she sang like an eagle."

"She sang like an eagle?" Margaret could see Rita swooping down upon the microphone, crooning over the shiny metal stick with sweeping arms and much tossing of her hair.

"Of course," Sullivan said. "Don't you know how talented our Rita is?"

Margaret wanted to laugh at all of them. They were passing the bottle as if this were an old B Western. Woody, the young upstart, was baiting Sullivan, the seasoned gunfighter, with that professional restraint and courtesy B movies made famous. Rita and she were the dancehall girls watching in the background with that curious fascination for violence and death that sends people to prizefights and car races. As in a B movie, the women weren't truly there; their bodies only occupied the dancehall costumes and held up the flowered curls of the hairdos. But they were all playing the wrong roles. Sullivan poured her shots into a glass; Woody handed the bottle to Rita and usually it would have been different— Woody beside her, Sullivan with Rita.

"The thing is," Sullivan said, "she's got no manners."

"Manners, again," Woody said.

"Yes. Manners. You two have gone and upset the whole applecart."

"Naw," Woody said. "No way." His eyes focused in on Sullivan.

"Yes," Sullivan said. "I'm going to do it to you. I don't like this kind of slop in my bar."

"It was all in fun," Woody said, looking at Rita. She kept her head down, studying her drink.

"Do you think it would be fun," Sullivan said to Maggie, "if Rita slept with Woody?"

Woody stood. "You're a bastard, Sullivan."

"I don't care for this slop in my bar."

Margaret's thoughts seemed to bounce back physically. Her mind circled the parts of it but could not visualize the whole of it. Rita and Woody: it changed too many things. Rita was her friend, the only woman Margaret truly enjoyed. Rita's childhood with her brother James on the Reservation seemed more real to Margaret than her own childhood in the factory section of the Bronx. They shared that with Margaret's children; Rita dressed up in her beaded buckskins, handing out presents like Santa Claus as they observed the Celebration of the Winter Spirit for Christmas. Rita gave Margaret that stone, cooked Woody that ham. Rita who had not come to the dinner so she could sing with Woody. Rita who ... Margaret could not think any closer to it. She could not imagine Woody and Rita together.

"Who are you," Woody said, "to pull this kind of shit on me?"

"I got no right," Sullivan agreed. "But I warned you. It's got to be done."

"It sure is done now," Rita said, still not looking up.

Margaret should have been warned. This was not her ground. Margaret never fought a frontal attack. Woody used to joke about it, saying that if Margaret were mugged she would have to have a few days to think about kicking the guy in the balls. But after thinking about it Margaret wouldn't kick some mugger in the balls. Her attacks were from unexpected angles. She might piss on the mugger, shit in his hand. Or tweak his nose, smash his windpipe.

She had to get out of here. As she looked across the room at the people who remained at this party that had somehow gone all wrong, she saw Adam sipping a can of 7-Up and playing poker with Silent Sam. She was on her feet and halfway across the room before she noticed Sullivan following her.

"I thought I put you to bed," Margaret said. She stood directly behind Adam, Sullivan at her side. Adam ducked his head and pulled in his shoulders as if afraid she would hit him. Silent Sam gestured at the cards, pointed at his watch.

"You shut up," Margaret said. "Where's Allison?"

"Woody said it was okay," Adam said miserably.

"Woody is not your mother. I put you to bed. Is Allison in the truck?" Margaret knew the answer to that before she asked. If Adam wasn't in the truck, Allison wouldn't be either.

Adam crawled out of his chair and ran for the door.

Silent Sam began to gesture again, pulling the little blue notebook from his breast pocket and quickly writing out an explanation.

"It's okay," Sullivan said, closing the notebook and patting Sam's shoulder.

Margaret looked at Sullivan. "Why?" she said. She wanted to say more, but it was as if her mind had stopped. She didn't know whether to curse or thank him. "I'll look for Allison," she said, her eyes never quite meeting his.

She walked back toward the card room, ducking down several times to see if Allison was curled up asleep on a chair. Somewhere in the circle of her thoughts was a picture of how Allison and Adam would feel if . . . She couldn't say what followed that if.

Margaret kept to the dark corners of the bar before realizing how silly she must look. There was no reason why Allison should be in a corner. She took a deep breath and tried to clear her head. As she climbed the short step to the card room Margaret heard Birdheart's voice.

". . . and when the old man knew the marlin was dead he began to row for shore, which was almost out of sight by now. It was dark and he was tired, but he was very happy about his fish. And then he spotted a fin in the water." Birdheart sat in the dark of the card room with his feet propped on the table and Allison sound asleep in his arms. Diane dozed on the floor, curled up like a big blond dog.

"Hi, Maggie," Birdheart said. "Looks like it's time for this little lady to go home." He rose gracefully, stepping over Diane, and followed Margaret back into the bar. Margaret gathered her dishes and bowl, keeping her back to Rita and Woody, who were still sitting at the table.

Sullivan lifted Allison from Birdheart's arms and walked toward the back door. There was no more time now and Margaret turned to face them. She watched Rita, knowing that if Rita looked up, something would be better, something could be saved. But Rita kept staring at her fingernails, which she ran up and down the side of a bar glass. Margaret heard the door close behind Sullivan.

She knew she should say something as she stared at Rita, aware of Woody staring at her. Yet the lines in her mind sounded so stupid. She felt so stupid, standing before them as if on trial. She could not look at Woody, and at last turned and followed Sullivan out the door.

six

Sullivan knew that by the time he walked back from Maggie's the party at Shelly's Leg should have been over. He was mostly right. Rita and Woody were gone and Sullivan could bet they were over at Rita's. Valgaardson was asleep on one of the little tables and Amos and Randa were sitting on either side of the bar, Amos with his back to the mirrors, wagging his finger at Randa as he lectured her about economics. Sullivan woke Valgaardson and walked him to his room next to Birdheart's. "I love her," Valgaardson mumbled, more asleep than awake. "Isn't that right, Sport?" Sullivan closed the door to Valgaardson's room and headed toward the bar.

"Let me put it to you this way," Amos was saying.

"No," Sullivan said. "We'll put it this way. Go home." He stepped behind the bar and took a half empty bottle of Tanqueray from the shelf. "Here," he said. "Finish your arguing at home."

"Now this might interest you," Randa said. "You're a businessman."

"I'm just interested in closing this joint. It's past your bedtime," Sullivan replied.

"What if we get sober?" Amos said. "It'll be your fault."

"Come back in the morning. I want to lock up."

"Actually," Randa said, "you're only sort of a businessman."

"Please," Sullivan said, although there was no begging in his voice.

Amos said to Randa: "I think he's throwing us out."

Randa picked up her purse. "He's not throwing me out. I'm leaving. I'm not putting up with any more of your bullshit."

Amos looked at Sullivan. "Now see what you've done."

"Out." Sullivan herded them toward the door.

With the door locked and the lights off, Sullivan seated himself behind the bar opposite Shelly's picture. In the morning he would have Valgaardson or Deadeye clean because they were behind on their tabs. It was a technique Shelly had used and Sullivan continued it whenever there was something he didn't feel like doing himself. Tonight he didn't want to sweep the spilled food and drinks off the floor, haul the beer kegs back into the cooler. He probably wouldn't want to do it in the morning either. If he felt generous and they did a good job, he might even square with them on the rent too.

They danced, holding each other close and drifting in time to sad country tunes. "I can only dance with you," Shelly would whisper in his ear. "Paul and I can't dance. Our bodies don't fit together." She pushed herself into him, warm and smelling of sweet apples. "See? Your body is built for me. My head here," and she nuzzled into his shoulders, "my arms here," and she stroked the back of his neck. "And so forth," she said pushing her pelvis against him.

"Bitch," Sullivan said. "Offer a man love with your body and take it away with your mouth." He kissed her deeply, long, his teeth hard against her lips. Her mouth was stale with the taste of vodka.

She laughed and pinched his ear. "Your perfect woman would be divorced and mute."

"Just divorced."

She laughed again, the laugh Sullivan still hears in his sleep and sometimes when he is drunk behind her bar. "You're in the wrong line of business, Sullivan," she said. "You should have been a con man. Or a used car salesman. You always go for the hard bargains."

"Nope. Those types are willing to compromise. I'm too single-minded for that."

"You've been compromised for years."

The band stopped playing but they continued to stand on the dance floor, their arms draped over each other's shoulders as couples moved past them back to tables for drinks and cigarettes. Sullivan began dancing again, although the band was leaving the stage for its break. The tune in his mind was "Room Full of Roses" and he waltzed Shelly around the empty dance floor, not even humming or singing to her, just letting the music flow over his mind and his hands wander over her body.

"I've driven you crazy," she whispered. "We're the only ones out here."

"Always," Sullivan said. "You and me. The only ones out here."

"With you," Shelly said, "it's like living on an island. Water all around us."

Sullivan poured another shot of Chivas into his glass and set the bottle back in the bar well where the ice was melting slowly. He knows the order of his memories and fought to keep the next memory of their dancing away from his mind. He concentrated on dancing with Maggie earlier in the evening, the smell of her hair and the way his hand fit around the small of her back. He hadn't danced with anyone since Shelly died, since she lost her leg. That's eighteen years, Sullivan thought, trying to forget the night they danced in this bar, holding only to the memory of those years they danced in Seattle. Drunk and laughing that night Sullivan held Shelly tightly, holding her up as her foot dragged along the floor. "I can't live without dancing," she had told him when she bought this bar. "If I can't dance I want to be where others can."

That night Sullivan picked her up and two-stepped across the floor with her in his arms. "This isn't dancing," Shelly laughed. "It's flying. Do a spin." Sullivan twirled round and round on the dance floor, holding Shelly tightly in his arms, her laughter in his ears. He circled tighter and tighter until he made himself dizzy and fell, Shelly sprawled in a heap on top of him.

Sullivan concentrated on the smell of Maggie's hair, the feel of her breasts against his chest. She had been so quiet on the way home, no tears, no questions. If Shelly were alive, she would give him holy hell for mixing into Maggie and Woody's troubles. Shelly had never understood how he hated the lies and his own cowardice.

In Sullivan's mind the problem had always been the sneaking around and the lying. As the years went by he felt more and more strongly about it until one night his father, Old Ernie, accused him of thinking like his mother, a strict Irish Catholic who seemed to have more feeling for the Bible and its characters than she did for her husband and son. "All that religion," Old Ernie had said, "just mucks up people's lives. This world is complicated enough without adding a bunch of rules and judgments."

But Sullivan believes it would have been better if he had confronted Paul directly. Driving along in his pickup truck with an open beer and some country-western song slipping out of the radio speaker, Sullivan would imagine how he could go up to Paul's big house, park his truck in the circular driveway and walk to the big double front doors. Maybe a butler or maid would let him in. Of course, Paul would offer him a drink. They would be very civilized about this. The two men would stand in the living room, which Sullivan didn't dare to imagine, and finally Shelly would come in. The next clear image Sullivan would have would be how he would load her leather suitcases into his pickup and drive Shelly away.

Sullivan had these thoughts rarely before the accident, but they became more frequent and more vivid as he watched Shelly moving through her bar on her crutches. Once she was dead and he had only her picture to talk to, he got so he could imagine the living room, the look in Paul's vacant eyes. In some way Sullivan felt the accident was his fault. If he had been man enough to take her from Paul, things would have been different.

"You know," Sullivan had said to Rita one night as she sat in the bar as if she had forgotten to go home, "if you are lucky you only fall in love once. It's sad never to fall in love at all. But if you do it too often the thrill wears off."

"Trash," Rita said. "You take what you can get. There's monuments to the dead all over the world and they don't keep no one warm at night."

* * *

Shelly was pouring pancake batter onto the grill when Paul knocked at the door. Sullivan knew it was Paul, had always known that Paul would come to him. Looking out the window at Paul's new 1959 green Mercedes parked behind his truck, Sullivan debated whether to put his pants on. Screw it, he thought as he went toward the door.

"This is it," he told Shelly as she flipped a pancake.

"Who's at the door?"

"This is the moment we've been waiting for." He looked into her face for a clue to her feelings. He wondered if she would laugh or cry, become angry. Sullivan imagined that if he saw Shelly and Paul at a party or in a bar, she would ignore him at first, waiting for him to make the first move. But Sullivan knew he would never make that first move and sooner or later Shelly would figure some way the three of them could be introduced. She would never let an opportunity like that pass.

Shelly patted at her hair, pulled the tie on her brown kimono. "Aren't you going to get dressed?"

"No."

She touched his arm as he moved past her toward the door. "Do him that favor."

Paul wore a business suit, dark gray, with a pale blue shirt and no tie. Merely glancing at Sullivan's body, naked except for his jockey shorts, Paul said: "It's an emergency. Is Shelly dressed?"

Shelly stood behind Sullivan, her body silky in the kimono, her arms around his waist. "Have you all met? Want some breakfast, Paul?"

"Your mother had another stroke. I'll wait for you in the car." Paul walked back across the yard to his new Mercedes.

He has empty eyes, Sullivan thought.

Haloes of black smoke rose from the charred pancakes. "So much for breakfast," Shelly said as she tossed the mess into the garbage and went into the bedroom for her clothes.

Sullivan followed her. "How does he know where I live? That you're here?" He was frowning as he settled himself on the bed to watch Shelly dress.

"He knows everything. We've never had any secrets."

"All along?"

"He found out sometime during the first year." She stepped into her panties. "I remember," she said as she reached for her bra lying on a chair. "It was when we took that trip to San Francisco. The first time." Her arms looked like bird wings as she hooked the bra behind her.

"That long," Sullivan said.

"I think he used a detective. It was our only fight."

"Why didn't you tell me?"

"What good would it have done?" She slipped her sweater over her head. "It wouldn't have made any difference."

Sullivan handed her the skirt and he can still remember it, the navy blue and white herringbone pattern of the wool. "It makes a difference," he said. "No secrets from Paul but secrets from me."

"You must have known he knew. All this time? Come on. Don't be dumb."

Embarrassed at his own nakedness as he watched Shelly dress, Sullivan thought the idea through again. Of course Paul must have known. They hadn't been exactly subtle about things. But what bothered Sullivan most was the knowledge that their affair wasn't secret. Sullivan had treasured that notion through all the years. He could think of Shelly in her bed at home with Paul, but Paul could not think of him. It was painful to let it go, to acknowledge Paul as a person who allowed his wife to have a seven year affair.

"Screw it," Sullivan said as he watched Shelly brush her hair.

"Stay close," Shelly said. "This is her second attack. I never thought she would come through the first one. I'll call you as soon as I know."

"I'm going to Portland."

She turned from the mirror to face him. "You didn't tell me you were going to Portland. You can't. What if she dies?"

With his back to her, Sullivan took a shirt from his closet. "I just decided."

"Don't," Shelly said. "I need you."

"You don't. And if you do, I won't be here."

Sullivan remembers now, sitting behind Shelly's bar and sipping his Chivas, his body remembers the two of them standing in his bedroom in Seattle. Shelly all dressed but for her stockings and shoes, her hair mostly combed and shining, and in this memory Shelly is caught as a still photograph, the brush raised to her hair and reflected in the mirror. Sullivan stood in his jockey shorts and unbuttoned shirt. She had time only to drop the brush before Sullivan had her on the bed, her skirt bunched up around her waist, the silk of her panties curling around her right ankle.

Sullivan feels the warmth of his own hand against his fly, the hard throbbing that beats like a pulse through his palm. He remembers the feel of her wool skirt on his stomach as he made love to her, her husband waiting in the green Mercedes, her mother dying of a stroke. He pushed into her roughly and made love to her as if it were rape. He can still feel her fingernails in his hair.

She called it selfish screwing. "You didn't wait for me," she said years later. But Sullivan could never bring himself to explain, although he can remember as clearly as the moment he first thought of it. He was leaving Shelly and that moment on his bed in Seattle was his goodbye present. He wanted her to remember it as the end of their affair. Pushing into her with all his strength, Sullivan was tempted to leave bruises on her body, liver-colored spots to remind Paul he had been there. He grabbed her hair with his teeth, breathing in the smell of shampoo mingled with cigarette smoke. Shelly scratched his skin, bit his cheek. Her heels came down on his back, kicking.

When he finished with her he rolled off quickly. He paced the room, his head so light he felt wind in his ears. He went into the bathroom and closed the door, hoping she would be gone when he came out. He would leave Seattle, maybe go back to his father's ranch in Montana because Portland was too close, too tempting. Holding his head under the tap, Sullivan felt the water sliding across his open eyes, pulling at his eyelashes. Water ran into his nose, beat through his ears like the beginnings of thunder.

Shelly turned off the tap. "This is a hell of a note to end on," she said. "If you go, I'll find you." She left the bathroom and Sullivan listened as she let herself out of the house. He waited for the sound of the door of the green Mercedes and imagined he might hear Paul turn the key in the ignition and drive the car away.

Rubbing his head dry with a towel, Sullivan walked into the living room and looked out the window. The green Mercedes was gone. He truly believed at that moment he had left Shelly and felt like he wanted to laugh, but knew the sound would ring hollow in the room. He wished he were in some bar and could lean over to a drunk and share this. You know, he would say, and perhaps buy the man a drink, you know how long it takes to end an affair? An affair lasts as long as a circle. Once the circle is closed, the affair is over. Meeting Paul had closed the circle. Shelly rode away with him. There was no secret, no moment except in Sullivan's mind when he could claim Shelly as his own. Sullivan believed he would never see Shelly again.

Sullivan heard the sparrows in the trees along the alley. It was still dark, the blue black before sunrise that is the only color Sullivan ever wanted to paint. It has a hold on his imagination like the depths of the oceans have on sailors. Sullivan believes he can feel the earth turning when the sky is dark before dawn. If he does not go to bed during this darkest time of night, if he stays up to watch the sunrise dilute the blackness of night, a new day will begin full of the endless Montana sunshine and the transparent blue of the skies. He would like to go to bed, to mount the steps behind the cooler and lie in the bed he shared so many years with Shelly. Most nights when he closes this bar and talks to Shelly's picture above the jukebox, the sparrows are his signal. He believes it gives form to his days. But Sullivan knows which nights give him bad dreams and a cold sweat will break out over his body. Even now, three years later, remembering the leathery stump of her right leg will make his hands sting, always did, those nights she wanted it rubbed. Sullivan would rub the stump, not sure what she was feeling, gently, as if afraid to touch the end of the bone. Then to restore feeling to his own body he would place his hand in the curve at the top of her thigh, his other hand on her breast and feel the softness of her body that was so healing.

His dreams are different now, but he does not trust they will stay this way. He no longer dreams of Paul's motorcycle, no longer sees it shining in the sun, the wind moving around it as the spokes of the wheels turn so fast they become liquid silver. He has stopped hearing the whir of the axle grinding through the flesh and upper thigh bone of Shelly's leg. Those nights when he awoke to his own screaming are behind him now. Shelly cannot calm him by kissing his forehead and stroking his hair. "It was nothing like that," she used to say. "I don't remember any pain."

Pouring another shot of Chivas and listening to the sparrows, Sullivan concentrated on Shelly, thought perhaps she might have winked at him from her frame above the jukebox, and tried to ignore the brightening sky.

Sullivan believes the only times he ever lied to Shelly were the stories he made up about where he went and what he did after he left Seattle. Of course, at first he didn't lie. In her hospital room Sullivan hadn't the heart to lie. He told her he had been waiting for that envelope, or perhaps it would have been a phone call. He said he believed she would find him, just as she had said she would that last morning in Seattle. "I'm easy," Sullivan said. "I didn't really make it hard. You found me." Shelly laughed at that, but Sullivan was not sure how she meant it.

It was only later when they were more settled with each other that Sullivan began to lie. And that lying still puzzles him, especially in the hours before dawn. Maybe that is why he shot her picture, but he can't remember for sure. He would make up women for her, fancy descriptions of them and what they did to his feelings. "Well, you know, this Juanita, maybe it was just her name; she was like a rose blooming in the desert."

Shelly asked: "Did I ever make you feel that way?"

Sullivan's answers changed as Shelly changed. In the hospital Sullivan told her she was a whole forest of blooming desert flowers and Juanita had only been a single rose. Later in Mexico he mentioned that roses have thorns. But when they moved to Montana and Shelly asked again about this Juanita, Sullivan confessed Shelly had always been the rose; Juanita made him feel there was sand slipping through his veins.

Sullivan still wonders where those envelopes went, how they managed to disappear from his life. Sometimes he suspects Shelly took them and imagines her burning them, one by one, the white paper curling black in the yellow flame. But it could have been his father, Old Ernie. Sullivan suspects Ernie never liked Shelly and might have thrown those envelopes away because he thought it was the right thing to do. Sullivan himself might have destroyed them on one of those nights he does not remember but have become stories people tell sitting around the bar.

He can no longer guess how many envelopes were sent, stuffed only with the newspaper clipping of the accident. The first one was handed to him in a bar in Lolo by a logger, Taylor Sullivan, who worked out of Darby.

"You know," Taylor said as he sat down next to Sullivan, "I'm glad I run into you. Been looking for you for a couple of days."

The bartender set up their drinks while Sullivan tried to understand why Taylor would be looking for him. Sullivan had never done any logging. He had been in the shipyards in Seattle, or running cattle for his father. Not cutting down trees.

Reaching into his breast pocket, Taylor handed Sullivan a folded envelope. It was addressed to T. Sullivan, the box number in Darby, the envelope typed and postmarked Seattle. Inside was the newspaper clipping, no note. Sullivan still sees those envelopes in his sleep, the typing and the postmark, but he can no longer remember the details of the clipping. Something about a truck and a Chevy Impala. He remembers how the words 'Mr. and Mrs. Paul Newhouse' looked in newsprint. He knows the bike was a Ducati 500 and it dragged Shelly across an embankment almost one hundred feet.

Taylor sipped his beer, eyeing Sullivan as he read through the article. "I thought it might be for you," Taylor said. "You spending so much time in Seattle."

Sullivan wondered if there were tears in his eyes. All he could hear was blood rushing through his ears, the pounding of his heart as he tried to understand what this meant. Who had sent this? Was Shelly dead? How could the story of a motorcycle accident in Seattle have reached Taylor Sullivan in Darby, Montana?

Taylor put a silver dollar on the bar and signaled the bartender to give Sullivan another drink. "You might as well keep it," Taylor said as he set down his beer mug and got up to leave. "It means nothing to me."

That night at the ranch his father said: "There was a call for you from Janie Sullivan up in Missoula. She said she might have a message for you if you know some people named Newhouse in Seattle." The next day his father, Ernest Sullivan, received an envelope, postmarked Seattle, with the clipping inside. Sullivan made some phone calls. Mrs. Shelly Newhouse was in serious condition in Angel Memorial Hospital in Seattle.

Always checking with the nurses to see if Shelly had visitors, Sullivan would wait if Paul was in her room. The waiting was based on fear of what he might do to Paul if he actually had to meet him again. Sitting with a magazine, Sullivan would watch Paul walk away from Shelly's room. Paul couldn't walk consistently. Sometimes the walk was tight-assed, mincing from the knees and stiff like a horse on ice. Other times he moved away down the hall with a long-legged stride. But sometimes the walk was all in Paul's shoulders, hunched over as if to protect himself. Sullivan studied Paul's walk, one leg in front of the other. Paul could run if he wanted to. Paul could dance.

"You should say something to him," Shelly told him one day. "It would make him feel better."

"Him? Feel better?" Sullivan began to pace the small room. "I'm liable to tear his legs off." He imagined snapping Paul's leg at the knee like a chicken bone.

Shelly began to sing softly; it was a joke with them.

> *"I know I'm only Shelly's winter love.*
> *She only seems to need me now and then.*
> *I know I'm only Shelly's winter love,*
> *But she's mine alone 'til springtime comes again."*

Sullivan sighed and sat beside her on the bed, on her good side where the leg remained. "How does he know I'm here?"

"You don't give him much credit, do you?"

"I'm liable to give him a couple of busted knees."

"Hush," Shelly said and she put her arms around his neck and let her fingertips wander under his collar and across his shoulders. "He sent you the letter. And he knew you were here when the flowers started coming."

Sullivan looked past her and around the room. The seven sprays of roses, each different and carefully chosen each morning, were all his.

"Paul doesn't notice flowers," Shelly said. "He thought the hospital supplied them. But when he realized they were all roses he knew it was you."

"He never even sent you flowers?"

Shelly smiled.

For the first time since talking to Taylor over a week ago, Sullivan understood the envelopes. What could Paul, or Shelly for that matter, have known about him? When he left Seattle a year ago he told Shelly he was going to Portland. That was all she knew, that and the fact his father owned a ranch in the Bitterroot Valley in Montana. Paul must have tried every Sullivan in the whole valley, every Sullivan in Portland, sending out the clippings, no message, in the hope one of them would reach him or someone he knew. Sullivan imagined Paul's panic. He wondered what Paul would have done if Sullivan had been his first name.

Shelly pulled him to her chest as his tears spilled down his face, making shadowy trails through the fine hairs on her neck. He did not know why he was crying as he lay in Shelly's arms, in her hospital room filled with his flowers. Maybe he was crying for Shelly, or maybe for himself. Maybe he was crying because Paul had brought him here, Paul who had lost control of his bike and maimed his wife. They would never dance again. Shelly's hands stroked through his hair, her arms wrapped around his back as he cried and breathed in the stale hospital smell, the bitterness of medicine.

Sullivan's Chivas was empty and it was full daylight now. Pretty soon someone would show up to tend bar for the day, clean up the mess after the party. Sullivan did not want to see them, Birdheart or Rita, whoever, hungover, making drinks. He rubbed his hand hard against his eyes, his fingers pushing at the sockets. He pulled his hand through his hair, feeling it bristle against his palm. Taking another bullet-shaped bottle of Chivas from the back bar, Sullivan went out into the morning light and climbed into his pickup. His pickup could do ninety-five on a mountain road and Sullivan tried to believe that would ease his pain.

seven

Adam screamed "I want to go! I want to go!" Margaret heard Woody yell "Shut up! You'll wake your mother!"

She threw her arm across the bed and felt the still-folded covers on Woody's side. There was more shouting from the kitchen, the banging of pots and pans, the slamming of cupboard doors. She tightened her eyes to make oil-spot colors appear behind her eyelids and followed the dull ache that spread from the bridge of her nose up to the roots of her hair. Another voice, maybe Lloyd's because it was so deep, said: "Don't you guys have any sugar?"

Margaret focused on the clock. It was 7:26 and there was a party or riot going on in her kitchen. Where would Adam want to go at seven thirty on a Sunday morning and why was he screaming about it? Adam was normally the quiet child; Allison was the screamer. Margaret knew she should go into the kitchen. Instead, she rolled over, burying her head in her hair tangled across the pillow and smelled the smokiness lingering in it from the party last night.

Woody was home. At best he could be trying to make breakfast. He had done that once after a fight, although he could barely boil water. He brought a tray into the bedroom with a burned English muffin, partially cooked bacon, cold coffee, and spilled orange juice. They had laughed about it and Woody had taken her out for a champagne brunch. But if Woody was making breakfast, why was Lloyd there and where did Adam want to go?

Sitting up in bed, Margaret felt the nausea of her hangover rising in her throat. She waited for her eyes to clear. On the night table was a half glass of vodka and diet ginger ale, a drink she mixed last night after Sullivan drove her home and helped her put the kids to bed. Searching in the drawer, Margaret found a bottle of vitamins and some Excedrins. A little hair of the dog. She downed them with the remains of her drink and stepped into the shower.

She put the water on as hot as it would go and stood soaking and sweating under the shower, the water beating on her head and streaming through her hair. There would be a scene and she didn't want to have it in front of Lloyd. Yet more than likely, that's why Woody had him here. She heard someone in the bedroom, pulling open drawers and slamming the door of the closet. She dried herself slowly and wound a towel around her hair turban style, waiting for Woody to come in. She rubbed moisturizing cream into her face to bring back some of the color. She put on her long terrycloth robe.

Adam was sitting in his pajamas at the kitchen table with a glass of orange juice and the cigar box in which he kept his savings. A five dollar bill was centered in the middle of his coins and the two dollar bills Woody saved for him. His money was sorted into stacks of different heights and arranged evenly around the lone five.

"Where's Woody?" she asked. There was coffee on the stove and two empty beer bottles on the counter.

"He's gone. He said I had to stay here and take care of you."

"What?"

"He gave me five dollars toward my pony. He said to take care of you and Allison. I wanted to go." Adam toyed with the bill in the center of his change.

"Where did he go?"

"I donno," Adam said.

"If you don't know, how do you know you want to go with him?" A quart of milk stood open on the counter which Margaret automatically closed and put in the refrigerator. She saw a folded note propped in the dish rack.

"It's man's stuff," Adam said. "You and Allison are girls."

There was a sneer in his voice that made Margaret want to slap him. Instead, she held the note in her hands and looked at her son, feeling sorry for him and angry at the same time. Adam was getting too old to hang out with his mother and sister. Still, he didn't have to remind her of that right now.

Suddenly Margaret was dizzy as the images of the party last night came back to her. Rita and Woody. She tightened the belt on her robe as if to steady herself. What would happen to Adam if Woody left them? Margaret ran into the living room. His chair was there, the pedal steel guitar, the picture over the mantel. But in the little utility room off the kitchen, cabinets were open, piles of gear and laundry were heaped in the middle of the floor. Margaret walked back out to the Morris chair and sat down to read the note.

> *Sweetheart,*
>
> *Things got a little out of hand last night but I guess you can figure that out for yourself. We really ought to talk about this and figure out what we are doing. Lloyd and I are going up to Quartz Lake and do some fishing. Will be gone a couple of days just to have some time to think about this. I guess you should do the same. I've left you the truck so you can get around. If Max calls to bitch, tell him you don't know a thing.*
>
> *Love*
> *Woody*

Margaret read the note over and over, concentrating less on what it said and more on Woody's handwriting. It was almost feminine in its precision. It slanted uniformly to the right, loops in the l's and f's graceful and narrow. It looked like the music he wrote, neat across the staff and spaced like the timing, the eighth, quarter and half notes spaced integrally across the page. When Lloyd wrote music it was just a scrawl, lines scribbled along the staff as mere indications of the tune. Woody's music could almost be heard as it sat on the page, the movement of the notes as precise as the beat.

Fishing my ass, Margaret thought. He's probably at Rita's right now. She went to the phone but did not pick it up. Whether Woody was there or not, Margaret could not imagine speaking to Rita. What would she say, how could she keep her voice smooth?

Margaret walked back into the kitchen, past Adam, whose eyes followed her as she stepped into the utility room. The expensive wicker creel she had given him for Christmas was gone, and the net, the stringer, and his waders. In the front closet she found his sleeping bag and the ice chest gone. In the bedroom she discovered his thermals missing, most of his socks, and his hiking boots. Woody had taken enough stuff for a month. She didn't have to check the refrigerator to know it was probably empty.

Max, the manager of Heart of the West, would know. But as she listened to the phone ring she remembered it was only eight o'clock on a Sunday morning and Max never went to bed before three. Max answered on the second ring, just as Margaret was about to hang up.

"I'm sorry to wake you," she said.

"You ain't the first. What do you want?"

Margaret wasn't sure why she had called. "Have you seen Woody?"

"I don't have visitors at these hours. Lloyd called though. Is that what you want?"

"I don't know."

"I know what you want, Maggie. Don't you guys ever talk?"

Margaret nodded, then realized that wouldn't help on the phone. "Sure," she said. "All the time."

"Well you tell him this," Max said. "I'm going to dock them. Maybe get that Fifties band in for Wednesday and Thursday."

"Wednesday and Thursday?"

"Yes sir," Max said. "I'm going to break them in in case your boys take that tour. They don't think I know about that tour, but I do."

"Wednesday and Thursday?"

"You guys don't talk, do you?"

Margaret was silent, hanging her head, her palm sweating against the black receiver.

Max's voice became softer. "Lloyd said they went fishing up to Glacier. But if you want to know what *I* think, I think they've got a job, maybe down the Bitterroot or up to Flathead. Someplace I won't see them."

"They've gone fishing," Margaret said.

"Then why did you call?"

"All the music stuff is here. They just took fishing gear."

"Then why did you call?"

"I don't know," Margaret said. "I'm sorry." She was silent for a moment, searching for a lie. "He forgot his sleeping bag. I thought I might catch him at your place."

"Well, it's a good thing he forgot his damn bag. Might get him back to work on time, frozen ass or not. You tell him that. I'm going to dock him. And if that band's hot, your boys are out on their asses."

"I'm sorry to bother you," Margaret said.

"Don't mention it. Just don't call again till afternoon. You or any of your friends." Max hung up.

Adam stood in the doorway staring at Margaret as she placed the receiver back in its cradle. She sat in the Morris chair and, surprisingly, Adam crawled into her lap. Adam, who had been going through a don't-touch-me phase because he thought it was girlish. Margaret wrapped her arms around her son and held him close to her for a moment. Adam seemed content in her arms; his small hands played with the terrycloth lapels of her robe.

"Woody's got his sleeping bag," Adam said.

"I know," Margaret said and she held him more closely and began to rock softly against the chair.

"I remember when Daddy left," Adam said.

"You couldn't. You were just a baby. Not even in school."

"I remember you cried and cried. We all slept in the same bed together and you told us stories."

"What brings all this up?" Margaret pulled back from him to bring his whole face into her line of vision.

"If Woody leaves," Adam was working the robe hard between his hands, "would you be mad if I went with him?"

"Jesus!" Margaret said. She laid her head back in the wing of the Morris chair, the towel turban slipping from her wet hair and sliding down her shoulders. "Oh God." She sat back and removed the towel, but did not know what to do with it.

"I'll come see you all the time. Allison too."

Margaret shut her eyes tight and put her head on Adam's shoulder.

Adam continued. "Tommy Apple lives with his dad. He has to go see his mother every week. He says it's not so bad. She cooks good food for him."

"Woody's not your dad."

"Almost. We go fishing and shoot pool. He's spanked me. And he's helping me save for my pony, maybe even a horse he says."

"Oh Adam." Margaret rocked him. "Woody might not be able to take care of you. He has no legal responsibility for you."

Adam pulled away from the circle of her arms. "That's mushy, Mom. This is business. Serious shit. You know."

Margaret straightened and reached over to the end table for a cigarette. She lit it slowly and blew a long line of smoke at the ceiling, carefully avoiding Adam's face. "Who says Woody's going anywhere?" she asked at last.

Adam hung his head and studied the belt on Margaret's robe.

"Come on now. Who says anyone is going anywhere?"

Adam studied the nubs in the terrycloth.

"Come on," Margaret said again, catching his hands in hers.

"Well." Adam would not raise his head. "Nobody *said* anything."

"Then what are you worried about?"

"It's just the same."

"The same as what?"

Adam looked her in the eye. "The same as when Daddy left."

Margaret thought she would cry and took a long drag on the cigarette, making a little hiccupping sound as she inhaled. "But it's not the same, don't you see?"

"I want to go with Woody."

"Don't you want to stay with me and Allison? Allison's your sister."

"I want to be like the guys. I want to go fishing and stuff."

"We go fishing and stuff."

"Yeah, but we go with Woody."

The problem with children, Margaret thought, was that they

grow up and time gets shorter. When Adam was younger a discussion like this could be put off for a day or so, even an hour would do. Margaret could cry and smoke, have a drink, and then be ready with something fine to say to her son. But Adam was growing up and could not be put off for that simple hour. She had to say something to him now and she could not imagine what it would be.

"You worry too much." Margaret tried to force a smile. "And you have an imagination as big as the planet Mars." Adam smiled at her. "I think you made all this up to scare me." Adam looked at her seriously again.

"Listen," Margaret said. She brushed his hair off his forehead with the palm of her hand. "Woody just went fishing. With Lloyd."

"He never gave me five dollars when he went fishing before."

"Oh that. He just wanted to do something nice for you. He'll be back in a day or so and tell you himself. Everything is okay. Just like always." She had ruined it. Adam saw the tears in her eyes.

"Then why are you crying?"

Margaret sniffed and felt small. She hated to tell practiced lies. "Because I don't think you love me."

Adam put his arms around her neck, nestling his head into her shoulder. "I love you, Mommy. Don't cry. If Woody leaves I'll stay here with you and Allison."

Margaret tried to smile but felt guilty. How was she to know when Adam would be old enough for her to express some of her real feelings to him and stop hiding them behind lies and false promises? "It's okay," she said and wished someone could tell *her* that. "You worry too much." She disentangled herself from his arms. "You go play and remember everything is fine. If you're still worried we'll talk about it again, okay?"

Adam said "Sure" and slipped off her lap. "I'm gonna play in the garage," he said. "Woody told me if I cleaned it out we might keep the pony there."

While Allison watched cartoons Margaret sipped vodka and orange juice. If there was a morning to be drinking, she thought, this must surely be it. She had often envied Rita's job, the morning light falling through the one window in front while Amos Espinosa read the paper aloud and ate the danishes Deadeye sometimes brought with the rose. She and Woody had spent a few mornings like that, banded together with the others to make the morning survivable as their hangovers passed easily into mild drunkenness again.

On each trip to the kitchen Margaret looked through the window and watched the growing pile of junk from the garage standing in the driveway. Bicycles, the baby carriage, the torn tarp for the boat Mike had bought before Allison was born. The boat he had sold when he went to Alaska. Adam was doing a thorough job, but Margaret knew they would never keep a pony in that garage.

She searched the house looking for other things Woody might have taken. When she realized his acoustic guitar was gone she felt sure he would never return. Someday she would come home from work and all the big things would be gone: the Morris chair, his footlocker, the pedal steel guitar, and in the front lawn would be the tire tracks of his pickup backed up to the front door.

There was a sign somewhere in these days that Margaret had not noticed and she did not know where to look for it. Rita would know. Rita had known all along. At noon Margaret called, hoping she could hear Rita's phone ring in an empty house. That was a sign she could understand. Rita answered on the third ring.

"Did I wake you?" Margaret asked and in her mind saw pictures of Rita and Woody lying on the bed.

"I was cleaning my aquarium," Rita said. "Are you hungover?"

"To say the least."

"You need a drink," Rita said.

"Maybe we should talk," Margaret said.

"Do you want me to come over?"

"No," Margaret said. She did not want Rita in her house. She wondered if Woody had slept with Rita in her house, or here. "No," Margaret said again. "I'll walk."

"Hell of a long walk for a person with a hangover."

"I'll walk," Margaret said and hung up.

The drink she mixed was over half vodka and much of it spilled on her coat sleeve. It was cold and threatening rain and within two blocks Margaret almost wished she had taken Woody's truck. Somehow, in spite of the cold and a light drizzle, walking seemed better. It gave her time to think, time to play over the pictures of Woody in her head. She saw his glittery eyes again and again, and remembered the night, drunk on his hands and knees, he had laid his head in her lap and cried.

Gradually, she began to remember Mike. Mike laughing. Mike holding the babies. Mike driving them through the country on a spring morning with the sky so blue it seemed iridescent. She still talked to Mike in her mind, the conversations more perfect than those they had had when they were together. In her mind Mike answered the way she wanted him to.

—I've had this guy living with me, you know. Adam is really fond of him and if we split Adam wants to stay with Woody.

—You guys won't split. Woody's into the kids too much. He realizes how they would feel.

—He keeps threatening and now he's done a thing with my best friend.

—Power tripping. Stay on top of it and he'll come around.

Margaret laughed to herself. Mike would never have said any of those things. He'd probably say: 'Let the damn kids go.' He always called them the damn kids. She wondered where Nondalton was in Alaska, the last address she had for him before he went off to work the pipeline. She should have looked it up. Mike used to study maps, imagining the routes in his mind as he daydreamed them around the country. That was ten years ago, Margaret realized. Ten years.

Rita managed to open the door and usher Margaret into the house without really looking at her. " 'Bout time," was all Rita said and then she turned her back to Margaret and walked into the kitchen. "What'll it be?" Rita called as if she were tending bar at Shelly's. "Scotch, Bourbon, White Wine. Or you can start the day with the liqueurs? Grand Marnier. Drambuie."

When Margaret first met Rita she had assumed the large, clear Mason jars full of booze were all stolen from Sullivan. Rita would pour the contents of a chipped or cracked bottle through cotton cloth into a Mason jar. "Part of my job," Rita always said. "Fringe benefits." Still, to Margaret, there seemed something faintly illegal about the Mason jars that were never labeled or kept in any order under Rita's kitchen counter. Rita knew each one and could pick out whiskeys and specific brands by merely looking at them.

"I see you brought your own glass," Rita said.

"Vodka," Margaret said. "I've already started my cure."

Rita picked out a Mason jar, clear like so many others under the counter. "Straight?"

Margaret shrugged.

"I'll give you a twist. And some good stuff. None of that Lewis and Clark rotgut."

Margaret shrugged again. Vodka was vodka.

Rita handed Margaret a drink. She lifted her own glass to make a toast. "Here's to life in the pits."

They sat in the living room, just like all the other times Margaret had sat in Rita's house, talking about the team, planning dinners or trips, passing the time in each other's company.

"The kids are alone," Margaret said. "I can't stay long." She kept looking for Woody or something that belonged to him. Some stamp that he had been in Rita's house. Had spent the night here.

"Precisely." Rita took a shallow little breath and brought her eyes up to look at Margaret's face. They could not hold each other's stare. Margaret thought she heard a bird outside the window and turned to look through the glass. Somewhere in those light green leaves sprouting on dark branches Margaret expected to see a brilliant colored bird in the cherry trees. Not a little brown bird like so many of the songbirds, but a Bird of Paradise, a Magnificent Frigate Bird with the red swelling throat. Rita sang like an eagle, Woody said.

Rita began to laugh. The laugh was long and clear, pure as a birdsong, and Margaret had to smile just at the sound of it. She turned back to Rita, Rita smiling at her and laughing.

"Now this isn't so hard," Rita said. Bruegel hopped up onto her lap. "Kind of funny, huh Bruegel?" She pulled softly on the Belgian hare's ears.

"Funny?" said Margaret, although she was still smiling.

"Us. We're so worried this is some big tragedy."

"We are, huh?"

"You think all this is serious?"

"You damn betcha."

Rita took a sip of her drink. "Do I have to start? Is that part of my official role as 'the other woman'?"

"The other woman," Margaret repeated. "Is he here?"

"He and Lloyd went fishing up to Glacier. He said he thought you and I should try to straighten this all out."

"You been taking orders from Woody long now?"

"Just recently."

"How recently?"

"Come on, Maggie. It was just last night. It was a mistake."

Margaret took a sip of her drink and tried to make her mind totally blank. She wanted no pictures of Rita and Woody. No images of them lying together on a bed, sitting side by side in an auditorium. No pictures, listen to the words. No pictures, listen to the words. She repeated this like a chant.

"This changes a lot of things, you know." Rita sounded businesslike.

Margaret didn't trust herself to say anything. No pictures.

"You, for instance." Rita took a little breath. "You must feel something. Betrayed. Abandoned. I don't know. But you're a serious little bitch and you probably don't think this is very funny."

"I'd like to pull each and every one of your teeth out with a pair of pliers."

"Jesus!" Rita stood, stepped nervously around the room. She picked up a softball and rolled it between her palms. "Let's try this again," she said. "Pretend this is like a therapy session."

"That's the problem," Margaret said. "Remember last winter when I thought Woody was messing with that little twat down at the West? I came over here, to you, my best friend, and I said: 'Rita, I got this problem.' And you listened and we talked and I felt better. You talked to Woody. You kept the kids while I went over to Portland with him when he did those gigs. But I can't talk to you like that now. You are that twat at the West."

"Sour owl shit," Rita said. "We can talk about this. We should. It's the only way we're ever going to get it straight."

"What's to get straight? Am I supposed to doubt you fucked Woody?"

Rita looked straight into Margaret's face as she placed the softball on the coffee table. "No. How do you feel about it?"

"I don't know. Like I want to talk to you and can't. And I can't talk to Woody. But you and Woody can talk. He can tell you to get things straight with me. I hate it." Margaret was surprised at her own words.

"The feeling is mutual," Rita said. "Woody loves you and he fucked me. I'm like his sister and we committed incest. We all have our needs."

"You seem to need an unnatural lot. Or am I supposed to take that as some kind of apology?"

"No apology. That won't help anything. Woody and I did a thing last night. He feels terrible. I feel terrible. You must feel terrible. But he's looking, Honey. If it ain't going to be me, it'll be somebody else. He feels you are driving him away."

Margaret felt her face tighten. "How?"

"The tour. Just go."

"That's blackmail. Emotional blackmail. He's jacking me around to make me go. I would think you would resent being used like this."

"I do. But I'll go with him if you don't."

There were tears in Margaret's eyes. "You can't do this to me."

"You're doing it to yourself." Rita sat next to Margaret and put her arms around Margaret's shoulders. Margaret was rocking, her face in her hands, as Rita held her and murmured in her ear. "That's all right. It's okay. It's all right." Rita's arms were hot. She smelled warm and dark, the mustiness of her body that spent smoky days in a bar, the warmth of being huddled into blankets on a cold night.

Margaret stood and walked to the window, still crying but wanting space between them. She didn't want Rita to see her like this. Rita and Woody. Woody and Adam. 'You cry like a baby,' Mike used to say. 'You are ugly when you cry.'

"Damn!" Margaret said and before she realized what she was doing she had picked up the softball and thrown it against the wall.

The aquarium exploded. Water poured out across the floor. "Oh my god."

Rita ran into the kitchen and brought back a roasting pan to try to catch the water. Margaret stood watching her, unable to believe she had done this. The softball bobbled in the tank as the fish swam frantically across the bottom. "Get more pans," Rita said.

Margaret seemed to be moving in slow motion, out to the kitchen, back into the living room with the pressure cooker and a casserole dish. Rita was trying to net the fish and put them in the roaster. Margaret saw a gourami lying on the floor. She picked it up gently and put it in the roaster, but it floated lifelessly to the bottom. Dempster Dumpster, the procostimus, still stuck to the side of the tank, his gills pumping air, as water dripped down his sides and off his tail.

Water ran off the entire front of the table. The softball had made a perfect round hole but hundreds of cracks spread out from it, leaking water. Rita removed the softball only to find the pulpy remains of the Veiled Angel, a delicate fish she had been raising for over three years. The silver and gold Mono was bleeding, its side torn from the glass.

Margaret was crying as she watched Rita work, netting the fish, even the dead ones or the ones that might be in shock. She put the dead ones along with the Veiled Angel in the casserole dish and put the live ones in the roaster. The Pictus Cat swam madly around the bottom while the New Guinea Rainbow hung motionless above him. Of the eighteen fish, Margaret counted nine dead ones in the casserole dish with the Veiled Angel. Five swam in the roaster while the other four Rita put in the pressure cooker: the Mono, Dempster Dumpster, and two Lyretails.

Rita said nothing as she worked, moving the pots and pans into the kitchen, setting up a filter and aerator, bringing back a mop and a bucket. She handed these to Margaret and took the broken tank into the bathroom. Margaret mopped and sponged at the carpet, seeming only to move more water across the floor, not really getting any of it off.

"Try the vacuum," Rita said as she went to look at her fish again. Margaret pushed the heavy machine across the floor, wondering if she could get electrocuted. It would be just what I deserve, she thought. Just what I deserve.

"Here," Rita said, handing Margaret a drink and a cigarette, lit and burning unevenly along the paper edge. "That's all we can do for now."

"I'll replace it," Margaret said. "All of it."

"You betcha," Rita said. "We'll have to get another tank this afternoon. Feel better?"

"I've killed all your fish."

"Only about half. Fish die," Rita said. "But not generally by being beaned with a softball." She laughed and sipped at her drink.

"You're taking this awfully well. I'd have killed me if I were you."

"We've had enough violence for one day."

"Do you want me to leave?"

"Suit yourself. I'm going to the fish store," Rita said. "At any rate, we've found out how you feel about all this."

"I guess," Margaret said. "What about you?"

"I'll get some new fish and a tank. Maybe some of them will pull through. It won't matter anyhow if I go on that tour with Woody."

Margaret's ears seemed to ring. "Woody ask you to do that tour?"

"Not yet," Rita said. "He wants you to go. But if you don't and he asks me, I'll do it."

"What makes you think he'll ask you?"

" 'Cause I'm working on it. Nothing personal, Maggie, but I got to get my ass out of the bars someday."

"You want my man to do that?"

"No," Rita said. "I wish it had been someone else's man. Or a man that could have just found me."

eight

Sullivan knew Huson Hydraulic was easy to beat, just what the Shelly's Leg women would want to start the season off right. Yet as they gathered in the card room before the game, the women decked out in their maroon and white uniforms, some of them with the sweet scent of perfume coming off their bodies, Sullivan was worried. They looked good, shining like new coins, and the shrill of their high voices bubbled in the air. But to Sullivan, softball wasn't a hitter's or a fielder's game, it was the pitcher and catcher that counted. Maggie and Rita were the team's secret to success. Rita had the ability to sense the way a hitter would go just from her stance in the box. And Maggie had an arm God couldn't stop if she would just concentrate and pay attention to Rita's signals.

Sullivan watched them: Maggie near the door with Edithanne, Rita at the card table with Coker and Miriam. He ran his palm over his head and a sigh came up from him like a cough. He could sense it; their troubles were going to louse up his team. Shelly would have known what to do about this. Sullivan could only coach the playing.

"This year," Coker said, "we ought to get some visual aids."

"We don't want to teach them to play ball," Lolie said, "we want to beat them!" She fussed with her earrings, those perennial gold loops.

"No, No," Coker said. "Stuff to distract them. Signs in the out-field."

"Like SWING BATTA!" Shirley raised her arms as if she were holding a sign.

"CLOSE BUT NO CIGAR!"

"You're all acting dumber than a barrel of hair," Sullivan said. He sat quietly in the dealer's station of the card table, the women fanned out in front of him shifting their weight and pacing so that their spiked shoes made little tapping noises on the concrete floor.

"We'll play better to music," Diane said. "We should set up a stereo. Songs to boost morale. Like 'Hit the Road Jack.' "

" 'I'll Be Seeing You.' "

Coker said: "Maybe a light show to shine in their eyes."

"Christ!" Sullivan said, disgusted by their silliness. "This is a softball game, not a rock concert. Right, ladies? We're going to play some ball, heavy softball. Start this year out proper. Kick their asses!" The women cheered, their soprano voices sounding like screams to Sullivan's ears.

"We need one more thing," Irene, the second baseman, said. "We need a mascot. An emblem or something."

"We've never had a mascot," Miriam said. "Why now?"

"Seven is a lucky number," Irene said. "We need something to show that."

"Oh for Christ sakes," said Rita.

"I got a chainsaw," Lolie said. "Would that do?"

"Sure!" Irene said. "The Shelley's Leg Chainsaw. All right!" She made a ratchety sound in the back of her throat. "Cut 'em up!"

The women began imitating chainsaws and cheering. From out in the bar the men shouted their encouragement. Sullivan noticed Rita smiling, Maggie looking bored.

"All right. Enough. You girls are giving me a hangover and I ain't even drunk yet. We'll get a damn chainsaw when you win this game. Now bust your asses over to that field. We sit here all night won't be no need for no mascot. Move!"

As the women walked into the bar, the men began to applaud.

"I'm giving the girls 8 to 5 to win," Valgaardson said.

"They'll take it 6 to 4." Deadeye looked over the softball field

as if he were eyeing horses on a racetrack. "6 to 4." He nodded
knowingly.

Sullivan kept his eye on Maggie and Rita warming up along the
third-base line. Although he had told them not to practice the sliders in front of other teams, they were practicing them anyhow. He
glanced over to the Huson team, but no one seemed to be paying
any attention. He let them go; it might be their way of working
this out. "You think she's going to be close, huh?"

"Huson looked pretty hot last year," Deadeye said.

"They're always out of shape in the spring," Valgaardson said.
"It's all those clothes. All that warm-up gear Big Bob lets them
wear. Slows them down too much." This point always pleased Valgaardson, as if he had thought it up himself. The Shelly's Leg team
never appeared on the field in more than their thin cotton uniforms. Even in drizzle or a late spring snow. Shelly had always believed the cold made them hustle. "8 to 5," Valgaardson said again.

Sullivan laughed. "I don't see how either of you can afford to bet
this game. I still need the rent and your bar tabs for this month."

"It's 'cause he cheats," Valgaardson said. "Keeps changing the
rules on me."

"I never," Deadeye said. "Same rules all the time. I win. You
lose. Five dollars a point."

"If you win big," Sullivan said, "I'll let you pay his bills too." He
kept watching Maggie's sliders. The sliders had started to take
shape last summer in practice, although they hadn't relied on them
in a game. Nobody could hit sliders; it was like having a secret
weapon. The few that did connect became grounders to third, and
Edithanne would play third this year. Her arm was good and Sullivan hoped she would boost the double plays.

From this angle the sliders looked solid but Sullivan decided he
didn't want them given away in the first game of the season. He
whistled at Rita. She tossed the ball back to Maggie and swiveled to
stare at him.

"You do that to dogs, Sullivan, not me." She turned her back to
him and caught another slider from Maggie.

The umpire blew his whistle as he dusted off the plate. Sullivan
watched as his team moved out onto the field. He wouldn't say any-

thing to Rita and Maggie unless they lost the game. That was the way Shelly would have handled it, quietly over drinks in the bar after the game.

Sullivan kept this team going for Shelly, but could imagine it only by seasons. He knew some year there might not be enough women, or something else might happen. But until then it was a way of conjuring her up in his mind. With a pint of Chivas and a bottle of Maalox, Sullivan would sit on the bench, watching and coaching the women, and sometimes he could hear her voice in the cheers of the crowd. Or she might sit with him in his mind and talk over how the game was going. It had been his secret until the year Rita broke her hand and sat on the bench, listening as he talked to Shelly. Rita hounded him about that, quiet arguments behind the bar when they weren't busy, telling him he needed therapy, that he should get on with his life. Rita was the only woman Sullivan had ever been tempted to strike. She must have sensed that one night when his hands fisted and he became quiet as he tried to contain his rage. She never mentioned it after that, but Sullivan has always been sorry it had to go so far.

The first three innings were stiff and of not much account. The women on both teams looked sluggish to Sullivan, overweight with winter flab. Even Edithanne looked heavy today, Edithanne who had the statistics of a pencil. Maggie looked good on the mound, but her pitches lacked the style of last summer. Maggie could wear a baseball uniform like she was dressed in a tailored suit. The flat buttons ran evenly down her chest, her breasts swelled gently to either side. She always looked tucked in, straightened up, buttoned down as she went through the pitch. The small of her back had fit exactly into Sullivan's palm when they danced.

When Maggie first joined the team three years ago, Sullivan had had a bartender who had been a signpainter for Versharon's Outdoor Advertising Company. Pete. Sullivan could not remember Pete's last name. But he remembered Pete's sketches and the drafts he worked on when things were slow. Pete had wanted to do a billboard of Maggie at the height of her wind-up. He sketched her constantly during the games or when she sat in the bar with

Woody. Pete had a billboard all picked out, one of the Versharon's that had been empty for over a year. It was unlit and in a field south of town. Stolen billboards were stolen billboards. You take what you can get. Pete showed Sullivan the final sketch and asked him only to pay for the paints and materials. In carnival loops and curlicues, burnt oranges and deep wine cranberry reds he had lettered the sign: SUPPORT SHELLY'S LEG BAR AND GRILL, MOTEL AND LAUNDROMAT, LADIES FASTPITCH SOFTBALL TEAM. STATE CHAMPS. Pete claimed there was no reason not to use the full name; he had nothing else to say on the billboard. Most of the space would be devoted to a picture of Maggie, arm back, left leg cocked before stepping down and releasing the pitch. In that stance she would be six feet eight inches tall. Sullivan liked it and gave Pete the money for paints and brushes. They are still in a tool chest under the bar because shortly after that Pete disappeared. Didn't even collect his last paycheck. Sullivan wishes Pete had left him that sketch. The hell with the billboard; there would just be trouble over that. But Sullivan still misses the sketch of Maggie stepping down for the pitch and the fancy letters spelling out the name of Shelly's bar.

By the fourth inning (Huson 2, Shelly's Leg 1), Sullivan's team had struck out three consecutive times: Coker, Miriam, Lolie, then Shirley, who managed to get a single to first base, got tagged out at second on a pop-up of Edithanne's. They were at the bottom of the order and the next two went down swinging, Irene and Diane, the new woman this year. Sullivan sensed the boredom of the crowd and cast a glance around the bleachers at the Shelly's Leg regulars as they huddled in down vests and wool shirts, sipping the official Shelly's Leg softball drink, Tank and Tonic. Tanqueray Gin and Schweppes Tonic with a shot of Rose's Lime Juice. It had been Shelly's favorite drink and before each game she made about ten gallons of it and passed it out in maroon pitchers with a fancy decal that said SHELLY'S LEG LICKS LUNCH, a slogan Sullivan never liked but amused Shelly no end as she coached the softball team and led their fans in cheers. Those pitchers were all lost now, but Sullivan still makes Tank and Tonic and fills large glass bottles, rusty thermoses, or plastic milk gallons for everyone before the games. Even

Deadeye abandons his usual red beer and drinks Tank and Tonic out of an old pickled egg jar, he and Valgaardson sipping through separate straws stuck through holes drilled in the metal lid.

At the bottom of the order Maggie chopped at a high outside ball. From behind Sullivan, Valgaardson said: "They start out tight then they get looser and looser."

"Sounds like a universal law to me," Deadeye said.

Sullivan walked away from them, keeping his eye on Rita, their best hitter at .428 last year. Judy Crow, the Huson pitcher, signaled her catcher for a pitch-out. They threw four balls and Rita walked to first. "Poops!" she called at them as she gave the bat to Coker. "You can't walk us all!"

Coker hit a pop fly to center. A little can of corn.

In the fifth, Irene at second, let a ground ball go through her legs that cost them two runs. Huson 4, Shelly's Leg 1. For the first time Sullivan began to think seriously about how to get his team out of this hole. Huson was just not that tough. His women were asleep on their feet.

"You're playing those positions like a bunch of rocks!" he hollered as they came in at the middle of the fifth. "You," he said to Irene, "we'll have to get you a Seeing Eye dog!" "Chainsaw my ass," he told Lolie. "You look like you been swinging an axe in that box! Don't let them see no light, ladies. Have a little rally!" He sat down and took a pull on his Chivas. He couldn't play the game for them, but he could give them hell about it.

Miriam and Lolie were both on base with grounders when Shirley swung at a wild pitch. Sullivan heard himself screaming "NO!" as the bat connected with the ball and bounced off into right field. Shirley stepped daintily across first, Lolie pulled into second, and Miriam, too heavy to be a good runner, puffed into third.

Sullivan took a hit on his Maalox and cautioned himself against saying anything to Edithanne as she stepped into the box. Edithanne was the nervous type; she would sometimes freeze at the plate, letting pitch after pitch go by as she tried to make up her mind to swing. Some pitchers knew this and could strike her out every time. Judy Crow wasn't one of them, but there was only one down for this inning and Irene would be up after Edithanne. If Edithanne was unpredictable, Irene wasn't. Irene would pop out.

Edithanne waited for her pitch, standing stolidly in the box, not twitching or shifting as she did when she could not decide to swing. Judy Crow pitched a curve that swung out too far. Ball. She pitched the curve again and although the umpire called it a strike, the pitch looked sloppy to Sullivan. Edithanne seemed bored in the box. Judy Crow's third pitch was a fast ball. Edithanne slammed it across the left-field fence. The leaves in the Lombardy poplars rustled. Sullivan could not believe his good fortune. Edithanne was going to make a ballplayer yet. There was this homer and the one against the Duck Inn in the championship last August. Sullivan felt proud of her.

Miriam panted in, followed closely by Lolie, her gold earrings flashing in the sun. Valgaardson and Deadeye slapped each other on the back and cheered. Silent Sam blew a few random notes on his trumpet before falling down the bleachers to land in the laps of Randa and Amos Espinosa. Shirley came in, running daintily. 'I'll play,' Shirley had told him when she joined the team four years ago, 'but I won't slide. My customers wouldn't like the bruises.' In the four seasons since then Shirley should have done some sliding, but preferred to be tagged out. 'Softball don't make me no money,' she would say.

The team lined up along the third-base line to slap hands with Edithanne as she trotted leisurely down the home stretch.

"Nice work," Sullivan said as she rounded third. Edithanne winked at him. It was 4 to 5, bottom of the fifth with only one down.

Irene popped out and Diane struck out. Sullivan decided Diane would need some batting practice if she was to stay on this team. She had a good arm and ran well, but her batting was pretty sorry. Still, batting was in the eye and maybe she could learn.

At the top of the seventh, Huson Hydraulic's third baseman hit a long drive that sent Lolie and Shirley scrambling across the outfield. Lolie fielded it and threw to Irene at second, but the runner was safe. Huson's shortstop hit a grounder to Coker at first. Coker booted it, maybe she was trying too hard on an easy play, but it put another runner on base and a runner on third. Huson's catcher singled to Miriam in deep right, enabling the third baseman to make the tying run. Only one out.

Maggie walked around the mound a moment before facing the next batter. She threw her slider. Strike. She threw another slider. Strike. Rita signaled for a change-up. Maggie threw another slider, but it hit the plate. Still, the batter had taken the swing, so that was two out.

The next batter was one of Huson's best. Rita gave her the signal for the riser. Maggie threw her slider. Strike. Sullivan watched as Maggie threw off each of Rita's signals, but she struck the last batter out in three.

Sullivan took a hit of Maalox. She had struck the batters out; that was all that counted. Still, she should be working with Rita, not against her. Whatever problems they were having, they shouldn't be having them on the field. He did like the look of those sliders, though. But it was too early to use them. If the league teams thought they had to deal with a slider pitcher all season they might start practicing up on them.

Sullivan would talk to her after her turn at bat. As the bottom of the order she would probably pop out. Maggie took a strike but her next swing connected for a nice base hit. Rita, as their best hitter, would pull her around. But Judy Crow pulled another pitch-out on her, four balls outside the box. The fans booed each pitch while Rita played with her fingernails, her bat resting against her thigh.

With Maggie on second and Rita on first, Judy Crow talked and signaled to her catcher endlessly. The umpire called two balls on her for not presenting the pitch to Coker. Trying for a sacrifice fly to move Maggie and Rita along, Coker went down too far on the ball and hit it directly into the third baseman's mitt. Miriam struck out and Lolie popped out, leaving Maggie and Rita on base at the end of the inning.

Rita did not signal Maggie once during the top of the eighth. She positioned herself well behind the plate and let Maggie do the work. Fastball, curveball, slider. Knuckleball, slider, knuckleball. Maggie put the first two women down quick. The first pitch to the third batter was a slider that hit the plate. So was the third. Sullivan called time and walked out to the mound.

"What the hell do you think you are doing?" Sullivan turned to look back at Rita, who rested on her haunches and played with the lacing in her glove. He motioned for her to come forward, to the mound. Rita began readjusting her chest straps.

He looked back at Maggie who was tucking in her jersey, head down. "Do you want me to get Coker in here?"

"Nope. I've got it."

"Bull! You're dropping pitches all over the infield. You're not letting Rita give you the signals. You ain't playing this game by yourself, you know!" Sullivan pushed his cap up and looked back into the bleachers. On the top row sat Woody and Lloyd.

Sullivan changed his tone. "You nervous? Tired?"

"I got it," Maggie said. She looked him in the eye. "Just let me pitch."

"You ain't working with Rita."

"She's not giving me signals."

"You've been ignoring them. Shape up."

Maggie smiled at him and shook out her arm. "Let's get this game over with."

"I'm going to start grooming Coker for this job if you don't get your shit together."

"Let me pitch," Maggie said and fired the ball off to Irene at second.

Sullivan walked back to the sidelines. The batter stepped into the box. Rita signaled for a fastball and Maggie complied, pitching a fastball that connected squarely with the bat. The ball sailed high into the air, a beautiful arc that ended in the palm of Lolie's glove in deep left. Sullivan knew luck when he saw it.

With the score still tied at the middle of the eighth, Sullivan sat quietly in the dugout and finished his pint of Chivas. Shelly had once figured the team scored at least one run in the last inning 63 percent of the time. Sullivan believed it as superstition and let the game play itself out. In the last inning he could always remember Shelly best, the maroon and white jersey tucked into the long striped skirt that came down to her ankle. He expected her to move toward him on her crutches, sit down and ask the score as if she had only been gone for a while. He could smell the sweetness of her perfume on the air and feel the specific pressure of her hand when she would grip his arm in excitement. 'Get down on it, girls,' she would say, and Sullivan believed his team could hear her too.

"You're going to owe me ten dollars," Deadeye told Valgaardson.

"Horse puckey. A tie. No money on ties."

"You watch," Deadeye said. "Ten dollars."

Shirley doubled to second. Edithanne sacrificed to move her to third. Irene hit a long ball deep into left field, bringing Shirley home and putting the Shelly's Leg team ahead 6 to 5. They had won the first one.

"Five dollars," Deadeye said. "Could have been more."

nine

Margaret left the cheering and backslapping of her teammates shortly after they walked the formal line, shaking hands with the Huson Hydraulic women. Judy Crow was the only one to speak to her. "Sliders," she said. Margaret smiled and shook hands and moved on to the next Huson player and another handshake. At the end of the line she walked toward the bleachers, looking for Adam and Allison. Woody and Lloyd were not in sight.

There was no one tending bar at Shelly's. The women were drawing their own beers from the tap while Randa roamed around the back bar mixing a few drinks. If someone handed her some money she placed it on the little shelf above the cash till. "I'm not into making change," she said. "I don't work this side of the bar."

Birdheart, who should have been tending bar, sat at the far end with Sullivan and Amos, taking long pulls on a bottle of tequila. Margaret gave Adam enough change to go play the shuffleboard game with Allison and grabbed a beer before going down the bar to join them. She looked around for Woody; she hadn't talked to him since the party last week.

Tilting back on his stool, Birdheart looped a long arm around her shoulders, hugging her to him in a rough, sloppy way. "Our little pitcher," he said and Margaret detected a definite slur. He lurched against her, bouncing from his hips. "Down in the Malay they got a plant just like you. Little red lip on the top, round little body." Birdheart slapped Margaret on the butt. "Pitcher Plant." He laughed and hugged her again. "Pitcher Plant. Eats insects. Carnivorous little bugger." Margaret tried to draw away from him. "The femme fatale of the vegetative world. Attracts those innocent little bugs with that soft red lip and then burns them up in the acids of her heart."

"Come on," Margaret said. She had seen Birdheart like this before. It never led to any good. "That's not a nice thing to say to the lady that just brought glory to her local bar."

"Oh yes it is," Birdheart said with a smile. "You ate that Huson team like they were bugs in the jungle." He laughed, throwing his head back to reveal his large even teeth. "That's what old Sullivan says."

"Bugs in a jungle?"

Sullivan smiled at her. "I didn't phrase it exactly that way."

"You didn't say it that way at all," Amos said. "As I recall you were bitching."

"Sliders, I bet," Margaret said.

"Bugs in a jungle," Birdheart said.

"Lay off that crap," Sullivan said.

Birdheart glowered at him. "What would you know. You order around a bunch of women." He took a hit from the tequila bottle, disdaining the three empty shot glasses on the bar.

"Let's be a little nice here," Amos said.

Birdheart turned on him. "What for? You're no better than him. All you can do is read a bunch of books."

Margaret tensed, sensing this was not one of Birdheart's better moods. Two or three times a year Birdheart would get mean, surly, and knock around Shelly's and the other places in town until he got his ass thoroughly kicked, which wasn't easy. Birdheart was a big man, hard to take down.

"I think," Sullivan said, "you're being rude to my customers."

"Your customers are a bunch of drunken assholes."

"Now now," Margaret said. "Such talk."

"You stay out of it," Birdheart said. "You are one of those women who don't have enough sense to know when they're well off."

"That's enough," Amos said.

Birdheart took another pull on the tequila. "You've probably dicked her too. You know, over in Nam what they would do with a fat fart like you? They'd put you in a big room or box and begin filling it slowly with water until you just drown. Cold water, old Cong trick."

"There are times," Sullivan said, "when I am tempted to simply shoot you in the face. Aim for your rotten mouth."

"I'd kill you by ramming a rod up your ass until your heart busts."

"Jesus," Margaret said. She began to draw away.

"You gentlemen sound like your conversation needs a bit of civilizing." Rita stood between them, smiling, smelling of jasmine perfume. While the other women would line up at the bar in their uniforms, Rita always showered first in the back of Shelly's Leg. Her damp black hair hung over the shoulders of her lime green sweater. She tossed it back and reached across the bar to take a sip of Birdheart's untouched beer.

He grabbed her arm by the wrist, held it tightly so the fingers dangled and looked broken. Rita twisted her hand, tried to move away. She couldn't shake loose.

"If you were truly civilized you'd buy your own fucking beer." He released her hand solemnly. "Liberated women," he said, drinking the beer off himself, "are only liberated when it's to their own advantage. I ain't been out with a broad yet that would buy my drinks."

"My mother always taught me liberated meant free," Margaret said. "Not foolish."

"Well, I've been generous," Rita said with a look at Margaret. "I let this man sit in my bar all day. Day after day. I give him free drinks by the hour. And he bitches."

"That's not all you give out by the hour."

Sullivan said: "You better not give this man free drinks. He works. He can pay. Nobody should be allowed to be this rude for free."

"He hauls garbage," Amos said.

"I'll tell you who's a bitch," Birdheart said. "I can tell you right now who is a little whoremongering bitch. A pussy-waving hole. A god-damned sewer who lets any man fall into it."

"That's enough," Sullivan said. He hefted his beer bottle with his right hand.

"You ought to know," Rita said. "You been there."

Birdheart laughed again. "Indeed I have. Oh yes." He took another hit off the tequila and leaned over to Rita as if to speak to her confidentially. "If I was going to kill you, I'd give you leprosy. Watch that ugly little Indian face of yours, your pussy too, peel off your bones like scaling a fish."

Margaret saw Woody come through the back door.

Rita leaned toward Birdheart, her chest out, her back straight. "Any particular reason for you being such an asshole today?" she asked. "You got an excuse for being on the rag like this?"

Birdheart moved quickly. All in one motion he grabbed one of the empty shot glasses from the bar. Not breaking that momentum, he caught Rita on the left side of the face, the glass encircled in his fist.

Margaret saw it all in slow motion, strange music in her ears. Woody running the length of the bar. Rita smiling, her lips slightly parted, as she floated to the floor, her arms thrown back from her body, loose as a doll's. Her shoulder, her arm, knocking against the side of a chair, toppling it over as her head hit the linoleum.

Sullivan pushed Birdheart off his bar stool and across the short space to the wall. He clubbed Birdheart with the glass bottle just above the ear and dropped the bottle to bring his fist back and into the point of Birdheart's chin. Blood, a dark line of it, slid across Birdheart's left eye.

Woody pulled Sullivan's arm out of the second punch and landed his own first in the hollow of Birdheart's jaw. Woody grabbed Birdheart by the shirt front and dragged him toward the door, pushing him out into the parking lot.

"Code of the West," Amos said as he knelt beside Rita and gently extracted her legs from the litter of the broken chair. Rita moaned. "There there," Amos said. "Don't tell me that wasn't exciting."

Rita rested in the circle of Amos's arms as he stroked her hair gently with his big hand. Randa handed him a shot of bourbon and some ice in a bar rag. "Make her drink that," she said. "Only cure for a punch in the jaw."

"Oh no. Don't," Diane said. "You might go into shock." She seemed to be fluttering around the edges of the group, dancing from one foot to the other.

"Nonsense," Randa replied. "When you've seen this more than once it's not so complicated. Put that ice on her cheek, Amos."

Amos daubed gently with the rag at the corners of Rita's face. She smiled at him. "You sure do know how to treat a lady," Rita said. With a little shudder she finished off the shot and took the rag from Amos. "My daddy was a boxer," she said. "He told me bruises gives a face character."

"Do you think it will bruise?" Margaret asked.

"What does it matter," Randa said. "If it bruises, he'll just have to remember it longer."

"Somebody better take him home," Rita said.

"Maybe we'll get lucky and someone will park their car on him."

"Remember when we left him tied up on the median?"

"But the best was when we dumped him in the Clark Fork." There was laughter now, nervous giggles from the women and deeper, heartier laughter from the men.

"Somebody better take him home," Rita said again.

Sullivan said: "I don't want him back in here until he's sober. And I don't want him out in my parking lot."

Deadeye laughed. "No one else wants him either."

Sullivan sucked the knuckles of his right hand. He turned to Woody. "Next time," Sullivan said, "I want to punch somebody out, I'm not going to be stopped by somebody like you. It's not your fight."

"You can't let him go around punching women."

"It's none of your business," Sullivan repeated. "Remember that."

"Don't start telling me what to do."

"Don't you think we've had enough fights for one day," Rita said.

Valgaardson spoke up: "I should think you've had *your* fair share."

"Stop this," Coker said. "You're just making all this worse."

"Don't worry, honey," Randa said. "Why don't some of you boys go load him up in something and take him to our house. We'll take care of him."

"You," Amos said. "I'd rather take care of Rita here."

Randa moved through the circle surrounding Amos and Rita. She bent over and peered closely at Rita, lifting the rag and looking at her cheek, deepening now from ivory to a light liver color.

"I'll be more interesting looking with a black eye," Rita said.

"You'll be fine," Randa said. "Sullivan, you get this girl drunk. Be the best thing for her."

"I ain't serving her on the floor," Sullivan said.

"Come on," Margaret said. "Let's sit over here." She offered Rita her hand as Amos guided her unsteadily to her feet.

"My daddy always said to keep your eyes above the punch. I never knew what he meant until now."

Amos seated Rita as if she were in a fancy restaurant. "Pretend you ladies are having tea."

Margaret pulled up a chair. "Nice. Real nice," she said.

"You ain't supposed to understand them," Rita said. "If you're smart, you stay out of the way."

"You just got to learn to duck," Amos said. "I'll be back. You just get a little drunk here." He gave Rita a kiss on the brow and then went over to the bar and pulled a bottle off the shelf. With a wave to Sullivan he followed Randa out the door.

Woody set three drinks on the table and handed Rita a clean rag with some ice. "You don't want to be nursing your cheek with a rummy rag," he said.

"When I was a little girl on the Res. I believed women had signs." She pointed to her cheekbone under her left eye. "Some of the women had little scars right here. I believed those women were signaling to each other with those scars, telling which of the men were bad. Women-beaters. If a woman had a man who beat her, then she would wear this little scar under her eye. I thought they were decorative, like freckles on white girls. It was so the other women would know not to mess with that dude, that he was a bad ass." She played with the rag at her cheek. "I wish I could believe

that they were just signs. Like I believed white girls took off their freckles at night. Just signs. Not cuts from rings or broken glasses."

"What did you do to piss him off?" Woody asked.

"I imagine you know," Margaret said. "You might say you're the primary cause."

"What an open mind you have," Woody said.

"We should form a terrorist group of wronged ladies," Margaret said. "Jilted ladies. Beat-up ladies. Fucked-over ladies. Teach you bastards a lesson."

"They'll never learn," Rita said. "We could blow up the whole US Army and they'd just wonder why there's nothing for dinner."

"I'm going to call it GILA," Margaret said. "The Grand Imitation Liberation Army. We'll sign all our communiqués with lizards."

"That ought to be fun," Woody said. "I can see you now, taking dynamite caps and brass wire from the spice rack over the stove. Reading directions for Molotov Cocktails out of the *Joy of Anarchy*."

Margaret wasn't sure how it happened. She sat with her hands curled around a tall bourbon ditch. She was not tense, her arms and legs ached only a little after eight innings. This was the first time she had seen Woody since the dinner last week. Since the last time they sat in this bar. She watched his eyes, still looking at the surface. Margaret could see nothing behind the glittery eyes, eyes that could have been staring at either herself, the woman he lived with, or Rita, the woman he . . . Margaret's mind withdrew from that question as it had all week long. She remembered the swing of his arm as he pulled Sullivan away from Birdheart and the force of the punch he landed on Birdheart's jaw. Margaret was as surprised as anyone when her fingers curled around the glass, raised it quickly and backhanded the full drink into Woody's face.

"Christ!" He sputtered, pushing back in his chair, standing now before the table watching the bourbon soak into his madras shirt, the colors bleeding down the front of his chest, little runs of alcohol dripping off his beard. "Jesus Christ!" He flopped his hands in the air a couple of times. His hands, so well formed. His fingers clattered at his side.

Woody looked at her with nothing in his eyes and began stroking his chest like soothing a cat, wiping softly, rhythmically, at the stain growing on his shirt. His fingers splayed, his cheeks shining and dripping as Margaret's bourbon ran off his face, his beard clumped together in vertical lines capped with clear drops.

Margaret could see nothing in his face, no emotion, not even noticeable interest in what had just happened. He seemed to be looking at something just behind her facial bones, studying it as something completely foreign. Woody blinked a few times and walked over to the bar.

Margaret began to make a water flower on the table, setting her glass on the rim of the last circle, carefully, until she had a full pattern in front of her. She felt too surprised to be sorry. Just as with Rita's aquarium, nothing seemed premeditated about it. She could feel Rita looking at her. She heard Sullivan laugh, the heels of Woody's cowboy boots as he returned to their table, a bar rag in his hand.

He mopped absently at the bourbon on the table. He wiped up the water flower with regular, symmetrical sweeps of the cloth.

Margaret was trying to apologize but the words would not come. She felt it was Woody's turn to say something, to explain his part in all this. But Margaret knew he wouldn't. She knew she should say something or laugh, but she didn't trust her voice.

Woody sat down and finished his drink. As he set the glass down on the table, he leaned back in his chair and looked at them. He smiled, the one move Margaret didn't expect. "Getting a little arrogant, aren't you, Maggie?"

Margaret watched his eyes, saw nothing.

"You know," Woody said, "throwing a drink in your lover's face isn't exactly a nice homecoming." He smiled again and tipped his chair back on its heels.

"Sleeping with my best friend isn't exactly a nice going away present."

"You might be right there," Woody said. "But I did some thinking up in Glacier. Lloyd and me planned it, just a short little tour before your kids start school. A big camping trip and then we'd come back. I thought that might suit you and we could both

be happy. But then I come back to town and I see you and Rita
aren't working together on the field. I see Birdheart punch Rita in
the face. Terrible thing to do to a woman. I sit down to talk to you
and you throw a drink on me." Woody wagged his finger at her.
"Not good."

Woody picked up his glass, in his fist, the way Birdheart had.
"Maybe there is no way to make you happy. Maybe I will quit
trying."

Margaret found her voice. "I'm sorry. Look. I didn't know I was
doing it."

"I don't hang around with people who don't know what they're
doing."

"It was a mistake," Margaret said.

"I'm sure it was a mistake," he said, "but not the kind you
think." He turned and smiled at Rita. "Maybe you'd feel better if I
took you home."

"That," Rita said, "might be a real mistake."

"I don't think so," Woody said. "I think you need someone to
take you home and I think I'm just the fellow to do it."

"No," Rita said. "Not now."

"Please," Margaret said.

Woody shook his head at her and placed his hand on Rita's
shoulder. "What do you want to drink, Love? I think Sullivan will
stand us to a bottle."

"No," Margaret said. "No. Wait."

"Too late, Sweetheart. The tune's been called. All we do now is
finish the dance."

"I didn't mean it," Margaret said. "I don't want you to go off."

"Save the begging," Woody said. "Try to keep from embarrass-
ing yourself."

Margaret's eyes filled with tears. "Please," she said. "Don't. At
least until we've talked."

"We'll talk," Woody said. "But right now me and Rita are in-
jured parties. We have to go lick our wounds."

"Christ, it was only a drink. You'll live."

Woody stood over Margaret, his eyes flitting over her features for
a long moment. Then he leaned down and kissed her on the

mouth, his hand cupped behind her head, the kiss warm and powerful. He straightened, but his hand stayed on her hair.

"Maybe this will work things out. You think about it. When you want me, call me at Rita's."

"You don't have to go to Rita's. Please, come home."

"No," Woody said. He gave her hair one last lingering pat and turned back to Rita. "Are you coming or are you going to give me some kind of loyalty crap?"

Rita stared at the table. "Take me home," she said. "There's nothing else for it now."

ten

Men must have a different sense of timing, Margaret thought. Or maybe they have no sense of time at all. She watched Allison pick the black olives off her last piece of pizza, setting them carefully aside. Allison saved all her black olives for dessert. She ate them in one big handful when the pizza was gone.

There had been no call from Woody. Three days now. He had been there; Margaret knew that because she checked through his clothes each day when she came home from work. At least he has the decency to not leave me stacks of dirty laundry, she thought.

She expected Woody to simply show up, or at least call. That Sunday night after the game Margaret had listened for the sound of his boots on the porch, dreamed of his footsteps as she slept. Monday she made dinner for the four of them, but there was no word from Woody. Same on Tuesday. Tonight Margaret had given up and ordered a pizza. She sipped her drink and watched her children. They had been quiet and suspicious these last few days, asking no questions, but looking at her with questions in their eyes.

Maybe it was better to let Woody go off with Rita. Maybe she and Woody were traveling separate paths. Rita was free to roam the entire country if that's what they wanted to do. Margaret wasn't free, that was all there was to that. She couldn't pretend Adam and Allison could be hauled around the country like amplifiers, microphones, electric pianos, and pedal steel guitars. There were people who had done that: carted their children around in the backs of vans, camping to save money on motels, going vegetarian, and trying to educate their children without the benefit of schools. Margaret had read about those people, leftovers from the late Sixties, and the children they raised. She remembered one little girl particularly. A commune child who had managed to build a room of her own. While the rest of the children ran wild over the Kentucky hills, this little girl spent her time furnishing her room much the way Margaret's mother had furnished a room for Margaret: a frilly dressing table cut in the shape of the top of a heart, flounces around the fourposter bed, dolls lined up along the windowsill waiting for tea. Margaret could see this little girl clearly. Polka dot and gingham dresses instead of the all-purpose blue jeans. Ribbons in her hair, hair that she brushed one hundred strokes each night. And she saw the girl's mother, braless and wearing men's thermal underwear, surrounded by manuals that had the word *People's* somewhere in the title. Maybe the woman had learned to be a plumber or was trying to make her living selling macramé.

I'm old-fashioned, Margaret thought. The Sixties drifted right over me. I didn't blow up any buildings. I have no radical ideas about raising children. I let Mike lead me around like a pampered dog, run my life as if it were his instead of my own. She watched Adam wordlessly clear the table and her eyes followed him as he moved off to the living room. She heard the noise of a TV gunfight.

When Margaret was six months pregnant with Adam, she and Mike had taken a trip to San Francisco to visit friends. Stoned on the best 'organic' to honor Margaret's pregnancy, they lay naked on a dirty rug watching the light of the day fall through madras curtains and listened to music. Mike and his friends dropped 'windowpane' and rubbed Mazola oil on each other's bodies. The round dome of Margaret's belly shone in the California light and the women and men took turns rubbing their hands over it, making circles with their palms and feeling the warmth and movement of the unborn child. A long-titted woman placed herself over Margaret so that the slope of her oiled breasts glided over Margaret's taut belly. This frightened Margaret, but Mike held her hands and told her to be cool, to go with the flow, that this was love. Margaret felt pinned to the floor, Mike holding her wrists as she lay in the center of a circle of naked, oiled people. Mike's friend Greg worked up an erection and placed it inside Margaret's dry canal. She cried, begged Mike to make him stop, to get her out of there. "He won't come," Mike had said, as if that was all that mattered. Flat on her back, Greg knelt over her, crooning "This is life, man. I can feel it." She wished for a gun to shoot them all in the very spots where they lay or sprawled around the room. Her mother had never had to suffer this. The long-breasted woman held Margaret's ankles as Margaret cried and begged them to stop. Each man put his erection into her body, held it reverently and felt the life inside her.

By the next morning Margaret was determined to get a divorce and go to a home, like one of her girlfriends in high school, to have her baby. Mike pleaded with her, apologizing for his behavior and the desires of his friends. They were leaving San Francisco at Margaret's demand, and as they stopped for a light in the Haight district, Margaret saw a backpacking hippie couple loitering at the corner to change the diaper on their child.

She screamed at Mike: "Do you see that! Do you see that! Do you want me to do that on a street corner? Do you want your kid to be fed in bus stations, to sleep on the ground?" Mike bought this house when they returned to Montana.

Woody had never put her through anything like that. But Woody had slept with Rita, her best friend. Woody was probably living with Rita right now. She would have to talk to Woody, make him understand. It's funny, she thought. Woody and I have never talked about this tour. Or Rita. We have only argued.

Margaret shook her head and watched her kitchen curtains swim before her eyes. So simple, she thought. So god-damned simple. I'll go talk to Woody. Straighten all this out. Timing. A man's sense of time. While I have been waiting for Woody to come home to me, he has been waiting for me. It was like with Mike and the decisions she had had to make for him. So simple. It explains everything. Everything.

Margaret slopped more bourbon into her glass and asked herself how drunk she was. "Can we get down to Heart of the West in one piece?" She seemed to be speaking to the kitchen sink. "Should we walk?" She sipped at her new drink. "Bad strategy," she said. "Take a cab. Have some class." She looked at the clock, both fuzzy images of it floating against the wall. "A cab," she said again. She squinted her eyes to bring the clock back into focus. Eight o'clock, more or less, she figured. Woody would be at work in an hour.

She went into the living room, pausing a moment in the doorway to look at Allison, who was busy with a coloring book, and Adam, who was dealing himself a game of solitaire. Pictures moved smoothly across the television's face. A foreign language seemed to drift in the air.

"You have a choice," Margaret said slowly, so they could hear each word. The children looked up at her, long, serious expressions on their faces.

"Either," she said, holding up one finger, "you can go to bed right now, or," she held up another finger, "you can be good."

"Aren't we being good?" Allison asked.

"Of course," Margaret said. She smiled.

Allison seemed satisfied with that answer and turned back to her coloring book. Margaret realized she would have to explain a little more clearly.

"I have to go out," Margaret said and she noticed Adam still staring at her. "I was just wondering if I should put you to bed first."

"Where are you going?" Adam asked.

"What would Woody say to that?"

Allison looked up. "Timbuktu," and she giggled.

"Right," Margaret said. "You kids will have to take care of yourselves. How about that?"

Allison's eyes brightened while Adam began to look worried. "Can we stay up late?"

"You can go to bed whenever you want."

Adam bent back over his card game.

After watching them for a moment Margaret began to have second thoughts. "You'll be all right, won't you? You won't do anything bad like try to light the stove or something?"

Adam looked up at her. "I'll take care," he said. "Just like Woody told me to."

Margaret fled back to the kitchen. She knew she should say something to Adam but hadn't the heart for it right now. While she was dialing for the cab she noticed Adam herding Allison into the bed-room.

She sat in the Morris chair, trying to organize her thoughts and to phrase some speech for Woody. The television pictures drifted before her eyes and the sound still seemed to be some foreign language, although if she concentrated she knew it was English, a commercial for dogfood. She couldn't think of anything to say to Woody. There seemed to be no beginning to her thoughts.

It was this house, that's what was wrong. Margaret felt she couldn't breathe in Mike's house, filled with Woody's gear. Her own home was suffocating her, muddling her mind. She sipped at her drink. She wanted to go to some clean and anonymous place. Some place where the memories of Mike and the sight of Woody's stuff would not overwhelm her. She just wanted to think for a while in some distant place so that her thoughts would be clear. Then she would go see Woody.

She decided to go to a motel. As simple as that, check into a motel. She would check out when she knew what to say.

By the time the cab arrived Margaret was dressed in her best velvet pants and the leather coat Woody had given her for Christmas. In her flight bag was a mostly gone bottle of bourbon and a carton of cigarettes. She kissed Allison and Adam and told them to be good. She asked the cab driver to take her to the Holiday Inn, where she registered as Margaret Pedersen, from New York, the name and identity she had had as a child.

The walls were white and the rest of the room was done in shades of blue. Blue tapestry curtains hung over the windows, a matching spread on the double bed in the middle of the room. Across from the bed on a low Mediterranean piece sat a big color television set, chained to the wall like a large sleeping animal. Perfect, thought Margaret. Just like any other motel room in America. And in the morning a maid will come clean up after me and the room will look perfect again, day after day. Even the faked scrolls on the Mediterranean piece pleased Margaret. Mediterranean, she had once read, was the most popular American furniture style.

She got ice from the machine down the hall and made herself

another drink in a plastic cup. Kicking off her boots, she sprawled across the bed and stared at the blank television. Maybe she could just stay here until her thoughts cleared. She could go home and put the children to bed then. If her thoughts were in order she could talk to Woody any time.

In an anonymous place like a Holiday Inn, Margaret was sure she would come to some decision. A decision that would be right for all of them. For herself, her children. For Rita. For Woody. With an immense sense of relief Margaret believed some perfect knowledge would come to her here.

Woody called this the 'Hour of the Wolf,' when those fears you can't face are suddenly staring you down. There's no place to go then, though everyone tries to hide. Margaret remembered a woman she had known when Mike was still at home. Susan. Susan's husband was having an affair and Susan faked a nervous breakdown in the hope her husband would feel sorry for her. She checked into a hospital. But with his wife in the hospital, the husband had more time for his lover. Once Susan realized her plan had backfired she began picking up the shreds of her life and tried to determine what new angle to attack it from. Susan learned in the hospital that there was no hiding.

Could the problem be as simple as Woody made it sound? Could they tour for a month or so and come back to what they had left? A month or six weeks on the road, staying up late to hear the same music over and over again, spending the days on the highway listening to the idiotic chatter of Lloyd and Chuck. And what about Margaret and her softball, the only thing she felt was uniquely hers? She felt that was the only time people seemed to notice just her, standing on the mound ready to strike the batter out. And she would lose her job at the printing plant. "What about that, Woody?" she said to the air in the room. "That's money. Don't tell me we don't need money."

'You and Woody are not fighting about a band tour,' Sullivan had told her. 'You both want to be the power.' She would call Sullivan. He would know what to do.

Margaret took a slug straight from the bottle and felt her mouth go numb as if she had been sucking on ice. When Deadeye answered the phone she heard laughter in the background.

"What do you want?" Deadeye said. "This is a private party."

"Hello," Margaret said. "Is Sullivan there?" She heard the phone drop and Deadeye shout above the bar noise.

"What can I do for you?" Sullivan said.

"Talk to me."

"Who is this?"

"It's me," Margaret said. "The lady who wants to be the power."

"Why don't you come down and have a drink and we'll talk about it."

"I'm hiding."

"You can't be too well hidden if I have you on the phone."

"I don't know what to do, Sullivan," Margaret wondered if this was true, or if she had the answer spinning somewhere in her mind but just couldn't recognize it.

"I thought you were the lady who told me she had to save her own life."

Margaret sighed. Maybe this was one way of doing it.

"Where are you?" Sullivan asked again.

"I'm hiding."

"Yeah," Sullivan said. "But where?"

Margaret spoke as if she were playing a game with Allison. "I won't tell."

"Maggie." Sullivan sounded impatient. "Is Woody with you?"

Like watching a movie, Margaret saw Woody squatting beside Rita at the party, his back to her and his elbow on Rita's thigh. She could see everything, the creases in his jeans, the way his hair lay across the back of his neck. She blinked hard to try to put the pictures away from her mind. She began to see other pictures, the freckles on Woody's back. "Right now," she said, straightening her shoulders, "Woody is probably sticking his dick into Rita's hot box."

"You can't argue with the truth, can you?"

Margaret's body slumped as if the air had gone out of it. She felt tears welling in her eyes and sniffed loudly into the receiver.

"You know," Sullivan said, his tone more kindly now, "if this was a hundred years ago, you would be sitting on a divan by a window. There'd be this little lap desk across your knees and you would be writing this long, mournful letter and decorating the inked pages with big, fat teardrops."

"If this was a hundred years ago," Margaret said, "it would be fashionable to die of a broken heart."

"Broken hearts have never been in fashion. They have always been a pain in the ass."

"What am I going to do, Sullivan?"

"I'd say you're just lonely and sad. Do you want me to come by?"

"I'm not home," Margaret said. "I'm hiding."

"I know that. But where?"

"Cleveland." It was the first word in her head. "I'm hiding."

"Where are the kids?" Sullivan's tone was more abrupt.

"You got to call Woody for me. I shouldn't have left the kids alone."

"Listen," Sullivan said. "I'll come get you. Where are you?"

"I want you to make Woody go home."

Sullivan was quiet for a moment and Margaret wondered what he was thinking. She looked at the phone and imagined his face, framed by his baseball cap.

"I'll do that," Sullivan said at last, "if you will let me come get you. We don't want anything to happen to you."

"Nothing will, Sullivan," Margaret said. "Nothing ever will." With her index finger she depressed the clear plastic button. There was absolutely no sound, which seemed to Margaret different than silence.

"You see, Sullivan," Margaret tipped her head back so that the tears ran into the corners of her eyes, "it's more complicated if you are in love with someone who is alive." But the truth of this bothered her. In many ways being in love with his memory of Shelly must be in some way like her feelings for Mike. She still believed she could walk back into Mike's life at any time. Not that he could walk into hers, open the door to the house he had bought and step into the living room filled with Woody's chair, his music, the pedal steel guitar. But she believed she could walk into Mike's life. She could take the children up to Alaska and say: 'Here we are.' That must be the reason she didn't want to send Adam and Allison up there. It would be as if she were saying: 'I'll be along shortly. Get ready.' She didn't know why, but Margaret clung to this idea even though there had not been one word from Mike in four years. It was just a feeling she had. Someday she would be standing on the mound waiting for the batter and she would look up and see Mike sitting in the bleachers. He wouldn't come to the house. He would just find her out there on the ball diamond, even though she had not played ball when they were married. He would find her in her own place. A place apart from Woody.

Margaret stretched out on the bed and folded her hands over her breasts as if she were a corpse lying in state. Maybe you only fall in love once in your life. Maybe she had fallen in love with Mike and was trying to repeat those feelings with Woody. They looked very different, Mike dark, Woody a rusty blond. But their spirits were the same. The traveling. The desire to see new places. And what they wanted from her was the same, a base, a home.

She got up quickly and placed her leather coat over the phone as if afraid it could see her thoughts. She made herself another drink and paced in her motel room, running her hand along the smooth plastic finish of the furniture.

Maybe that was why she would not have Woody's child. Adam was Mike's child, Allison her own. There seemed to be no room in her heart for any more. Some part of her had closed up somehow and Woody would have to be Woody, not a replacement for Mike. She couldn't do the things with Woody she had done with Mike. No more miles of empty traveling, their only home some suitcases strewn across the back of a van. No more children to chain her to the house just because some man wanted a son. Things had to be different with Woody or else she would be stuck.

But she might be stuck alone. She could always picture herself in bed with Woody, as if she were standing in the doorway to the bedroom observing the couple on the bed. She could see the way her hair fell across her forehead as she dozed to the sound of Woody's voice, his soft, beautiful voice, as he read to her the current bestsellers, the journals of Lewis and Clark. She could see herself making love with Woody, her hands on his shoulders and naked back. Memories of Mike in bed were of his sleeping, his mouth slightly open like a child's. More often in her mind Mike was standing or walking, driving the van, in his flannel shirts and heavy logger boots. She remembered Woody naked and playing, scratching his belly and laughing.

She took a drink straight from the bottle, then another sip to finish off the fifth. Sliding down on the bed, she placed her hands between her thighs, her forearms along the V of her belly. She wanted Woody to walk in, put his arms around her and warm her from on top. Her hands closed over her pelvis, making her belly hot. She opened her thighs and slipped her hands under the waistband of her pants. It was pleasant, the pressure of her hands caught against her body, trapped beneath her clothes. Woody had taught her to masturbate, a generous, courtly gesture she always thought. Moments after he came he would roll back to her and place his hand in her crotch, playing with her tiny clit through the long pubic hairs. He would rub her with two fingers. He placed the cool, dry palm of his other hand flat on her belly. He massaged her, following her own rhythms, building with her until she could no longer move.

They had done this together and Margaret thought of masturbation that way, a communal act. She felt sorry for women who had learned to masturbate alone; the isolation of the act always bothered her. Fully clothed in the motel bed, Margaret touched herself, imitating Woody's strokings. She knew it was not the same. She felt cold beneath her shoulderblades where Woody's hands should have been. Rocking and moaning to herself, her hands worked busily against her body. She felt her frustration building, the sure knowledge that alone she could not come. There was a bone creaking in her wrist, her heart racing against herself.

Sliding her pants down off her ass, she reached for the empty bourbon bottle. It was cold and she held it tightly between her thighs, working the smooth sides against her sweating legs. She teased herself, waiting for her body to open, for her muscles to ex-

pand and contract of their own. At last she pushed the neck of the
bottle up inside and remembered high school stories of girls who
had broken Coke bottles, leaving shards of glass and ragged-edged
cuts along the soft vagina.

When she stopped, it was because she believed she was tired. Her
arms ached and her shoulderblades were still cold. Withdrawing
the bottle, she studied the whitish mucus on the neck. The room
smelled like sex and antiseptic. Her fingers smelled musty.

This is what motel rooms are for, Margaret thought. "Self-indul-
gent crap," she said aloud. "Low-rent rendezvous."

She threw away the bottle and washed her hands. After she rearranged her clothes neatly on her body, she studied herself in the
mirror as if checking for something missing. "Ain't going to solve
nothing this way," she said to her reflection in the mirror. She removed her coat from the phone and dialed home.

Woody answered on the second ring. "Where are you?" he said.

"This isn't going to solve anything," Margaret said. She could
see herself in the mirror, the phone flowering at her ear like a
growth.

"Where are you?" Woody repeated.

"What are you doing? Is Rita there?"

"No. No. Sullivan called. He was worried."

"Somebody should be. Things are a mess."

"Are you in trouble?"

Margaret looked around the room. All the troubles in a place like
this would have to be imported. She wondered what had happened
in this room last night, what would happen in here tomorrow.
"How are the kids?" she said.

"They're fine," Woody said. "They were having a great time
until I showed up. Sullivan was telling them stories. Where are
you? I know you're not in jail."

"How do you know that?" It amused Margaret to think of herself in jail. She wondered if Woody had called the hospitals too, or
if jail was just his logical conclusion.

"I called," Woody said. "They asked if I wanted to put out a po-
lice bulletin on you."

"I'm in Cleveland," Margaret said.

"Cleveland?"

"Sure. Ever been to Cleveland? Things look much different in Cleveland."

"Maggie, please. I want to come get you. Bring you home. This is no way for us to be acting."

"Okay. So I'm not in Cleveland."

"Come on. Tell me where you are and I'll come get you." Woody sounded as if he were in a hurry.

"And then go right out again. In that case I'm better off in Cleveland."

"Cut the Cleveland crap." Woody's voice was rising. "We'll stay right here. Things will be fine."

Margaret lit a cigarette and said nothing. Her fingers still smelled musty.

"Maggie? Are you there?"

"I'm here."

"Then talk to me. Tell me what's the matter."

She was amazed Woody could ask a question like that. "Everything's the matter," she said. "You. Me. Rita. Adam."

"Adam? What's the matter with Adam?"

"Nothing," Margaret said. "Nothing at all. Except if you leave us he wants to go with you." She felt small and wished she could bring that statement back. Using the kids was emotional blackmail.

"That's nonsense. I can't take him, just him."

"I know."

In the long silence Margaret searched for some word to erase what she had said about Adam. It was one thing for Adam to speak directly to Woody, altogether another thing for her to have done it for him.

Woody asked: "Are you with a man?"

"Would that make a difference?"

"Yes." He was quiet for a moment. "No. I'll still come get you if you want. I don't want to hurt you, Maggie."

"But you already have."

"Enough," Woody said. "Let me bring you home. We'll get it straight. I promise." Woody was begging.

"Okay," Margaret said. "Come get me." She felt tired, as if she had done something very physical.

"That's better," Woody said. "Where are you?"

"The Holiday Inn."

"I'll be right there." He hung up quickly.

"Woody?" Margaret felt her heart racing. "I love you."

eleven

It seemed to always happen on the nights when Woody came home late from work, so late the birds had started singing during that darkest hour right before dawn. Heart of the West closed three hours ago.

On those nights when Margaret heard Woody let himself into the house she awoke from the same dream. In her dream the sun was shining, music drifted through the air. Dozens, maybe hundreds, of couples ambled off toward the horizon. Each couple strolled slowly, hand in hand, to the strains of soft melodies. Everyone was rich, young, beautiful, and in love. She and Woody acted like adolescents in a soft-focus movie, walking barefooted along some beach. Sometimes the frame would freeze and she and Woody looked like a sentimental California poster. Margaret felt euphoric and knew her life would never end. As if in a fairy tale, everyone would live happily ever after. Then she would hear Woody let himself into the house, feel his body as he crawled into bed next to her.

"Jamming," Woody would say. "Trying out some jazz." Her dreams would flash behind her eyes and Margaret would fall back asleep, depressed. Two hours later when she got up to get ready to go to work the dreams and her suspicions fused. The dreams seemed dirtied and the suspicions seemed real. Some mornings she found herself crying.

"What's with you?" Woody would say, turning over to her and gathering her in his arms. "What's the matter?"

"I think I've become allergic to you," Margaret told him one morning. "Maybe it's that new perfume you're wearing."

"Perfume?"

"You smell different at night."

"You're just being paranoid. Suspicious."

Margaret looked into his pale eyes. "Should I be?"

Woody rolled away from her and pulled the blankets up around his shoulders. "Yes."

In the paste-up room in the back of the printing plant Margaret had plenty of time to think. The presses rocketed all day, the big press pounding out a rhythm that had always sounded to Margaret like the words 'Wolf Point Wolf Point.' But lately as the thumping press beat Margaret's thoughts into its pattern she heard it saying 'Stu-pid Stu-pid' or 'They Did They Did.' Sometimes Margaret would have to walk outside, away from the beat of the presses, to try and clear her head.

At home, over dinner, Adam and Allison would tell her about the treehouse Woody was building for them, a dangerous looking collection of boards and planks that never seemed to quite take form in the big maple in the side yard.

"Why are you doing this?" Margaret asked him one night.

"Every kid should have a treehouse," he said. "Didn't you have one?"

"We lived in an apartment. Trees belonged in parks."

"I should build you one too," Woody said. "Things always seem better sitting in a treehouse."

"I already have a house," Margaret said.

"I know," Woody said. "That seems to be part of the problem."

Somehow, they never got around to talking about the tour, or about all the nights Woody stayed out 'jamming.' Margaret occasionally tried to bring it up, but could see Woody neatly side-stepping the topic. Sometimes he would launch into a story about some long-ago summer when he listened to his father and the music on the Northeast jazz circuit. But more often, any attempt to talk about their future sent Woody into the bathroom or off to the kitchen for a sandwich.

That was the hardest part for Margaret, the lack of a future. A year ago she and Woody had spent endless time imagining the future. They planned a horseback trip through the upper circle of Glacier Park, a day trip to see the eagles feeding on salmon in Mac-Donald Creek. They discussed whether they should buy a new house, a three bedroom house so the kids could have separate rooms. But now when Woody spoke she felt confident only when he was speaking of the present, or the past. If he said 'I wish' or 'I would like to,' even a little word like 'Someday,' Margaret felt a ringing in her ears, numbness in her hands. Woody's futures didn't necessarily include Margaret, band tour or no.

By the first part of July the Shelly's Leg team had lost only two games, one to the Duck Inn, their major competition for the city championship, and one to the Pit Stop by a run on an error in the seventh. Rita and Margaret worked together on the field and sometimes spent afternoons practicing the sliders. Rita admired them, the clean arc of the ball as it fell through the air down almost to the plate. They planned to get together for drinks, yet somehow neither of them could find the time.

Sullivan bitched. "You're overdoing it," he told them during one game. "Save that slider for when we need it. Don't use it every time you're bored." But Rita came to rely on them, signaling up for one when she knew there was a good, strong hitter at bat.

Summer light lasted until almost ten o'clock. On evenings when Margaret didn't have a game or a practice she and Woody would play ball with the children in the backyard. At the heart of the season Margaret felt her arm and shoulder tightening into a perpetual ache located somewhere beneath her muscles. She felt good and loose only when pitching and for a few hours right after. She wondered about professional pitchers; they must hurt all the time, their muscles bound in tight knots until the arm was being used.

Woody caught and called the imaginary hits. If the whiffle bat connected with one of Margaret's pitches, the ball dropped like a shot pigeon. The kids always swung past the pitch. Woody invented the plays for them, giving them a lot of triples and home runs.

Adam had been talking about trying out for Little League next summer and he started concentrating on hitting Margaret's curves, slowballs, and sliders. Sometimes he would just stand holding the bat and watch the arc of the ball as it left Margaret's hand and sailed toward him, across the car mat they used for home plate, and into Woody's glove.

Margaret pitched a riser. Adam swung. The bat whistled through the air. "A double!" Woody yelled, expecting Adam to run to the maple tree, first base, and pull up at the garage corner, second base.

Adam stood with the bat resting in his arms. "Don't do that," he said. "Do that for Allison, not for me."

Woody looked at him quizzically. "Don't you want to run?"

"No. I mean yes. But I only want to run if I hit the ball. Then you can tell me if it's a double or something."

"I get all the home runs!" Allison yelled.

"Okay," Woody said. "You sure? It'll be easier to hit a Little League pitcher than one of Maggie's."

"I know," Adam said. "But I want to really hit them. Not just pretend."

Woody studied the boy. He seemed to be measuring Adam's height with his eyes. "There's more to it than that," Woody said. "You got to lob them into holes in the outfield."

"Woody." Margaret didn't like Woody trying to dampen Adam's enthusiasm. In some way Adam's seriousness about pretend ballgames seemed to her an indication he was growing up.

"We don't have an outfield," Allison said.

"I'll tell you what," Margaret said. "I'll give you seven pitches." "Seven?"

"Sure. Four balls, three strikes." Margaret smiled. "It will give you a chance to practice."

Adam grinned. "Okay!"

Allison pouted. "I'll never get to bat."

Woody touched her hair. "But you'll get all the home runs."

Margaret's first pitch was a nice, slow ball, directly across the plate.

Adam did not swing and stood to the side and watched the ball sail by. "That's a little kid's pitch, Mom. Do your regular stuff."

"You sure?" Woody asked. "It might take a while to get a hit."

Adam glared at Woody. "I'm not going to be a little kid for-ever."

Margaret pitched Adam three slowballs and four risers. He missed them all. As he handed the bat to his sister, Adam looked at Woody, over to Margaret, then back to Woody. "It's just kid's stuff the other way," he said.

Allison stood next to Woody, the whifflebat held high in the air. She wiggled her butt the way she had seen the women on the Shelly's Leg team shift when they settled their feet into the box. "I'm ready," she said. Woody, crouched behind the car mat, looked to be exactly her height.

"This will be a double home run," Allison said. "I've got Billie Jean King on second."

Margaret practiced another slider. Allison swung after the ball landed in Woody's mitt. "A home run!" Allison yelled.

Woody played the announcer. "Look at that, folks! That ball's gone right out of the park! A cute little girl in the second bleachers is going to catch that ball and take it home as a souvenir."

Allison slapped her hand against the tree trunk. "We've got the second-base runner coming in," Woody called.

"Billie Jean King!" Allison screamed as she tagged the corner of the garage.

Woody tossed the ball back to Margaret. "Look at that girl run, ladies and gentlemen. In case you folks in the stands didn't know, Allison is also an Olympic short-sprinter."

Allison ran past the piece of cardboard at third.

"She's coming down the home stretch now." Woody held his hands up like a megaphone. "And here she comes! A home run for Allison and a run batted in!" Woody caught her up in his arms as she crossed the car mat and swung her as easily as an infant in a circle through the air. He kissed her loudly on the top of the head when he set her back on the ground.

Allison giggled and squirmed in his hands. "Too bad," she panted, "you can't kiss Billie Jean King too. She doesn't like boys."

Margaret worked on her knuckleball for the next seven pitches to Adam. She watched his small body standing by the plate, studying the first pitch as if he were concentrating for a test. He swung at the next five pitches, missing them all. As he watched the last pitch, he seemed to be memorizing its pattern through the air. Then he handed the bat to his sister.

"I'm going to beat you," Allison said. "I'm going to cream you." She told Woody she had Phyllis Schlafly and Gloria Steinem on bases this time.

"Christ!" Woody laughed. "You sure have one hell of a team."

"We're all famous," Allison said. "Even me. That's what makes us so good."

Woody gave Allison only a single, but allowed Gloria Steinem to score another run. "Just to keep things interesting," he told her when she looked disappointed. "You can't get a home run every time."

Adam varied his attack on the slowballs Margaret pitched. He lunged at the first two, studied the third, walked lazily through the fourth, and on the fifth slowball he tipped it. The ball dropped and rolled off toward Margaret in the center of the yard.

"Okay!" Woody said. "Mightyfine!"

Adam stopped running halfway to the maple tree. "What is it? What'd I hit?"

"A triple for sure," Woody shouted. "Maybe you can steal into home. There's a muff-up in the outfield."

Adam ran hard past the maple.

"Hurry!" Allison shouted. "They're gaining on you!"

Adam slapped past second at the garage and ran, head down, toward the piece of cardboard at third. Sticking his arms straight ahead of him, he dove to the ground five feet in front of the car mat and scrambled in on his hands and knees.

"An in the park homer, folks!" Woody called as he stood Adam up, dusted him off, and patted him professionally on the shoulder. "That was all right. Mightyfine!"

Adam beamed at him. "See? I can do it. Someday me and Mom will have a real game."

Woody put the kids to bed while Margaret sat in the evening twilight weeding the rose garden. A stupid thing to do, she thought. I can't even see the weeds. But it pleased her to sit on the soft ground and spade through the earth, still warm from the long hours of sun. She could hear birds calling to each other, settling into their trees for the night. Above her the sky still held the mauve-pink of sunset.

In the back of her mind was the same nagging worry: how could they have such a fine evening when any day now Woody might just pack up and move out? Not just merely out, move all the way to California or New Mexico. Margaret tried to concentrate on the good times like tonight. She wanted to remember the smile on Woody's face as he swung Allison in the air and kissed her, the way he patted Adam as if Woody were personally proud of that tipped slowball. Later, if Woody left, there would be plenty of time to re-member the sadness and hurt.

"I have an idea," Woody said. He stood behind her and placed his hands on her shoulders. "Or rather I had to come up with one to get the kids in bed."

Margaret turned and looked up at him, the last colors of the sunset coming through his hair.

"Tomorrow we're going fishing for our breakfast, okay?"

"What?" Margaret said. "What are you talking about?"

Woody stretched out on the lawn beside her. His hand cupped her knees. "You've got to be inventive when you deal with kids."

"Oh boy," Margaret said. "Is this news?"

"I couldn't get Adam to shut up about Little League, so I prom-ised him if he would go to sleep we would get up early and go fish for our breakfast in the Blackfoot."

"A picnic for breakfast?"

"Sure. You and me and the kids. We'll take coffee and eggs and the skillet and see if we can get some trout." Woody's hand was making small circles on the inside of Margaret's thigh. He winked at her. "We haven't made love in the grass for a long time."

Margaret looked at the trowel in her hand. 'Made love' seemed such an odd phrase to her. Since the night of the party, almost two months ago, sex with Woody had been awkward sometimes, al-most unpleasant because it seemed to give so much and at the same time threatened to take so much away. Sometimes Margaret wanted to cry, to release her fear that this would be the last time.

"How about it?" Woody said. His fingers stroked her leg with a little more pressure, the circles slower and wider.

"Okay," Margaret said, more pleased with the idea than she was willing to admit. "It'll be nice to do something all together like that."

Woody kissed her quickly on the cheek. "I've got to go to work," he said as he stood up. "But I'll try to get off early. If you're still up, I'll help you get ready." And then he was off. Margaret heard him start the engine of the pickup and drive away.

She paced more than packed for the rest of the evening. Occasionally she would hunt up the old coffee pot or the iron skillet. Finally, to settle herself, she baked blueberry muffins. Still, she wasn't comfortable with this idea. Woody was just the type to plan a lovely day then spoil it by dropping some piece of bad news on her. She saw the scene over and over in her mind. Sitting by the fire, a blueberry muffin halfway to her mouth, Woody might say: 'By the way, I'll be leaving tomorrow.'

When Woody came home, shortly after one o'clock, he had a sack of ice for the ice chest and a bottle of Bushmill's. "Irish coffee," he told her. "A grand tradition in fishing."

They loaded the ice chest together, Woody packing in everything including some cold chicken and a bottle of ketchup. They could all live for a week on the stuff Woody packed.

"You know," Margaret said, "I feel like this is Christmas Eve."

"Sure," Woody said. "Why not? In Australia they have Christmas in July. Come on." He grabbed an old coffee can and her trowel and went out to the garden.

"Worms," he said. "The kids will need worms."

Margaret watched him spading through the rose bed. He seemed to pick each worm individually. "Ah, here's a nice one. . . . Look at this dandy." Margaret held the flashlight while he worked.

When the coffee can was full he reached out and took her hand, flicking off the flashlight. "Come here," he said and led her to the back of the garden. He placed his shirt on the ground and slipped out of his jeans. In the moonlight his jockey shorts seemed to glow. "You know," he said, "when I was in high school it always seemed more fun this way."

He undressed Margaret gently as if she were some delicate china doll. They made love to the sounds of the crickets and night warblers. Margaret concentrated on the warmth of Woody's body and the tickling of the grass against her back and the bottoms of her feet. She watched the face of the full moon, dusted with wispy swirls, as it shone down on them through the clear night. Woody's hair brushed her eyelids. She tried to keep her fears away.

The sun hadn't been up long when they parked the pickup at the edge of the Blackfoot. The air around the Ponderosa pines seemed more gold than blue, almost a topaz, Margaret thought. She imagined space as this quiet golden color, filled with the sounds of invisible birds speaking in ancient tongues.

In the long grass still covered with dew Allison built a ring of stones for the fire while Woody and Adam rigged up the bamboo fly rods. Margaret set out the hampers filled with muffins, coffee, eggs, and the ice chest Woody had packed.

"Let's go, Sport," Woody said to Adam, and the two of them ambled down to the riverbank.

Margaret watched Allison deliberately constructing the fire inside the circle of gray stones. She collected dead twigs and dried grass and dragged broken branches over to the stone circle. She tore up the morning paper for tinder and laid on the charcoal briquettes they always brought to ensure the life of the fire. "Okay, Mom," she said. "One match. Watch this." Allison struck the wooden kitchen match on one of the stones in the fire ring and carefully touched the flame to various pieces of the paper. She blew on it, her round cheeks puffed out as if she were trying to blow out all the candles on a cake.

"When I grow up," Allison said, "I'm going to have a house with a fireplace in every room." She watched the fire spread, tilting her head and peering around to the far side. Margaret thought she looked like a bird hunting for insects. "Even the bathroom," Allison said.

"Even the bathroom?" Margaret laughed.

"Sure." Allison looked up at her. "Bathrooms are always cold. Even in school the bathroom is cold."

"That's a lot of wood to chop," Margaret said.

"No problem," Allison said. "I'll get a chainsaw too."

Margaret tried to remember what she had wanted when she was Allison's age. Certainly not a chainsaw. Margaret had been trained to want a man to take care of her, chop the wood, even by the time she was Allison's age. Her mother's fairy prince had been as real as Allison's dolls. Margaret wasn't sure whether she should find all of this silly or feel guilty. Her mother had taught her to look for the fairy prince. She was teaching Allison to realize she would have to chop her own wood.

And where was her fairy prince, Margaret wondered. This was just the kind of day Mike would have enjoyed with his family. The only difference was that Mike would probably have owned a Winnebago and four dirt bikes. But the idea was the same. The coolness of the morning air, the sun playing through the leaves, animals and birds calling softly across the water. This was the kind of day Mike dreamed of. And she was spending this day with Woody.

"Hey Mom!" Margaret heard Adam calling her from the river. She watched Woody and Adam come up the bank, Adam holding a fair-sized brown trout by the gills. "I got the first one!" Adam shouted. "It must be a foot long."

Margaret found the tapemeasure and carefully stretched it along the body of the fish. Ten and a half inches. "Maybe the next one will be a foot," she told him.

"You bet," Adam said. "I'm just warming up for the big guys." He laid the trout on the ground next to his mother and turned to go back to the river.

"I want to fish," Allison said. She grabbed the little fiberglass rod, but the hook was unbaited.

"Don't you want a worm?" Woody called after her.

"Nope," Allison said. "I'm going to catch fish with my magic touch."

Woody and Margaret watched Adam and Allison disappear over the lip of the bank. "Diet breakfast," Woody said. "They'll horse around down there until one of them falls in."

"We've got plenty of stuff," Margaret said.

"Want to fish with me?" Woody asked. "I'll sit on the bank and admire your legs." He put his arm around her waist and walked her to the river.

Standing in the Blackfoot with her jeans rolled above her knees, Margaret played out the line and wached the Royal Coachman bobbing through a riffle. The smell of the pines seemed heavier over the water and appeared to be concentrated in patches of shade by the bank. She felt Woody staring at her, but ignored him as she watched the tension in the fly line. Her feet were numb from the cold water and her movements jerky as she slipped over the mossy stones in her tennis shoes. She wished she could believe in this day, all of them together in the early morning light. Down the river she heard Allison and Adam squealing in the thin air. They would never catch any fish this way. There was a tremble in the line. She jerked hard. Missed him. She pulled the line back to rebait the hook.

"Lose him?" Woody called from the bank. Then suddenly he was standing beside her, surefooted on the slick stones.

"We're never going to catch any fish this way," Margaret said. She heard Allison singing somewhere upstream. "Remember that book you gave me on trout fishing? The one that talked about sneaking up on the fish? With diagrams and all that? We've probably scared everything for three miles out of this creek."

"There's fish here," Woody said. "Don't you trust me?" He took the hook from her and smeared it with a piece of worm. "We'll get them."

She cast again, a sloppy bounce cast against a rock that landed in a deep pool. She picked her way carefully over the slick stones, downriver, away from Woody, who seemed to be crowding her. She still had that sense that any moment Woody would say 'By the way' and her day would be spoiled, her futures ruined. She couldn't think of anything to say to him to ease her mind about this. And she couldn't think of anything else. She felt this was a play with some invisible director, or perhaps Woody could see the director. He was just waiting for his cue to speak his line. Maybe this was some kind of modern theater where the director was relying on Margaret's spontaneous response. Whatever that response would be would surprise her as much as the director. If Margaret were a betting woman, she would only give herself a 30–70 chance of being reassured by whatever Woody might say.

Woody said: "You've probably always been a better fisherman than me. You've got the patience. You could stand there all day playing with those fish. Me, I'm getting hungry."

There was a tremble in the line. Margaret pulled back hard to set the hook. She had him, could feel the weight of him in the drag of the line. Now she just had to land him. He was a tricky fighter, somersaulting underneath the water, trying to dislodge the hook, break the thin line. He headed for a driftwood snag and if he got under there, Margaret knew she would lose him. The rod bent, the line pulled, and the air seemed filled with the fine, sparkling mist thrown up by the thrashing fish and the line cutting through the water. He jumped once, a full, arcing curve that displayed the silver on his belly. Margaret worked him back through the riffles, letting out on the line only when she felt it might snap. The line slacked for a moment and Margaret reeled in quickly, afraid he was gone. Then the rod bent again and she pulled him into the shallows, where he hung twisting in the water at her feet.

Woody slipped the net under him. "A beauty! A god-damned beauty! Breakfast, here we come."

Margaret examined the fish, a native cutthroat probably a little over a foot long. She looked at the hook of the jaw and the bright rose spots splashed like paint on his cheeks. Woody killed him easily, tapping his head against a rock.

"Let's go, Mama," Woody said. "Let's eat this devil before his color fades."

Margaret began rebaiting the hook. "Two fish," she said. "Two fish won't feed us all. Maybe he's got a brother down there." She didn't want to eat the fish. At that moment, more than anything, Margaret wanted to stand in the river tricking the fish with artificial lures and pieces of worm. She wanted to fight the fish up to her feet, gently remove the hook from their mouths, and release them. She wished the fish were finite, numbered, so that she could try to catch each one and turn them loose again. She smeared the hook with worm and arched her arm back for another cast.

"Wait," Woody said, catching her hand by the wrist. "Keep that brother hungry for a while." He cupped his fingers through the cutthroat's gills and worked his way back across the river and over to a willow tangle. The tree closed over him for a minute and then he re-emerged, the stringer held in his other hand. Two brown trout and a rainbow hung skewered through their gills.

"Breakfast," he said, holding the fish up proudly and dwarfing Margaret's cutthroat. "All these and Adam's spell breakfast."

"Where did they come from?"

"Got them when I first hit the stream. One two three. Magic touch."

"I thought Adam caught the first fish."

Woody grinned at her. "You don't know nothing about children. Children always catch the first fish or the biggest fish. Spoils their fun otherwise." He took her hand and walked her back up the river to the bank.

twelve

Irene stayed in the bar until closing and Sullivan had been tempted to let her keep drinking with him. But that was early. At closing he called a cab for her. Irene was a big woman, square and horsy. Her voice was pleasant, but she knew nothing of silence. It was as if she talked to keep her fears away, as though the power of her voice could command a strength she didn't have. At least not tonight.

Sullivan always believed it was important to sit with his people when they were in pain. Tonight Irene's father had died, a sawyer who lived not fifty miles away. But Irene, who was only in her middle thirties, had not seen him in over fifteen years. She hadn't been called when he fell ill, only once he was dead. She sat on the stool at the end and told Sullivan stories about her father, as if that would bring them together once again. Sullivan decided he wouldn't have liked Irene's father, a man who threw his sixteen year old daughter out of the house for getting caught with her boyfriend, a kid who later married Irene and left her within two years. Her father had never taken her back, and sometime in her early twenties Irene quit trying to go home. Now he was dead and Irene had no more 'somedays' when she might be reconciled with him.

Birdheart hadn't listened. He mixed the drinks, made the change, and stayed at the other end of the bar. Sullivan turned off the outside lights while Birdheart mopped up the tables. Sullivan counted the till while Birdheart cleaned the coffee pot and stacked the ashtrays. Then Birdheart reached around Sullivan and pulled a bullet-shaped bottle of Chivas off the back bar and, after taking a hit, offered it to Sullivan.

Christ, Sullivan thought. Two in one night. Generally Sullivan offered the Chivas to Birdheart if he wanted company in the hours before dawn. But occasionally it happened this way, and Sullivan couldn't really complain. Birdheart, unlike Irene, was a quiet drinker, like himself. They had sat through many nights and only rarely did Sullivan wonder what Birdheart thought or dreamed through the scotch.

Sullivan tried to remember if it had been quite like this when Shelly was alive. Sometimes he thought they all seemed happier then, but if he thought about it enough he would remember a night or two when Shelly sat in the bar until dawn talking to some woman who had found a lump in her breast, whose husband had left her, whose baby had died. With a little smile to himself Sullivan realized things were more equal now. Men and women could share this bar after closing.

Like Amos. Once or twice a year Amos would sit with him. As if telling some shameful secret that had never been shared before, Amos would talk about the day he came back from a long, rolling drunk through the little bars strung out across the Nevada desert and found a moving van in his driveway, his first wife's car packed, and his children pulling handfuls of grass out of the lawn because they did not believe there would be grass in the city. By dawn Amos would be in tears and it would be a week or ten days before he showed up back here. Randa would call or stop in to look for him every day, but Sullivan wouldn't meddle with that. Sullivan knows Amos is drinking at the Hotel Palace, his beaten up Ford parked in the alley with the dumpsters. But when he returns Amos will always say he's been out of town and Randa will only say that she thinks she deserves a vacation every once in a while too.

Sullivan thinks it might have been February of 1962. Lying on the Mexican beach with the incoming tide curling only a yard or so from their feet, Sullivan played with the coppery strands of Shelly's hair. She was propped on her elbows and her foot traced small cir-

cles in the sand. "I don't really miss Paul," she said. "But I feel guilty somehow, as if it were my fault." She laughed, and Sullivan remembers that laugh specifically, as if it were an original sound. "My fault," she said again.

"Will you go back to him?" Sullivan was afraid to touch anything more personal than her hair and worked it through his fingers, kneading it against the base of his thumb. Her hair felt the way silk must before it is woven into cloth.

"I don't think he wants me back." She studied the sand at the edge of their blanket. "But I guess he didn't want it to end this way."

Sullivan laughed, the sound catching in his throat. Even if Shelly would wear the artificial leg, it would never be the same. Paul let them live together now. They traveled down to Texas to look for Whooping Cranes, to this beach at Puerta Vallarta, picking up money orders for Shelly, from Paul, in cities all across the continent.

"He wasn't a bad fellow," Shelly said. "I mean the marriage wasn't bad. Look at what he let us get away with." She turned her head to smile at him and her hair slipped out of his fingers. Her smile faded as she watched his face. "The accident was just an accident. It could have happened to you and me."

"No," Sullivan said. "It couldn't have happened to us. I wouldn't have let it."

She reached over and traced his nose, ran her fingertips through his eyebrows. "Just pretend it didn't happen."

Sullivan rolled away from her over to the edge of the blanket. "It's just done. That's all."

"Listen," she said, wriggling her body over until it touched his again, leaving that shadowy space where her right leg had been. "I have a plan." She winked.

Sullivan pressed his eyes shut against the sun. "There are some plans I don't want to know about."

"You don't want to hear my plan?"

Opening his eyes, Sullivan watched the flight of a gull wheeling above the waves. The sun hurt his eyes, made them tear. At last he said: "If you are going back to Paul, I don't want to know until the day you're ready to leave. I want you to wake up in the morning and say: 'This is it. I'm going today.' Nothing more than that. I'll get you all set up. Train. Plane. But I don't want to count off the days. Only prisoners count days. I don't want to think of myself that way."

"I'm going to tell you my plan."

Sullivan clasped his hands around his neck and stretched himself out full length in the sand. He closed his eyes against the sun. "Shoot," he said.

"I'm going to open a dancehall."

Sullivan shifted his shoulders deeper into the sand. "A dancehall. How are you going to do that?"

"I'll get the money from Paul. He would love to give me money. It would make him feel better."

"How much does he think that leg of yours was worth?"

"I think he'll let me set the price. He can afford it."

"I think that accident scrambled your brains." Sullivan looked at her, the hearts of her eyes bright with secrets and pleasures, a slight smile set into her lips.

"Don't you like dancehalls?" she asked. "Well, do you?"

"I've been a sailor and a rancher. Those types, dancehalls just gives them a place to fight on Saturday night."

"Good. Maybe they need a dancehall in Montana."

He understood, but slowly, the idea seeping through his mind like sleep, calming and drowsy. The beginning of a good dream. "Montana," he said. "You and me?"

She smiled, broadly now, her teeth strong against the softness of her face. She kissed him, her tongue sliding inside his mouth. Wrapping his arms around her, he settled her onto his chest, the sand scratching at his skin.

They lay on the sand under the sun and Sullivan listened to the details of her plan, the problems she had already thought of, the ideas she had for the type of bar she would own. "Just the thing for a one-legged woman," she said. "Be my own boss. Have people around. And if you're nice to me, I'll give you free drinks." She wanted a good day bar with some steady regulars, a dance band in the evening.

"You sure you don't want to go back to Seattle?" Sullivan asked.

"I've never been to Montana. Cowboys. And Indians."

Sullivan tried to remember the women who first drank in Shelly's bar. As their clothes washed and dried in the laundromat next door, or while they helped Shelly put the finishing touches on the place, Sullivan served them drinks. He could remember their drinks and their faces, but not many of their names. Shelly and Rita would sometimes play chess. Some afternoons four or five women would take a table out by the dance floor and play Monopoly or cards. "Hey Sullivan," they would shout, "this place out of wine?"

Sullivan watched them, the women drinking and playing games in the afternoons, the men who stopped by after work to watch the women. When the band started playing Shelly would sit with him behind the bar, serving drinks and watching the dancing, close together until two.

There was one woman, the first baseman on Shelly's original team, who drank whiskey sours and had a birthmark to the side of her left eye. Sullivan always thought her features would have been perfect, like a model of a human face, if he could just brush that birthmark off with his hand. Just a little gesture like chasing away a dust mote. He was trying to remember her name when Birdheart got up and punched a dollar's worth of music in the jukebox.

"What the hell?" yelled Sullivan. "Can't a man drink in peace?"

Birdheart walked behind the bar and slid the volume control down low so that the music was only a whisper, not the raucous country and western the midnight crowd liked. "Better?" Birdheart asked. He took the Chivas from Sullivan's hand and helped himself to another drink.

"You got a problem?" Sullivan asked.

"Yeah. Can't sleep."

"That music going to be your lullaby?"

"No," Birdheart said. "It's going to orchestrate my thoughts."

"Hell. Your mind's so scatter-shot the London Symphony couldn't pull it together for you."

Birdheart took another hit on the bottle. "Yeah," he said. "That's the problem."

"Okay." Sullivan reached for the bottle and took a sip himself. "I got ears. You got until our birds start to sing."

Birdheart moved to his place on the back bar, stretching his long legs out to rest on the counter underneath. "There's the colored flares. Tracer bullets in the night sky cutting through rainbows of rising smoke. There's the blood that looks like your body is made of shit or river mud. Heat and bugs. Air so foul you can feel it clogging your breath. And the music. The music." He reached for Sullivan's bottle again. "You know," he said, "I could sit with you every night until one of us dies and tell you a different story. But it's all the same story. All the lights and the music and the surprising silences that mean you are going to die."

Jimmy Buffett sang "Wasting Away Again in Margaritaville."

"You wouldn't be any happier dead," Sullivan said. He reached behind him and grabbed a separate bottle of Chivas. He knew these nights with Birdheart, not the easy sharing of a bottle of scotch, but a bottle apiece.

"There was this kid from Philadelphia and I swear if he was a woman I would have fallen right in love with him. He was beautiful. Give him some tits and he would break your heart. His eyes were clear and deep like smoked glass." Birdheart sipped at his Chivas. "I'll tell you a first-time story, you tell me one."

"Done," Sullivan said.

"This is about the first time I lost my squad." Birdheart looked straight ahead, to the sign on the door of his room. "This kid, we called him Diamond, because he was pretty, and tough, and hard. Maybe he was crazy. Maybe I was his friend. Diamond used to tell me, he'd say: 'You know, the gooks ain't the enemy. They're not even each other's enemy. We are the enemy.' Churchill or someone. 'We have met the enemy and they are us.'" Birdheart dropped his eyes and fingered the gold label on the Chivas bottle. In his hands the bottle looked small and delicate as an egg. The amber fluid rolled ever so slightly, like a breeze on still water.

"I was on watch one night, before Khe Sanh. Before Khe Sanh the noise was different. Less is more, you know. After Khe Sanh it was all noise and it didn't mean so much." Birdheart took a sip of the scotch.

"Diamond, like I say, was smart. He conned us. He said we were a piece of shit squad except in one area. He said we were all terrific lovers. He said he could prove it by the mail we got. We got more love letters than any other squad in the area. The problem was, no-body knew it but us. And our job, since we were such a piece of shit squad, was to prove where our real talents lay." Birdheart chuckled at his pun. "So he got us to writing love letters. And he kept them. Said he wasn't going to mail any of them out until we had a whole body bag of them. Christ, we wrote letters. Made up packages of souvenirs. We fell for the little bastard's scam. And he put them in the body bag and we watched that sucker fill up. I don't think my hand could ever write another letter."

Sullivan wanted to say something, something like: Did you write to all the names in the New York phone book? But he said noth-ing because he knew the story was not about love letters.

"Diamond and I, we were on watch one night, just about when the body bag was full. It was real late. Quiet. Of course, there's supposed to be hundreds of VC in the area just waiting for Diamond and I to slack off and then the gooks would come in and blow us to pieces in our sleep. Diamond says he's got to go take a leak. I should have known something was fishy right then. Hell, he could have whipped it out right there. Couldn't have gotten any wetter in that god-damned spot. But I let him wander off. I was smoking and didn't give a rat's ass what Diamond did."

Birdheart placed the Chivas bottle on the bar, squaring it into his line of sight. "Next thing I know," Birdheart adjusted the bottle again, as if he couldn't see the pictures of his story without the bullet-shaped bottle filling his field of vision, "I hear it. God, he was fast. There were only nine of us, you know." For the first time Birdheart turned to face Sullivan in the darkened bar.

"I knew it was over even before I had my piece ready. He blew them all away in their sleep. Diamond come walking back to me and he says: 'You just make sure that body bag gets mailed.' And then he stepped off into the jungle."

"How come you didn't get your ass hung for that?" Sullivan asked.

"Well, I didn't hang it on Diamond, if that's what you mean," Birdheart said. "Diamond believed we were the enemy. It was kind of like a mercy killing. No torture. No pain. And he gave them that last reprieve, all those letters to folks who knew and loved those guys. If Diamond was going to go around that part of the country blowing away American squads, I wasn't going to stop him. He didn't shoot me. I got busted for sleeping on duty. They listed Diamond as AWOL. Some VC did the whole number. Hell," Birdheart laughed. "I wouldn't have even got busted if I hadn't mailed that body bag."

Sullivan was silent, trying to imagine being shot in your sleep. Did you wake for just that instant to feel the pain roaring through your body? Did you stay locked forever in that last second dream? Did your body die and your mind float, as those Eastern people believed, trapped in your thoughts throughout time? He imagined a row of Army issue sleeping bags, the first and second men dead, while the third through last wake just long enough to realize what is happening to them. He could see their eyes behind their sleeping eyelids, the pupils darkening like some animal's as the life drained out of their bodies.

Willie Nelson began to sing "Blue Skies."

Birdheart said: "You got more whiskey in your tank than I do."

Sullivan said: "One nice thing about drinking in a bar is that they always seem to have some whiskey." It was an old line with them. It meant Sullivan should tell his story. But Sullivan stayed quiet for a while, letting his mind drift.

Birdheart said: "The only difference between being a grownup and a kid is when you're a kid you don't get to tell the stories."

It was another old line and Sullivan knew Birdheart was getting impatient. Birdheart seemed to have some law or code about telling stories: each one had to be paired. It was as if one story left the teller too exposed.

"Well," Sullivan said as Willie Nelson sang the closing strains to his song. "You want a first-time story." The next tune was Tony Bennett. "I Left My Heart in San Francisco."

"Before I joined the Navy," Sullivan said, "I was working on a horse ranch outside of Seattle. Had a little room in one of the sheds. I'd quit boarding school but Old Ernie didn't know that, so I stayed around Seattle doing the only thing I knew how to do, working with horses. I'd been thinking about my life, what I was going to do with it and all. I hadn't decided to join the Navy yet. Maybe this is what made me do it, I don't know. That was, oh, thirty-five years ago now." Sullivan wished Birdheart did not have his own bottle for this story. He liked the pauses, the silence, when they passed the bottle back and forth. But Birdheart could drink at his leisure and Sullivan would have to create the silences in the story for himself.

"It was a plug ranch, the only thing a kid skipping school could get. A lot of nags. The guy who owned it was a teacher or something, I forget now, but he ran this ranch for dudes in the summer. I don't recall a horse worth a shit on the place. Except for the Tennessee Walker. A big long-legged bay. Deep-chested. But, of course, there was something wrong with him too. The guy had just gotten him because he had the worst case of lice in his ears I've ever seen in fifty years of ranching."

"You ain't a rancher no more," Birdheart said. "Haven't been as long as I've known you."

"It's all in how you think," Sullivan said. "You ain't a kid no more. You probably never were one. But you might think there's something out there."

"Wrong," Birdheart said. "I ain't waiting for something to happen. It's all been done."

Sullivan recognized the truth of this, always had, but it saddened him to remember this about Birdheart. He wanted a future for Birdheart, something ahead of him. If wishes were horses, beggars would ride. Birdheart, like himself, seemed to be merely waiting. Sullivan wondered why Diamond hadn't shot Birdheart too. He felt the cruelty of it.

"There was a light snow," Sullivan continued. He didn't want to think about Birdheart right now. "Just enough to cover the stubble in the fields and lace the orchard. We had the Walker penned in an old, rotted-out shed so he wouldn't infect the other plugs. I guess I was shoveling shit or something like that when Shelly stepped into the barn. She was fourteen, not full grown and her breasts were just barely rounded under her boarding school uniform. She didn't have a coat on and I thought she must be cold."

The next song was "Fräulein," one that Sullivan had hummed in the Navy back when it was new. "I asked her what she was doing out there and she says: 'I've left school.' I say: 'You can't do that.' And she says to me: 'Why not? You did it. You think only boys can quit school? Besides, I can go back any time I want and right now I want to be here.'

"I told her I never met a girl yet who preferred shoveling shit to sitting on her fancy ass staring out the window dreaming about movie stars. And she said to me that she wasn't out there to shovel shit and she didn't spend all her time dreaming about movie stars."

Sullivan stood and walked out to the bluish light of the jukebox, right underneath Shelly's photograph. He remembered the small brown mole at the nape of her neck. "I asked her if she was cold, offered her a coat. And she said she'd rather go into my room. She knew I had a room out there and she bet it was warm. I put down my shovel and walked her over to my room, noticing it was just about dark and how even the snow looked on the hills and fields. Not spotty at all; it seemed to have covered everything as evenly as air. When we get in my room she sits down on my bed and tells me she's spending the night. I'm pretty surprised and offer to give her a ride back to town, although unless I put her on one of those plug mares I'd have to walk her."

Sullivan went to the bar and leaned over it, as if he were the customer. He fingered the scotch bottle. "She says to me: 'I'm fourteen now and I'm a woman. I'm not a child, but I've got one last bit of my childhood to get rid of before I'm really there.' She unbuttons the little navy blue sweater.

"I didn't know much more than she did, to be truthful. I'd been with a couple of whores, but never had a decent girl. I'm scared but, Christ, I'd wanted her for two years already. I'm afraid if I ask her anything she'll change her mind. But I don't know really what to do with her. Then she unbuttons the white school blouse and she says: 'Just pretend it's like a movie, only we're going to do the stuff they don't show.' I say: 'What don't they show?' And she says: 'I don't know, but you do. I know you do.' Then she comes over and sits on my lap."

Birdheart laughed, deep and hearty. "I guess she didn't know. That would've blue-balled me for the rest of my life."

Sullivan smiled and walked back to the jukebox. "Well," he said, "she finally convinced me. I tried to be as gentle as I could to her and still not go crazy at the same time. We lay there in that old metal cot and after a couple of hours I remembered a whore I'd been with who told me when I was old enough to not need a whore and had found a decent girl, to play with her. The whore showed me how. I was trying it out on Shelly, wanting to please her, although she seemed happy enough. I didn't know dip shit about women then."

Sullivan returned to the bar and took the stool where Irene had sat earlier in the evening. Linda Ronstadt was singing "Love Is a Rose." "Then," Sullivan said, "we heard this crashing and banging, a god-awful racket. There had been no noise, except us in that squeaky metal bed, for all those hours. No owls, the horses in the barn had been quiet. You could feel the moon rise and see it come through the one window. But all of a sudden there was this beating and cracking and slamming going on just outside. We both froze for a moment, then stark naked, we got up and ran outside."

"Not me," Birdheart said. "I would've figured it was her daddy with a shotgun."

Sullivan moved back to the jukebox, annoyed at the interruption. "We stood in the snow, barefooted, yet it didn't seem that cold. I remember more how the stubble of grass underneath sort of tickled my feet than the cold from the snow. And I remember our smell seemed to hang on the air. We stood there and she grabbed my hand as the Tennessee Walker made his last kick and busted out of that rotted shed. He turned and faced us. It was like we all looked at each other. Then he took off up a slight rise covered with fresh snow. He twisted and bucked and sunfished all up that slope, leaving crazy trails in the new snow. It was like his feet were hardly on the ground at all. The moon was so high and full it was like daylight. I could see our shadows, tall across the ground, his shadow bouncing in the moonlight.

"At the top of the rise he stopped. I had just started to think about catching him. I remember at the time I had just begun the thought, like the beginning of a sentence, when I knew I wasn't going to catch him. I would just watch him with Shelly holding my hand. It seemed like she wasn't even breathing."

Sullivan took a long pull on his Chivas and returned to the wheeled stool behind the bar. "He stood at the crest of the hill, moving his head slowly as if he were looking around. His shadow was terrific, coming halfway down the slope. Then he began to run, not crazy this time. Straight down the hill in a long, hard race. He came close by us. He ran down the hill like he was breaking for the home stretch. He headed into the orchard, tearing down limbs, scattering branches, until he hung up in the crook of a tree, breaking his neck and pulling the tree down with him as he died."

Sullivan took the rose out of the cut crystal vase and twirled it in his fingers. He gave a little laugh as if embarrassed at what he was going to say next. "I always thought," he said at last, "that that horse was always between us."

Birdheart walked over and pulled the plug on the jukebox. "You know Sullivan," he said, "you should have never joined the Navy. It was right there for you the minute that horse died."

Sullivan said nothing. He was listening for the sparrows in the trees along the alley. He thought maybe he heard them, although it seemed a little early. Maybe he did hear them, just one or two. Without another word he grabbed a fresh bottle of Chivas and walked out the back door, fishing in his pocket for the keys to his black pickup.

thirteen

Margaret enjoyed the idea of the Blackfoot Ball, an all day outdoor concert and picnic that had been a tradition in town for the past several years. Sitting in the sun, sharing food with your neighbors while the local musicians played against the background of the river and the pines, made Margaret long for a simpler age. She imagined ice cream socials, kids taking turns cranking up the fresh ice cream. In her mind it was always peach. She wanted to see women wearing aprons as they doled out fried chicken, men in straw hats and arm gaiters pitching horseshoes. She wished for boys in caps and short pants, girls in frilly dresses with long white stockings. But today she was content watching the blue-jeaned people strolling along the riverbank or disappearing off into the trees. Children looked like miniature grownups in the standard uniform of her time. She watched two babies, perhaps three or four years old, playing in the fire circle Allison had constructed a few weeks ago for their fishing breakfast. Only the chubby, baby hands and round faces gave away the fact they were so young. They had the concentration of archeologists as they sifted through the dead coals.

The Old Time Fiddlers played first, since they did not need all the electrical rigging A Little Left of Center used, nor the piano the jazz band demanded. The fiddlers, some of them not so old, played on the riverbank while Woody and his boys bucked equipment around the jerry-rigged stage. Adam was helping, stringing electrical lines from the platform out to a mobile generator hidden back in a cottonwood clump. Allison and Margaret lay in the sun and took turns rubbing each other with sun-tan lotion. A boy of about twelve with a miniature fiddle played "Salty Dog" and his father joined him in a duet version of "Shine On, Harvest Moon." Margaret listened to the squeal of the bow across the strings and remembered a concert her parents had taken her to when she was about Allison's age. Margaret heard violins; Allison was beating time to the sorrowful sounds of a fiddle.

"Do 'Deliverance,'" someone shouted. "Just like in the movie." The father and his son did not know "Deliverance" and began "My Old Kentucky Home" to some applause and the booing of a drunk.

Margaret saw Birdheart and Rita working their way through the crowd. Birdheart wore his usual jeans and cowboy shirt, his hands thrust back deep in his hip pockets. But Rita was dressed up like some country and western Indian princess. Her long black hair was braided and the ends were spangled with porcupine quills and beads. She wore a halter top that barely covered her breasts and tight black pants caught below the waist with a hammered silver concho belt. She held herself with her chin out; the top of her head did not reach Birdheart's shoulder.

They saw Margaret and waved. Rita did a little Indian dance step and patted her mouth like a war whoop, then continued on toward the bandstand. Birdheart peeled away from her to come sprawl on the grass next to Allison.

"Where's Rita going?" Margaret asked.

Birdheart laughed. "The Indian Queen," he said. "Dress her up and she thinks she's Pocahontas."

"Sacajawea led Lewis and Clark right by our house, huh Mom?" Allison said, proud to be showing off her knowledge.

Birdheart said: "She might think she's Sacajawea too, for that matter."

"Right by our house," Allison said again. "Of course, our house wasn't there then."

"There wasn't nothing here then," Birdheart said. "Nothing but owl shit and buffalo turds."

Allison ran her thumbnail along the vein of a leaf. "Aw," she said, "there was more than that." She shredded at the leaf, then looked up at Birdheart. "Birds and stuff." She was searching for a stronger answer. Her eyes lit up. "Bears!" she said.

"What would you do if you saw a bear?" Birdheart asked. His mirrored sunglasses reflected two funhouse images of Allison sitting tailor fashion on the grass.

Allison giggled. "Tell him to get his ass to a zoo. He'd be safer."

Birdheart and Margaret laughed. "Yeah," Birdheart said, "I suppose we'd all be safer in a zoo."

"What's Rita all flashed up for?" Margaret asked again.

"Beats me," Birdheart said. "Custer's Last Stand, for all I know. Where's Woody?"

"Setting up."

"And Adam's helping," Allison said.

Birdheart poked her with a twig. "Well why are you lying on your buns, girl? Don't you know you're supposed to be liberated? You should be over there felling trees with a cross-cut saw, helping them make a stage. Men and women are equal now, don't you know. You better give this girl an education, Maggie." Birdheart smiled.

Allison giggled. "They're not cutting down trees, silly. They brought a stage with them. On a truck."

There was more applause for the fiddlers, and through the clapping Margaret could hear Woody tuning his pedal steel. Chuck ran a scale or two on his rhythm guitar and Lloyd did a drumroll. Wood smoke drifted on the air.

"Sounds like we're going to have some electrical music here right directly," Birdheart said.

"They should wait until the fiddlers are through," Margaret said.

"You sure don't know much about musicians," Birdheart said. "None of these bands knows the others are here."

Margaret cocked her eyebrow. "You going to tell me about musicians?"

Birdheart shrugged. "It's always been a philosophy of mine," he said, "that you should only get involved in something you understand."

Margaret smiled and saw her face flashing back at her from his sunglasses. "That's news," she said. "You, having a philosophy."

Another set of fiddlers began and Birdheart offered to take Margaret and Allison down to the fire where there was a roasting pig. Allison agreed but cautioned Birdheart against offering Gloria Steinem, the doll she had brought today, any of the roasted pork. "She's a vegetarian, you know," Allison told him.

They ate the hot, sweet pork, the grease and barbecue sauce coating their fingers, and drank a beer before A Little Left of Center began to play. Margaret stood next to Birdheart at the foot of the bandstand, looking up at Woody, who smiled and blew her a kiss. "I want to do something special with this first number," he said to the crowd. "This is for a good friend of mine. Maybe my best friend, a wonderful woman. This is for you, Maggie."

The song was one of Margaret's favorites, a rocking tune Woody had composed about old-fashioned hearted women. It painted the standard country and western ideals of Tammy Wynette and "Stand By Your Man," but from the point of view of a questing knight, the modern cowboy. Underneath the jazzy beat he wanted simple things, order that had vanished from the world at large. Margaret was pleased, warmed by the song, but somewhat confused. It wasn't A Little Left of Center's regular opening and not one of their more popular songs. She felt she was fighting that fear again, the one she couldn't name.

And then she could name it. For the second number Woody called Rita up. "Now I want you all to listen to the best honky-tonk singer since EmmyLou Harris." It wasn't the singing that troubled Margaret, it was watching Rita and Woody on the stage. She clapped her hands in time, not so much to be part of the music as to keep the circulation going through her fingers. It was hot, but Margaret felt as if every bit of moisture in her body had evaporated, leaving only cinders of pain. Her eyes were dry, her hands were numb, and it felt like her heart was pumping sand through her veins.

Rita sang with her face close to Woody's, their eyes on each other. The air smelled of smoke and sweat and sex as Rita's body shifted in time to the tune, the quills and beads in her hair swaying with her body, which moved like a woman on a bed. When Rita sang there was no sun and sky. The tight black pants with the big silver belt moved around the shadow of a man. And that man was Woody, seated at his pedal steel, staring up at Rita, shining on her.

Suddenly Margaret was going to vomit. She ran for the willow clump where Woody had hidden his trout a few weeks before. Pushing past the soft, stringy leaves, Margaret retched into the river, a part of her clear and detached, watching the pink worms of the pork sandwich clotting in the washing willow leaves.

She heard him stomping through the underbrush, the splashing as Birdheart came up behind her in the center of the willows and put his arm around her waist, his palm on her forehead, as she vomited into the water. She continued to heave, arched over Birdheart's arm, her hands crossed over her breasts and clutching at her shoulder bones. With the clear part of her mind she heard Birdheart crooning to her, his voice like the purring of a cat. "There there now. That's okay. Hang on now. It's going to be all right."

The chant seemed to work and Margaret gradually ceased and leaned back against Birdheart's shoulder for support. She coughed. Her legs seemed to have melted from her body. Her chest felt like an open sore.

"Had enough?" Birdheart held her against him.

Margaret nodded. Spots of light flicked through her field of vision.

"Let's clean you up then. Can you walk?"

Margaret nodded again and held tightly to Birdheart's arm as he led her upstream away from the willows. The sunlight on the water hurt her eyes. She blinked back the tears as her knees and Birdheart's arm floated in front of her.

Birdheart waded her out to a boulder not far from shore. He picked her up and placed her like a child on the rock, her toes trailing in the cold water. Drifting over the river were the muted sounds of Rita's and Woody's voices, the faint music of the band. Margaret could distinguish the beat of the bass drum punctuating the rush of the river over the rocks. She was glad she didn't know what song they were singing. It sounded foreign, pasted on top of the water noise.

From his pocket Birdheart took a bandana handkerchief and washed her face with cold river water. His large hands reached up

under her hair and gently followed the line of her scalp. He applied
the cold bandana behind her ears, along the back of her neck, across
her brow, careful not to wet her hair.

"Hold out your arms," Birdheart said, and Margaret stretched
her arms out mechanically. Downstream, swallows flitted over the
water before disappearing into the cliff face on the far shore.

He placed the wet bandana in the crook of her elbow, massaging
her arm in a smooth circle. Margaret felt the cold surging through
her veins, moving up her arms and into her back and shoulders. He
pressed the wet cloth to her wrists and she felt the cold in her fingers. She might have been perfectly relaxed; at this point she could
no longer distinguish what she was feeling.

Birdheart smiled at her. "Better?"

"I'm okay." She wondered if this was true.

"Let's get you back to town then."

He must have seen the confusion on her face, the flash of her
thoughts as she remembered this morning's ride in Woody's
pickup with the kids. "Sit still. I'll be right back," Birdheart said.
He left her with the cold bandana held between her wrists as if she
were wearing handcuffs.

Margaret watched the swallows, thinking of Rita and Woody.
Of course she knew they had been together. Their singing was the
product of hours of practice. Woody had been spending the nights
until dawn with her. There was still that band tour, although
Woody never talked about it now. Rita was going on that tour
with Woody. She had said so and now Margaret could see it. In the
last few weeks Margaret had circled all of this, but never confronted
it directly. Now when she could finally say this to herself Margaret
was surprised that something didn't physically shatter or break.
Swallows drifted over the river, touching down to the water for
only a fraction of a second.

"The kids'll be okay," Birdheart said when he returned with her
boots and purse and guided her off the rock and over to his car.
Margaret didn't bother to ask what arrangements he had made.
Maybe he had talked to Woody, although she had heard no break
in the faraway music. She believed him; the kids would be okay.

They sat in Shelly's Leg, the only customers this afternoon, while the bartender, a new kid, dusted bottles for lack of anything better to do. A fifth of Wild Turkey sat on the bar between their glasses. There was nothing to say and Margaret made water flowers on the bar.

She felt warm inside her body, but her skin was touched by the cold of the air-conditioning. Her bones and muscles seemed soft while her shoulders and arms goosebumped. She could see the fine hairs standing up. There are places on your body your own hands cannot touch, she thought. You can't hold your own back, touch yourself beneath the shoulderblades. You can't rub your own legs with satisfaction. The knowledge of your hand won't let you anticipate the pleasure of being touched.

Birdheart placed his hand on the small of her back and stroked gently along her spine. It was as if that space on her body had been needing something and Birdheart's hand was just what had been missing. Okay, Margaret thought, two can play this game. Woody and Rita. Margaret and Birdheart.

Birdheart's room was small, just big enough for the double bed under the high, tiny window, a straight-backed chair, and the little corner sink. To Margaret it seemed like a cage or cell, only large enough to turn around a couple of times. The weak sunlight falling through the window made the room seem colder than the bar. He kept a chest of drawers in the alcove at the foot of the bed and Margaret put her clothes on top of it, under the hanging folds of Birdheart's shirts. The bed smelled musty and there was only one pillow, fisted into a ball. On her back Margaret's stretch-marked breasts sagged off her chest. She was aware of all her scars and mars, the chipped tooth that had never been capped, the white lines strewn randomly across her body that were signs of errors and mistakes. They were visual reminders from her past, a childhood spent growing up on concrete, her lack of care as an adult. Margaret wanted to hide her body underneath Birdheart's sheets.

Birdheart was on top of her, the sweetish, sweaty smell of his body pressing down on her. He did not kiss her; he would not touch her breasts. His hands massaged the inside of her thighs, his knees keeping her legs apart. He buried his stubbly face in her belly so she could see only the top of his head, his sandy hair. His hands were cold and the hair on his chest itched against her skin. He kissed her navel, sucking it into his mouth. She was moving with him, sweat curling down her spine, her hips rocking into his shoulders. As he moved up on her she noticed he was heavier than Woody, his back thick with taut muscles. He was bigger than Woody too, and she felt the inside of her body opening to him. She waited for the fluttering, that most pleasurable part of sex when her body moved without the reasoning of her mind. But she was still forcing it, willing her muscles to ride against Birdheart's body. There was not that great blackness behind her eyes when her body responded with a life of its own and her mind seemed to have fallen away.

Birdheart was lost within her, moaning to himself, his hands framing her face. He pushed and strained against her, making Margaret want to slide up the bed away from the thrust of his body. Faster and faster he pushed against her retreating body until her head jammed against the wall and there was no farther to go.

She felt nothing when he came, not that tingling that would flood the bottom of her ribcage like sparkler fire. Nothing like with Woody. She knew only by the great sigh and the slope of his shoulders edging away from her. Sweat beaded and dripped down his arms, following the knotted paths of the veins and muscles. His hair seemed to lose its shine as he laid his head on her chest. Sad, Margaret thought. I should have been better for him, touched his shoulders or hair. She wondered what color his eyes were.

Birdheart rose from the bed and grabbed the Wild Turkey. He tipped it toward her and arched his brow. With an effort, Margaret smiled at him and drank directly from the bottle, the bourbon burning warm and brown down the middle of her spine.

She awoke to the sounds of Birdheart rummaging through his dresser and saw it was dark outside. He shoved the drawer back in its slot and sat on the edge of the chair to pull his socks on. His boots banged against the floor as he stuffed his feet into them. Out in the bar, the jukebox was playing.

"On your feet, lady," Birdheart said. He smiled and looked up and down the length of her body. "Might as well take them by storm."

Margaret wanted to hide the soft places of her body, to cover up her sagging breasts. She thought her toes looked broken.

"You plan to spend the night?" Birdheart put his mirrored sunglasses back on.

Margaret considered this. Rita and Woody were probably out in the bar, waiting for her. How could she tell Woody where she had been? Would a lie work? What if Woody had asked that new kid, the bartender?

Margaret huddled into the corner of the bed, away from the wet leaf of sex on the sheet, and pulled the blanket up around her breasts. I must look like an orphan, a refugee, she thought and remembered pictures of children hiding in small rooms. She recognized this as the final move in the card game. She had shown her hand. If Woody was in the bar, the game would be over. She thought she could hear his laugh in the noise outside.

"Come on," Birdheart said. He sat in the chair watching her from behind his sunglasses. "No point lying about this. Time to face the music." He tossed her jeans and shirt toward the bed.

Margaret stared at the heap of her clothes. "What will we do?"

"You can't hide in this hole," Birdheart said. "Walk out like a movie star. Stand tall, maybe pause to make a more dramatic entrance. Then walk over to the bar. I'll be right with you."

Margaret looked at him, trying to imagine his eyes behind the mirrors. What did he mean, 'I'll be right with you'? She was nothing to him. It was Rita and Woody who led them to this. Margaret felt as if her spirit had left her, drifted out of her body like a sigh and floated through the tiny window. Birdheart was nothing to her. It was all Rita and Woody. She didn't count to any of them.

The door leading to the bar was the only way out except for the window above the bed. Margaret imagined smashing that window with her fist, dropping ten feet through the air to land on the slivers of glass. She imagined the lace of blood on her body, the cuts from the tiny shards. She couldn't imagine the pain, but wished that she could. If she could imagine the pain of the glass tearing at her skin, perhaps she would not try the window.

For one moment Margaret thought maybe Woody would not be in the bar. But that was more horrible than what would happen if he was. If he was not in the bar, he would be in bed with Rita. He wouldn't even notice that she had done this, to spite him, to hurt him. This episode with Birdheart would drift over him like dust, unnoticed and unremarked upon. She decided it would be better if he were out there. The game would be over. They would all know where they stood.

She tried to think this through again and find her own responsibility in what was going to happen when she walked through that door. She hadn't seduced Birdheart, but she hadn't resisted either. Her thoughts wove back and forth between total responsibility and none at all. She could find no middle ground.

"When we get to the bar," Birdheart said, "I'll buy you a double." He tipped the last of the Wild Turkey into his mouth and set the bottle down next to his chair.

"You might have to buy me a new life."

Birdheart smiled. "Maybe. Maybe you could use one."

As Margaret climbed off the bed she felt the pains inside her bones again. There was no hope Woody would not be in the bar; he had the children with him. Margaret tried to wash her inner thighs at the corner sink and felt weak as she ran the grimy towel up and down her legs. Her eyes seemed puffy and she spent a long time patting them with cold water, her back to Birdheart, who watched her as if she were a private porno movie being screened in his room. She tried not to think, not to rehearse the scene when she and Birdheart would finally walk through that door and into the bar. Anything was possible; Birdheart might push her before him into the arena of the bar, like a Christian into the lions, a hostage before a bandit.

She tucked in her shirt and fluffed at her hair. Birdheart opened the door with a flourish and said: "After you."

The music from the jukebox assaulted her and she felt the eyes of the people who swiveled on their bar stools to turn and stare at her.

Some might have been facing Birdheart's room all evening, their backs to the bar, waiting. Shirley and Miriam were at the Keno table with Deadeye and Valgaardson. Amos and Randa talked with Sullivan, and at the far end of the bar sat Rita and Woody. Only Adam and Allison did not seem to notice her as they stood behind the belling pinball machine.

She chose the stools near the front door, next to the wall, and waited with her eyes down as Birdheart slipped onto the stool next to her. Sullivan said nothing as he placed two drinks in front of them and turned his back to talk to Amos and Randa.

"That," Birdheart said, "is Sullivan's way of saying he don't approve."

Margaret tried to rally. Maybe Woody would think they'd just been smoking a joint, or talking things over. Although she wanted to lay her head down on the bar and cry, she felt she should try to stand up to this. She managed a smile and her face did not crumble into hundreds of little broken pieces as she suspected it might. "What's to approve?" she said, testing her voice. "If we wanted his approval we would have asked."

Birdheart chucked her under the chin. "That's the spirit," he said. "Keep up that smile and this act is home free." He grinned at her broadly and took off his sunglasses so she could see his eyes. They were blue, darker than Woody's. Margaret felt herself smiling back at him, almost laughing for no reason she could name.

"Well kiss the crack of my ass," Woody said. He stood beside them with a drink in his hand. "Here's my little sweetheart with Old Junglerot, the garbage collector. You sure did collect some real ripe garbage here."

Birdheart placed his sunglasses back over his eyes. "You got it all wrong, man," he said. "I'm talking to the garbage."

Sullivan was between them as if he dropped from the sky. Margaret noticed the jukebox had stopped. Her hands were getting numb.

"You know," Sullivan said, "I've been in this business so long I can almost predict how things are going to happen." He looked at Margaret as if he were going to tell this all to her, as if she were the only one who didn't know. "I'll bet you old Birdheart was going to lean over and tap Woody here right on the chest. Like this." Sullivan reached out an arm and touched Woody above the heart. Woody stiffened and pulled away.

Sullivan stood back from them and looked at each one individually for a long moment. His eyes rested on Margaret. "Sometimes," he said at last, "we all get to know each other too well." He turned back to Woody and Birdheart. "Another fight in this bar between you guys. I don't want that. Neither of these ladies is worth fighting over. And I don't want your faces beat into my parking lot either. So," Sullivan set a bottle on the bar, "I'm keeping my eye on you people. You might say I'm buying you off." He turned and walked away.

Woody drained the last of his drink, sucking it through the ice cubes tilted back against his teeth. He reached for Sullivan's bottle. "Sullivan would make a great mother," he said.

"It's too bad," Birdheart said. "I was kinda looking forward to wiping that red beard off your face. As I recall, I owe you one."

Woody laughed. "You know, Birdheart, we got it all wrong. We should be beating the crap out of these ladies. They're the ones causing all the trouble."

"Oh no," Margaret said. Her ears were ringing. She tried to look at Woody but her eyes slid over to Birdheart's glasses. "You're the one started all this. Birdheart and I were perfectly happy until you started whoring around." In the mirrors of Birdheart's glasses her face looked tired and drawn. She thought she might look this way as an old woman.

"Now this is a fun game," Birdheart said. "Call it 'Catch the Guilt.' We used to play it in Nam. 'If you didn't have to take a shit, Pancho Peso wouldn't have stood guard and got blown away by that sniper gook.' Woody gets to go first. You fucked my squeeze and it broke this lady's heart."

"Stay out of this," Woody said. "We aren't playing war games here."

"Oh no?" Birdheart said. "Sex is the biggest war game of all."

"If Rita means so damn much to you, go down the bar and keep her company," Woody said. "This is between Maggie and me."

"You telling me what to do?" Birdheart pulled his shoulders back and sat straighter on his bar stool. Even seated, he was taller than Woody.

"I'd rather you stay," Margaret said, hoping in that way Birdheart would not punch Woody. She wished Sullivan would return. He would know what to do. "Our affairs have gotten pretty public these days." She refilled her glass, trying to think of something else to say. Maybe the smile would work again. "The more the merrier," she said, as if this were a joke. She didn't know if she was smiling or not.

"I want to talk to you, Maggie."

A man's got to do what a man's got to do, Margaret thought. If she didn't stand up to Woody now, he would have her buffaloed forever. It was her choice: if he got the best of her now she would end up on that tour, following Woody until he got tired of her or realized the hassles of traveling with children. Then he would dump her in Tucumcari or wherever. But if she stood up to him, she might lose him anyway, and then she would be alone again. Her stomach seemed to drop at that thought, slipping through her body with a slight shudder. If she had to be alone she wanted it to be in a place she understood. She simply had to make her choice and take her chances.

"So talk," she said, but she could not bring herself to look at him. "What are you going to say? I'm getting like Sullivan, you know. I bet I know what you're going to say. Listen to this." She poked Birdheart in the arm and saw her face in his glasses again. "Woody's going to tell me he loves me. Isn't that sweet? But then he's going to slip in his own shit and hedge around about this tacky affair with Rita. And somehow by the end of the speech it will be all my fault because I won't go on his damned tour. Isn't that what you were going to say, Dear?" She finally turned to look at Woody and, as always, could read nothing in his eyes.

"You know," Woody said, waving his glass, "if I was as ill-mannered as our friend Birdheart here, I'd haul off and crack you one right across your dirty mouth."

Margaret hoped to see some light in his eyes, some reflection of his voice. "You're wrong," she said, "and you know it." She toyed with her glass. "Besides, your true love Rita is just taking you for a free ride out of town."

"At least," Woody said, "she's going to have some fun. You, you can sit on your fat ass and call that life. Your idea of perfection is when everything stops. Nail it down, stick it in a museum and we've reached heaven."

"Life ain't all fun," Margaret said. "You don't even think about how you've hurt us. Me and the kids. All you care about is your own self. Having fun. Everything just to please you." She felt tears standing in her eyes.

"So far," Birdheart said, "this is a low scoring game."

Together, Woody and Margaret turned on him. "Shut up!" "Stay out of this." Birdheart merely reached for the bottle.

They were silent for a moment before Woody spoke. "It's supposed to be a compromise, Maggie. A compromise you're not willing to make."

Margaret pulled herself up on the bar stool, her shoulders back, her spine tucked in, the pose Rita assumed when angry. "I won't share my man with another woman." She felt her voice rising. "I ain't no liberated lady and this ain't no liberated life. I don't call that compromise. That's betrayal. Insult. Low-life." Margaret felt she would snap, begin to cry and scream all at the same time. She thought her hands might fly to his face, tearing at his skin. She took a deep breath and felt the air swelling her chest and shoulders. She wished for some sign in Woody's eyes that would call this whole thing off before she crumbled into those hundreds of broken pieces, some wanting to surrender, some wanting to win. She was like Woody; it had to go her way. She envisioned no other possible solution. There was nothing in his face, nothing in his eyes that said they would go home together. Only his blue stare coming back at her.

"Of course," Woody said, "fucking Birdheart here wasn't anything like that. That was moral. Or maybe you're going to tell me he raped you."

"She came willingly," Birdheart said.

Woody cocked his glass at Birdheart. "For the last time, mother. Stay out of this."

"This is horseshit," Birdheart said. "You guys are posturing like a couple of drunk peacocks. Kiss and make up. Everyone would be happier for it." He watched them for a moment, their postures frozen like dogs before a fight. "Hell," he said. "Sometimes I can't stand the sadness." He picked up his glass and walked across the bar to his room.

It hadn't been this way with Mike, Margaret thought. With Mike she had no choices. He had simply announced one day that he was leaving. Or maybe she had made all her choices before he decided to go. But there had never been a scene like this where she played a specific part, said certain words, and the outcome depended on how she behaved. With one part of her mind she wanted to ask Woody's advice, have him tell her what the next move would be.

Suddenly Margaret was tired, not just tired but aching with what felt like physical exhaustion. She poured some bourbon into her glass and waited with her eyes down while Woody slid onto Birdheart's stool. "I'm confused," she said and looked up at Woody. "I don't know what I want."

"You better figure it out," Woody said. "Real quick."

"Mike and I had an agreement," Margaret said. Her eyes felt too heavy to continue looking out at him. "We would fight, but we always knew in the back of our minds that it was our job or duty to make it up sometime. The point was to get it straight and go on. But you and I just live together. We've got no such agreement. Any day one of us can make a mistake and the other doesn't have to forgive. Any day either one of us can make the decision that it's over." She studied the way her numb hands curled around her glass and tried to concentrate on keeping them there. She was not going to throw another drink at Woody.

"Well," Woody said, "that worked out real well, didn't it, my little divorcee of the spirits?"

"Maybe it was just a theory," she said. Somehow she was losing her way. This was not coming out the way it should. Woody's voice was wrong. She turned to look at him, hoping he could see into her eyes. "Do you know why he finally left me?"

Woody's voice was cold. "I got some good ideas."

Some part of Margaret's mind still believed she could talk him out of this, whatever this was, if she only said the right thing. "Mayonnaise," she said. "I forgot to put mayonnaise on his turkey sandwich and he said I always forgot the mayonnaise and he was going somewhere where he didn't have to worry about not getting any mayonnaise on his sandwiches." She wasn't going to tell Woody the rest of the story, the way Mike always talked about ultimate mistakes, the ones you can't come back from. Mayonnaise had been her ultimate mistake. The last one in a long line of mistakes.

"Well," Woody said, "if you don't know what you want, maybe I do. Maybe it's good for both of us." He peeled at the label on the bourbon bottle. "According to you, that little story you told me in the bathroom," he looked over to her, then back to the bottle, "you got one act and you pull it with every man you know. It's called 'Things Go My Way' and you'll trot it out and run it as fast as you can blink your eyes." He pushed his glass and the bottle away from him, across the bar. "So you'll get your way. You'll get your house and your kids. And I'll get my way. I'll be getting the hell out of this town. Be moving on to better things." He stood and rested his foot on the bar rail. "Don't ever tell anyone I left you for mayonnaise. It's something more basic than that."

He moved away from the bar and gave her a salute with his hand. "Take my name off the mailbox," he said. "I don't live there no more."

He walked across the bar and pounded on Birdheart's door. "Hey Birdshit," he yelled. "You've become the consolation prize."

fourteen

With the lights off and the children in bed Margaret listened to the night sounds. She heard cars driving by, sometimes a tune playing on the radio or a laugh passing by her house as if tossed into the air. Crickets chirped and once in a while she could hear the mournful cry of an owl or the screech of a nighthawk. She wondered if the nights had been quiet these last three years. The last time she had listened to the night sounds was when Mike left. She would put her babies to bed and sit in the darkened living room memorizing the noises. She imagined her life as a blind person, seeing the movements in the dark with only her ears. She fantasized sounds she wanted to hear, the ringing of the telephone or a van pulling into the driveway. In some ways she felt she got to know Mike better after he left her. As the night moved toward morning she found herself talking out loud, saying to Mike the things she never told him, listening as he replied in her mind.

She never had a chance to test this new knowledge with Mike. He had left on a Sunday morning over four years ago. She knew he wasn't dead. Mike was very thorough. When the divorce papers came for her to sign, there was a copy of Mike's will. Even if he remarried, Allison and Adam woud have half his estate. It was as if that settled everything between them.

Now she was listening to the night noises again. In the years with Woody she had never heard them. If she waited for him while he played at Heart of the West she kept busy and created her own noises. She might bake, do laundry, mend somehing on the sewing machine. The passing cars and shrieking nighthawks had disappeared. She couldn't remember hearing even rain or wind while she waited for Woody. Now the trees whispered and the birds cried. The laughter and the music from the passing cars was the most painful. She couldn't locate the pain, find its exact spot and cauterize it.

It had been Sullivan who noticed Adam crying, Allison standing forlornly at his side and patting him weakly on the shoulder. Margaret tried to take him in her arms, but he fought her off, crying about the loss of his dogs and pony. "That was our last fishing trip," he cried. Allison began to cry too in her loud, babyish bawling. From the bar Woody shouted: "This is no place for kids, you stupid bitch. Get them out of here!" Then he and Rita walked out the door, Rita pausing for a moment to glance back at the crying children and Margaret, standing by them with her arms hanging uselessly at her sides.

"I'll just drop you," Sullivan had said and Margaret knew he was afraid of the screaming children. She was afraid Adam would turn blue, the way he had as a baby. "I hate you! I hate you! I hate you!" Adam screamed. He ran directly to his room as soon as Sullivan stopped the pickup. She heard Adam sobbing for another hour, but she didn't dare go to him. She would not be able to comfort him tonight.

They were quiet now and Margaret walked into their room and stood staring at them for a long moment. They were both dressed, sprawled across their beds. She covered them and noticed that Allison clutched all her dolls tonight and Adam's hands were still fisted. She wanted Woody to see them this way. He was as much to blame as she was.

Sitting in the Morris chair, Margaret wished that she could yell 'I hate you' and cry herself to sleep. Adam wouldn't forget this night. It would stand between them; she knew it would be somewhere in the space behind his eyes. Margaret wondered if there would ever be a time when she could think of Woody without placing scars on her heart. She felt there was poison seeping through her veins.

Maybe things would have been different if she hadn't slept with

Birdheart. She tried to focus her mind on the morning and erase the afternoon and night. But she couldn't remember the morning, couldn't remember any of the three years Woody had lived with her. She saw Rita and Woody singing at each other under the sun. She smelled Birdheart's body and felt his weight on her. His bones were hard, set firmly beneath the muscles.

"We should have had it out at the dinner," she said aloud. "Woody would be on his damned tour now and my heart would be healed." But as she puzzled this over she couldn't make it come out right. The summer had been more than just tension, she knew that, but now she could find no other images, no pleasant memories. When she thought of their fishing breakfast she only saw herself with a blueberry muffin halfway to her mouth as Woody said: 'By the way.' Woody had never said anything that day, but it was still what Margaret remembered most clearly. Woody had called her a wonderful woman, his best friend, not twelve hours ago. But all she could see was Rita swaying on the bandstand, Woody's eyes looking up at her.

It was clear now what her future would be like, a repetition of the events and scenes after Mike left. She remembered the loneliness of the evenings after the children went to bed, the chill of the double bed with only herself lying there. Three plates for dinner, not four. And there would be odd things left over; men seemed to always forget something. Mike had left several wall-sized Forest Service maps and his barber shears. She wondered what Woody would leave, some scrap of him that he no longer considered to be important and would be easily overlooked.

There would be hollow spots in the living room where the Morris chair and the pedal steel guitar once sat. There would be empty drawers in the dresser and unused hangers in the closet. There would be hollow spots in the rest of her life too. Adam carried grudges; unlike most children who forgot things easily, Adam brooded over an insult or punishment for weeks. He would be scarred by this. His mother had broken his heart. Scars spell NO ONE LOVES ME and a child is different then. Margaret imagined Adam refusing to speak to her, ceasing to love her, and how his silence would weigh on their home. Margaret framed the scene: how

Adam might look at fourteen or fifteen, with Mike's hair and long arms, as he walked out the front door, perhaps to search every bar and recording studio for Woody, who would be drifting somewhere down the road.

She wanted Rita and Woody to leave right now, tonight, so she could get on with the patching process, redesigning her life and the lives of her children without Woody. How could she play softball with Rita for the next month, Woody sitting in the stands watching Rita, not her? Rita and Woody would walk away from the field together. They would sit together in Shelly's Leg. Where would she sit? Who would she talk to?

"Unfair," Margaret said. "So god-damned unfair!" She pitched her glass at the framed portrait of Woody's grandparents above the mantel. She watched in slow motion as the ice and whiskey spun away from the sailing glass. She saw the star pattern burst across the photographed faces. The falling glass rang like small bells.

She wanted to hurt Woody, hurt him as much as he had hurt her. She walked deliberately to the mantel and lifted the broken picture from the wall. There were tiny cuts in the faces of his grandparents, slivers of glass sliding across the frame. With all the strength in her shoulders she raised the wooden frame, felt the shower of glass as she brought it down on the corner of the reel-to-reel. The wooden backing broke and a tear slipped between the two faces in the frame. Again and again she brought the frame down on the corner of the tape machine, satisfied with the feeling of power in her shoulders and arms as the wooden frame splintered, the photograph tore, and the reel-to-reel rocked back and forth under the weight of her blows.

It crashed to the floor at her feet. Margaret stood with the remains of the picture frame in her hands. She hurled the pieces at Woody's Morris chair and kicked the reel-to-reel hard enough to hurt her foot, but the tape machine remained face down on the floor.

One part of her mind recognized how childish this was, but another part told her it made no difference now. She would destroy everything of Woody's, to punish him for what he had done to her. She would attack the things he had left in her house to hurt him for not caring about her, about her children. She wondered if her toe was broken as she hobbled over to the small desk where Woody worked on his music. She didn't care if she broke a toe; it would be some outside sign of the pain and brokenness she felt inside.

Gathering all the sheet music in her arms and picking up a couple of songbooks, Margaret went into the bathroom. She remembered the night Woody burned matchheads in the soap dish, the sulfuric smell like rotten eggs. She threw all the music into the bathtub and lit several pieces with a match. The smoke curled up around the showerhead and made Margaret wonder if she would stain the ceiling this way. Who cares, she thought. It's my house. Every time I take a bath I'll think of Woody. Men were always leaving pieces of themselves behind. The old boat tarp of Mike's was still in the garage, his maps on the walls in the children's room. The smoky filigree of Woody's music would hang above her bathtub.

She watched the yellow flames curling through the sheets of music, and somewhere in her mind she could hear the tunes as Woody played them. The song for her, something special for this first number. The music unraveled at the bottom of her bathtub, arcing into black commas before the flames consumed it. Bits of ash drifted in the air and the smoke swirled through the room.

Suddenly she was afraid her heart might stop, might just quit beating and the flames in the bathtub would consume her house and her children. She imagined the flames leaping to the curtains, crowning like a forest fire across to the towels, dropping burning ash on the carpet and snaking through her house on the draft of the night wind. She heard each separate beat of her heart and the silence between them. Could she die of a broken heart? A heart that literally tore, broke, ceased to function because of some pain in her life. Margaret reasoned that if her spirit had left her, as it had this evening in Birdheart's room, her heart might break. She reached quickly over the flames and turned on the shower. The fire hissed like thousands of wasps crawling in the bottom of her bathtub. Smoke rose in a circle and rolled through the room. At that moment Margaret didn't mind dying from a failure of her heart, her spirit, but she could not allow anything to happen to her children. It's funny, she thought. If I just quit living right now, Woody and Rita would probably take the kids on that tour with them. The tour and Woody always seemed to win.

The smoke burned her eyes and tore through her chest as she tried to breathe. She rushed out to the kitchen, her heart booming in her ears. She could feel the pressure of her pulse throbbing in her earlobes. She had to do something, something safer than fire, to contain all the energy in her body. She believed if she stopped moving for only an instant the pressure inside her would expand and scatter bits of her throughout the house. She was composed of millions of small pieces, held together only by motion.

She took the icepick from a drawer and ran into the living room. She felt she had phenomenal strength as she brought the icepick down on the seat of the Morris chair and, with both hands clenched to the handle, tore a gash straight through the seat, pulling toward her legs. She stabbed at the back and carved ragged patterns out onto the wings. White feathers floated through the room. They smelled like charcoal and dust as they burst out of the chair and drifted in the air. She pulled and tugged on the icepick, exposing large sections of the bowels of the chair and listening to the whisper of the shredding fabric. Heaps of feathers covered her feet, fine white curlicues of feathers settled in her hair, stuck to the sweat on her neck and face. Her heart pounded and banged like someone knocking on a door.

The white feather stuffing drifted and floated to the floor in slow, lazy arcs. Margaret watched one feather falling and turning in the air, hoping its wafting would calm her and stop the thudding in her heart. But as she watched the feather she realized the noise she was hearing was not inside her body. It was outside, behind her. Someone was pounding on the door.

Assuming it was Woody, Margaret opened the door and said: "See how you like this!" But it was Sullivan who stood on the porch.

Sullivan wrinkled his nose and looked quickly into the corners of the room. "Maggie. Your house is on fire." He moved past her into the living room. "Good Christ!"

for not caring about her, about her children. She wondered if her toe was broken as she hobbled over to the small desk where Woody worked on his music. She didn't care if she broke a toe; it would be some outside sign of the pain and brokenness she felt inside.

Gathering all the sheet music in her arms and picking up a couple of songbooks, Margaret went into the bathroom. She remembered the night Woody burned matchheads in the soap dish, the sulfuric smell like rotten eggs. She threw all the music into the bathtub and lit several pieces with a match. The smoke curled up around the showerhead and made Margaret wonder if she would stain the ceiling this way. Who cares, she thought. It's my house. Every time I take a bath I'll think of Woody. Men were always leaving pieces of themselves behind. The old boat tarp of Mike's was still in the garage, his maps on the walls in the children's room. The smoky filigree of Woody's music would hang above her bathtub.

She watched the yellow flames curling through the sheets of music, and somewhere in her mind she could hear the tunes as Woody played them. The song for her, something special for this first number. The music unraveled at the bottom of her bathtub, arcing into black commas before the flames consumed it. Bits of ash drifted in the air and the smoke swirled through the room.

Suddenly she was afraid her heart might stop, might just quit beating and the flames in the bathtub would consume her house and her children. She imagined the flames leaping to the curtains, crowning like a forest fire across to the towels, dropping burning ash on the carpet and snaking through her house on the draft of the night wind. She heard each separate beat of her heart and the silence between them. Could she die of a broken heart? A heart that literally tore, broke, ceased to function because of some pain in her life. Margaret reasoned that if her spirit had left her, as it had this evening in Birdheart's room, her heart might break. She reached quickly over the flames and turned on the shower. The fire hissed like thousands of wasps crawling in the bottom of her bathtub. Smoke rose in a circle and rolled through the room. At that moment Margaret didn't mind dying from a failure of her heart, her spirit, but she could not allow anything to happen to her children. It's funny, she thought. If I just quit living right now, Woody and Rita would probably take the kids on that tour with them. The tour and Woody always seemed to win.

The smoke burned her eyes and tore through her chest as she tried to breathe. She rushed out to the kitchen, her heart booming in her ears. She could feel the pressure of her pulse throbbing in her earlobes. She had to do something, something safer than fire, to contain all the energy in her body. She believed if she stopped moving for only an instant the pressure inside her would expand and scatter bits of her throughout the house. She was composed of millions of small pieces, held together only by motion.

She took the icepick from a drawer and ran into the living room. She felt she had phenomenal strength as she brought the icepick down on the seat of the Morris chair and, with both hands clenched to the handle, tore a gash straight through the seat, pulling toward her legs. She stabbed at the back and carved ragged patterns out onto the wings. White feathers floated through the room. They smelled like charcoal and dust as they burst out of the chair and drifted in the air. She pulled and tugged on the icepick, exposing large sections of the bowels of the chair and listening to the whisper of the shredding fabric. Heaps of feathers covered her feet, fine white curlicues of feathers settled in her hair, stuck to the sweat on her neck and face. Her heart pounded and banged like someone knocking on a door.

The white feather stuffing drifted and floated to the floor in slow, lazy arcs. Margaret watched one feather falling and turning in the air, hoping its wafting would calm her and stop the thudding in her heart. But as she watched the feather she realized the noise she was hearing was not inside her body. It was outside, behind her. Someone was pounding on the door.

Assuming it was Woody, Margaret opened the door and said: "See how you like this!" But it was Sullivan who stood on the porch.

Sullivan wrinkled his nose and looked quickly into the corners of the room. "Maggie. Your house is on fire." He moved past her into the living room. "Good Christ!"

"Only the bathroom," Margaret said.

Sullivan ran into the bathroom and gazed down at the charred music floating in the bottom of the tub. "What the hell is going on here?" Margaret stood behind him, the icepick still in her hand. "Give me that." Sullivan took her wrist and pried the icepick out of her fingers. He walked her back to the living room and sat her on the couch. He sighed heavily, blowing the air through his cheeks. "Looks like I'm a little late," he said.

"You're just in time," Margaret said. "I've got the footlocker next and then the pedal steel."

"I think you've done enough for one night."

"This is like a movie. You've come to save me from myself. Where's your horse, Cowboy? Hey, White Knight, where's your charger breathing fire?" Her laughter sounded like the screaming of a small child.

Sullivan was washing her face with cold water and she had a shot of bourbon curled in her hands. "Oh my," she said when she recognized the cuts and blood on her hands. Her face felt sticky and wherever Sullivan touched her there was a needle of pain. "Oh my. Am I all right?"

"You'll live," Sullivan said. "But some of this stuff is done for." He looked around the room again, at the disemboweled chair, the shattered frame, the capsized tape machine.

"Well, at least they'll say I done it in style." Margaret began to cry and Sullivan pulled her onto his lap like a child, rocking her and stroking her hair. Through her tears Margaret could see blood from her face smeared across Sullivan's white polo shirt. There was no longer that clear part of her mind that observed her actions. There was just the deep burning, the air gagging through her body, the fire in her eyes.

Sullivan held her against his chest, her legs thrown over his lap. He stroked the back of her head, his hand running through her hair. Her hair smelled of smoke and a lemony shampoo. It was soft in his hands but every once in a while he caught slivers of glass which he picked out carefully and dropped in an ashtray.

"Go ahead and cry," he told her in a soft voice. "Get it all out of your system."

"It's all such a mess," Margaret sobbed. "It just gets worse and worse."

"No," Sullivan said, "I think the worst is over now. I think you've probably bottomed out."

Adam stood in the doorway, clutching his shirt together at the throat. Sullivan motioned for him to come over to the couch, to sit with them.

Adam looked around the room, tears standing in his eyes. "Shoot her!" he shouted. "Shoot her like you would a dog!" He ran sobbing back to the bedroom.

"A lot of unhappy people tonight," Sullivan said.

Margaret cried, the words sticking in her throat. "Even my son hates me."

"Now, now. That's enough of that. Can't let these things get out of proportion. It just takes some time."

"I should be shot," Margaret said. "Like that dog. I'm rabid. Crazy."

Sullivan laughed and patted her shoulder. "The old woman-scorned routine. Buck up now. You'll give yourself a hangover or something."

Margaret cried until her eyes were dry and burning, until she knew she must stop because there was nothing left to cry out any longer. But she continued to sit on Sullivan's lap, letting his hand run through her hair. She felt arrows of pain stabbing through her chest, swelling in her eyes puffed tight from her tears. Her heart still pounded but now she recognized she would not be lucky enough to die. She would not even lose consciousness and feared these feelings would be with her even in her sleep. She would live through this as she had lived when Mike left her. Hang on to this moment, she told herself. There's going to be lots of lonesome nights when no one will be kind enough to hold you.

Sullivan sensed she was becoming calmer. He felt her breathing less ragged against his chest. Her hands still clutched his shirt collar and he reached up and loosened her grip, holding her hand in his. "You're going to be all right," he said. "Nothing in this life is permanent. Even pain."

Margaret was afraid if she shifted on his lap or started to cry again he would leave her. 'You are ugly when you cry.' Mike used to say. She kept her head down so Sullivan could not see her tear-stained face. She wondered how women in movies could cry and not get puffy-eyed.

"Pain's real funny," Sullivan said. "There's no way to describe it. One of the few words in the language with no other word to help it out. My broken arm can't be described in terms of your pulled tooth. Or, maybe, your broken heart." He shifted her a bit on his lap. "Pain's private and all we can do for one another is to wait with them until it passes."

"Sullivan." Margaret's voice was very small. "Sometimes it doesn't pass." Maybe part of the pain she felt tonight had to do with Mike. Pain she had bottled up for years. She had never done anything like this when Mike left. She had become catatonic, sitting in the dark, silent tears streaming down her face. Nothing had been broken then but herself.

"It passes," Sullivan said. His chin rested on the crown of her head. "You don't notice when it's gone. And sometimes it surprises you when it comes back. Like malaria. You think you're over it. You've forgotten you even had it. Then one day it's back and there's no reason you can name for it."

"I never did this when Mike left," Margaret said. It seemed important to convince Sullivan that this was true.

"I know," Sullivan said. "Probably whatever you did then didn't work either."

Margaret sighed and felt the air all through her body. "I should have lived in my mother's world," she said. "They had standards then. You had rules. You made a commitment. You didn't go down every time you had an itch."

"It's always been the same," Sullivan said. He shifted her over and reached out for cigarettes on the coffee table. He lit two and handed one to Margaret. "The rules are just private now, not pasted up on billboards like when I was a kid."

Margaret sat back against his shoulder, dragging slowly on the cigarette. Feathers still floated in the air near the door and her eye caught pieces of glass and fragments of wood lying on the floor out to the kitchen. "Not me," she said. "Not Woody. He went off with Rita to hurt me. I went off with Birdheart to hurt him." Margaret suddenly felt very calm, as if all her problems were solved. "Maybe we hurt them," she said. "Or maybe even you. We got everybody involved in this because we couldn't make any commitments to each other."

"I'd say all this is some kind of commitment." Sullivan waved his cigarette at the room. "This certainly doesn't suggest you don't care."

"You know," Margaret said, "I feel like I've got it all figured out now. Maybe I do. Or maybe it's just another piece of dumbness like trying to destroy Woody's stuff."

Sullivan blew a smoke ring. "You think you got it all figured out, huh?"

"Yeah," Margaret said. "It seems like I do." She laughed. "But you know, Sullivan, all my life I've been afraid I lack just about three IQ points of being able to run my own life."

Sullivan squeezed her hand and smiled. "You're luckier than most if it's only three."

A vision of order came to Margaret's mind, as if all the thoughts and feelings she had been circling for the last few weeks assumed a shape now. It wasn't as clear and simple as beads on a string. It wasn't one perfect line. To her, it looked more like a suspension bridge, ideas looping down to support and hold the main thought. "I just never cared in the right way," she said. She reached forward and took a sip of the bourbon Sullivan had set on the table. There was a fluttering inside her, some fear or excitement she couldn't name, but could recognize as being important to this moment. "I'm selfish," she said at last. "I was selfish with Mike. I wanted my own life, not just to be some possession of his."

"Shelly used to say it was always a loss when some woman began thinking of herself as somebody's wife." Sullivan said. "She always hated that word. Wife. Said it even sounded ugly. She wanted everyone to be Ralph or Sue or whoever they were. She didn't think it was fair to ask someone else to be responsible for you."

"I know," Margaret said and turned to him, her eyes excited by this discovery. "I always hated it too. 'This is my wife,' Mike would say, and no one would call me by my name all evening. I hated it.

But I was too young. I didn't know any power but sex and children. And I thought I could be something, someone, with just that."

"Well," Sullivan said. "There's nothing wrong with that. Lots of women do it."

"There's something wrong if you hate it."

Sullivan shrugged. "You're not Woody's wife."

"That's it," Margaret said. "I was selfish with Woody too. Only in a different way. I wouldn't share myself with him." She feared she would cry again. "I was so afraid he would run off and leave me, like Mike did, that I made him run off and leave me."

"You can take all the blame if you want to," Sullivan said, "but I'd parcel some of it out to Woody. He baited you. It should have never come to this."

Margaret collapsed back against his shoulder. "I don't know," she said. "Now that I've got it all figured out I still lack those three IQ points to know what to do with it."

"You're the lady who told me she had to take care of herself. Who wanted to be the power, save her own life."

"All this for a stupid tour." Margaret sighed. "I should have just gone."

"You're taking care as best you can." Sullivan patted her shoulder. "It'll all work out. You'll see."

"My father," Margaret said, "he took care of my mother until the day he died. And then she remarried and that guy took care of her. She didn't have to do everything for herself. And she never taught me to." Margaret was angry, but tried to recognize how easily she could step out of this, blame everything on someone else. It wouldn't work that way. She had always blamed Mike, now she blamed Woody. At some point she would have to accept some of the blame herself.

"I bet she did," Sullivan said. "It's harder to see because there were more secrets then. Hell, I thought my mother and father had a picture-book marriage. It wasn't until Ernie started to go a little senile that I found out the truth. I think I would have liked my mother a lot better if I had known she had that kind of spunk."

They sat in silence for a moment. Margaret kept her eyes closed so she would not have to see the destruction in her living room. She tried to imagine Sullivan as a child, a boy like Adam. It was impossible. She was aware of the way her legs were slung over Sullivan's thighs, his arm around her shoulder and his chin resting on her head. It would be nice to sit this way forever, Margaret thought, and she felt herself drifting, as relaxed and comfortable as she had ever been.

Sullivan shifted a bit. "I'll tell you a story," he said, "then I'm going to put you to bed. You've been a bit of a child tonight so I'll tell you a bedtime story." He tipped her face up to his and looked at her slowly, all the various parts of her face. He kissed her softly on the brow.

"Did I ever tell you why Shelly wanted that motel in the bar?" Sullivan asked.

"It's not much of a motel," Margaret said. "I always suspected it was just a place for drunks to sleep." She tried to laugh at herself. "And for ladies to go crazy."

"Not quite," Sullivan said. "Women are funny about how they look." He decided not to say anything about the cuts on Maggie's face. She would discover them for herself tomorrow. Tomorrow, he thought, will be a bad day for her. He wished she and Rita were still friends.

"You should have seen Shelly," he said. "Of course, I'm biased. But I truly thought she was the most beautiful woman I'd ever seen. She was even beautiful as a young girl. She was lucky like that, or maybe I was. Some women are only beautiful at certain ages. Some when they're young, and then they fade. Some grow into their beauty. But Shelly was beautiful until the day she died." Sullivan concentrated on seeing Shelly as a young girl. He remembered the long legs, thin and coltish he always thought. The roundness of her breasts that fit so perfectly into the palms of his hands. He knew if he closed his eyes he could see her clear stare, the fringe of her long lashes around the open eyes.

"But when she lost her leg in that accident she became frightened." He remembered how she looked lying in the hospital, the rusty scabs and liver-colored bruises scattered on her face and arms.

And the shadowy space in the bed where her leg had been. "Paul was a funny one," he said. "I only talked to him once, before the accident, when Shelly's mother died. After that I never spoke to him, although I'd catch a glimpse of him sometimes in the hospital. Maybe I should have said something to him, I don't know. But one day right before Shelly was going to be released she asked me what I was going to do. That question had had me terrified for weeks. Hell, I didn't know. I figured once Shelly got out of that hospital I'd lost her for good. And I couldn't bear that."

Without a word, Margaret reached over to the table and handed Sullivan the bourbon bottle. Sullivan smiled when he accepted it; it was just what he wanted. Maybe some night Maggie would drink with him in the bar, he thought.

"I told her I didn't know and she asked me if I would like to take a trip with her. A trip with her." Sullivan smiled, his eyes wide, his eyebrows up. "It was beyond all my dreams. She explained that she and Paul had talked and he said she could do anything she wanted, go back to him, go off with me. Anything at all. He wasn't going to bribe her with money; she could have all she wanted. Anything. And she chose me." Sullivan shook his head with another small smile and handed the bottle to Margaret.

"We traveled. I always suspected she was just getting used to being without her leg and she would eventually go back to Paul. But she didn't. She wanted to come to Montana and open a dancehall. That's what it was back then, a dancehall with live music every night. Shelly loved to watch the dancing. It seemed to be the only thing she really regretted about losing her leg."

Sullivan was aware of his hand resting on Margaret's thigh, the full butteriness above her knee, almost the exact spot where Shelly had her stump. "That bar," he said, "used to be an old Ma and Pa grocery. The people were going to retire and move to New Mexico. Paul gave Shelly the money to buy it and turn it into her dancehall." Sullivan remembered the pale green check Paul sent. Cash outright, no payments. It was a sum of money Sullivan could not imagine. Some nights as he lay beside Shelly in bed he imagined the money as bills, fifty dollar bills, one hundred dollar bills, physical money he could hold in his hand. But as he counted those imaginary bills Sullivan would drift off to sleep and the amount would still not be reached.

"Those rooms, Birdheart's and Deadeye's and Valgaardson's, were just old storage rooms and Shelly wanted to make them into a motel. The Rio Montana Motel, she was going to call it. We were living in the apartment upstairs and working on the bar. I told her I didn't think we needed a motel. The bar was enough. And the laundromat. Women still used the laundromat then. But Shelly insisted. I kept asking her why, and she kept saying it was her place, and I'd agree with that, but I wanted to know why the god-damned motel seemed so important to her."

Margaret handed him the bottle and again Sullivan appreciated her sense of timing, the exact spots where he wanted silences in his stories. "One night she finally told me. She said she was afraid I was with her out of pity. Duty. She said pity was the sorriest emotion ever invented; she knew because she pitied Paul for feeling so guilty about the accident. It was a disgusting feeling that made her stomach crawl."

Sullivan took a sip of the bourbon. "I wasn't with her out of pity. I have pitied people, and it is disgusting. But I never once pitied her. There was something about her that just wouldn't allow it. Oh, sometimes I felt sorry about something specific, like the fact she couldn't dance anymore. But never pity. I couldn't convince her of that. She said I might pity her later. That's why she'd never marry me. She said it would tie her to me and someday I might get tired of living with a one-legged woman and if we were married it would be harder for me to leave." Sullivan brushed a feather off his knee.

"She wanted that motel to prove she was still an attractive woman, even without her leg. She reasoned very few women would ever take a motel room in a bar and she wasn't going to run whores, that wasn't her style. She wanted men in those rooms. She said if she began to feel that she was no longer an attractive woman she could test it out on those men in the rooms. She would be able to judge herself that way. If they didn't want her, then she would know and would try to adjust to that."

"That's crazy," Margaret said. "Didn't she know you loved her?"

"Oh sure," Sullivan said. "Before the accident. But after she lost her leg she just wasn't as sure of herself anymore. At least for a while." Sullivan ran his hand back over his hair and massaged the back of his neck for a moment. "Birdheart used to be a carpenter," he said. "Before he went to Vietnam and came back the crazy bastard he is now. He was real young then, just off a ranch in eastern Montana and drifting around looking for his life. He rented that first room when it was ready. He'd been there about six weeks and we were still working on the bar, just finishing it up. It had been over a year since the accident and Shelly got real depressed. I did everything I could, suggested we take another trip, get married, anything to bring her out of it. But I just couldn't. One night we were lying in bed and she said to me: 'I'm going to use that new room and the young fellow in it.'"

Margaret patted his hand. "Birdheart," she said.

"Yeah," Sullivan said. "Lord knows I didn't want her to do it. But she said she needed it, needed to know she was still attractive. She made me promise not to interfere and told me she loved me and that this was just a test. Birdheart was real moral then; the war changed all that, but then he thought it would be some kind of sin or something. It took her about a month. She made me promise not to tell him the real reason if he asked. Finally, he came up to me one night and said: 'You know, your woman has been putting the moves on me. It's driving me crazy.' I lied. It about killed me but I did it. I did it for Shelly, not really sure what would happen when she finally got him. I said it was okay, that I didn't mind. A little variety is good for the sex life. All crap as far as I'm concerned, but it meant a lot to Shelly."

Sullivan took another sip on the bottle, wondering if he would feel the pain again or if it had truly left him all those years ago. "I lay in our bed upstairs. I think I might have cried. All kinds of thoughts ran through my head that night. Like maybe she didn't love me. Maybe I wasn't good enough for her, hadn't satisfied her and she needed some young stud to get her rocks off with. I wanted to kill the bastard, young, pretty kid like that. He didn't have the hardness in his eyes then. He seemed innocent, asking me, being worried about it in the first place. That was a horrible night. But it worked out. Shelly came up the next morning to fix breakfast and she got in the bed and held me. At first I didn't think I could stand it, but she talked to me, trying to explain the difference between sex and love. I don't know you can explain that, maybe the meaning lies in the tone of the words, not the words themselves, just their tone and a look in the eyes and the touch of a hand. She and Birdheart had just had sex, and whatever it had given her she had needed. But with us, we had love. And she needed that, more than the sex. She said she hoped she'd never have to use that room again. And she didn't."

"What about Birdheart?"

"I guess after they were done Shelly told him the real reason she seduced him. He took it pretty well. We got along fine after that, became real good friends. The big problem was what Birdheart was going to do with his life. He traveled some but always came back to us. In a year or two he decided to join the war. That was where the action was, he said. And when he came back he was different. The man you slept with today. Sometimes I don't even remember what Birdheart was like before the war; I can't remember his real name. But he came back to us, back to that room, with a whole chunk of him missing. Sometimes Shelly could see what was gone, some part of his soul. Every once in a while I can see it. Only Birdheart knows what's really gone, what he left in the jungles of Vietnam, or what they took from him. He's not the boy we sent off. I don't know what he is now."

"Did he come back for Shelly?" Margaret held her breath, afraid that was the wrong question.

"In a way. He never tried to take her to bed again. But once he told her that we were his past, all of the past he wanted to deal with. And that he knew we would take him in because he knew Shelly's secret, her one fear. He said: 'As long as I'm in that room you'll never have to worry about being an attractive lady.' "

Margaret took the bottle from Sullivan's hand and sipped at it, the bourbon stinging her lips. She wondered what to do about a story like this, what she could say to comfort Sullivan. Hell, she thought, I can't even comfort myself. I think so damn slow. A couple of days from now I'll know what this means. Not tonight.

Sullivan lit another cigarette and offered it to her. "That was your bedtime story," he said. "It's almost morning. Listen." Outside, birds were chirping in the trees.

"I'm going to put you to bed," Sullivan said, "because you're not going to like what I've got to do next."

Margaret's eyes widened. "What?"

"I didn't come here to put out fires in your bathtub." He pulled a slip of paper from his breast pocket. "Woody wanted me to get some stuff."

Margaret sat stiffly in Sullivan's lap. She had been leaning against Woody's list for the last hour, his neat handwriting numbering out the things he wanted to take with him, to take out of her house.

"Come on," Sullivan said. "You don't have to watch."

Margaret continued to sit on his lap, searching in her mind for the right thing to do. Her thoughts tried to slip away from her as if they had a life of their own. But Margaret concentrated on pulling this back into focus. She blocked the sounds of the birds, the comfortable feeling of sitting on Sullivan's lap. Finally she said: "No."

"Come on, Maggie. We've had enough excitement for one night."

"I mean I'll help you." She turned to face him, her eyes searching his to see if this was the right thing to do. "It's the spaces," she said. "When someone leaves you, you discover all these spaces in your life. I don't want to be surprised by them in the morning. I want to watch them appear."

Together they moved through the house. They packed Woody's suitcases and stuck his boots in a plastic trash bag. They hauled the footlocker out onto the porch and lifted it into the back of Sullivan's pickup. Margaret took his books out of the bookcase and stacked them neatly in paper bags. She handed Sullivan the pliers and a screwdriver to take down the pedal steel guitar. They even laughed when Sullivan decided there was no point in moving the Morris chair. A monument, he told Margaret. A monument to passion.

Margaret felt like crying only once, when she gathered the wicker creel and the fishing gear out of the utility room. But she didn't cry, merely reflected that if she would cry, the wicker creel would be appropriate. There was no room for tears now. She watched the spaces appear in her house. She found dustpuppies in the corners where Woody had stored his ice chest, his footlocker. The books in the bookcase leaned against each other crookedly. Hangers rattled in the closet. The paper in his dresser drawers was rumpled. Margaret wanted to stuff these spaces with dirty clothes, old newspapers, shapeless objects to hide the defined space. But she forced herself to look at the places where Woody's things had been. She memorized them, the emptiness, the hollowness.

It was still early when they finished. The pickup was only half filled and Margaret thought it would be more complete in her mind if the pickup was packed, the pieces of Woody's life cluttered and jammed into every corner like a truck from the movie *Grapes of Wrath*. His things looked so small in Sullivan's pickup, not an accurate measure of what he was taking from here, no compensation for the spaces.

"Enough," Sullivan said. "There's no point doing more than this." They stood on the lawn, the grass damp with dew, and watched the sun crest the treeline, its colors moving through the spectrum from blue to gold. There were no clouds this morning and Margaret thought the sun looked painted on the sky. They listened to the warbling birds and watched the silhouettes dart across the quickening sky. Margaret wished she had a rooster to announce this day.

She didn't notice when the streetlights went out. One minute they were on, but when she looked again they were off. She regretted not seeing that exact moment when the lights flicked off. It would have been a sign she understood.

The sunrise moment was broken by a truck rumbling by. Sullivan took her hand and led her into the house, into her bedroom. He pulled the drapes and turned down the covers.

"Let me get you some breakfast," Margaret said. She wanted Sullivan to stay with her, help her keep the fears away. She wished he could sleep with her the way a child frightened in the night wants the warmth of another person beside him.

"No," Sullivan said. "Get some sleep. I'll talk to you after you've rested." He left her in the bedroom, standing by the bed, and closed the door on her. As she undressed she heard him straightening up the living room.

fifteen

Margaret was resigned to pitching against Moose Lodge on Thursday night. She couldn't think of a lie to tell her team about the scabs on her arms and face and was afraid the truth had become a bad bar joke. Then, unexpectedly, her boss asked her to work overtime on a rush job that had to be camera-ready by Friday morning. A little extra money never hurt anyone, her boss said. But Margaret knew it wasn't the money. She simply didn't have the heart to face the Shelly's Leg regulars until her cuts healed.

"Come on, Maggie," Sullivan said when she phoned. "I never thought you were a coward."

"Coward? What do you mean coward?"

"No one's even going to notice," he said.

"I know," Margaret said. "But I still have to work."

Sullivan volunteered to take the kids to the game. Maggie could come whenever she got through.

"No," Margaret said, wondering if Sullivan could hear the lie in her voice. "I'll be late. I'll bring them down here." When she called the bar at ten Valgaardson told her they had won. 15–9. Lots of good hitting, he said.

Allison and Adam played cards while Margaret pasted in prices on the sale shopper. Toilet paper—10 for $1.00. Grapes—39¢ a pound. It was mindless work and in the silence of the empty printing plant Margaret's thoughts kept drifting.

Over and over again Margaret saw Rita as she turned from the bar door to look back at Margaret and her crying children. She kept hoping that if she understood that look in Rita's eyes she would unlock some of this puzzle. She would know how to deal with Rita. At least once a week for the next month Margaret would have to spend an hour and a half looking at Rita, obeying her signals, working together against the other teams. The minutes on the mound wouldn't be bad; Margaret could concentrate on the batter, the type of pitch. But there would be those odd moments between innings, in the dugout, before and after the games, when Rita would be there, simply there. Unlike her children, Margaret was supposed to be grownup. Tonight she didn't feel very grown up. Tonight she felt she was playing hookey.

She could quit the team, as simple as that. But quitting would be self-punishing. She would deny herself the pleasure of standing on the mound, her slight smile when she outsmarted the batter. It would deny her the surprise and pride she felt when she connected with a good, solid swing. Enough had been taken from her already; to give up more seemed unfair. But what is fair? Margaret thought. Or real? Part of her mind still believed that what had happened was merely dramatic. Woody hadn't left her. Rita hadn't betrayed her. It was all part of a game they were playing, without knowing the rules or the reasons. It hung in the air around all of them and any one of them could call it off, quit playing, when the moment seemed right.

As she pasted in the prices on the sale items, she tried to find her role. She wished she could see the exact moment when she should have taken control and everyone and everything could have returned to normal. A whisper in her mind told her this was nonsense. But she brushed that thought away and concentrated on lining out the prices with her T square. She limited her thoughts to fractions of an inch. At least at the drawing board she was in control.

Margaret waited through the days, trying not to imagine what Rita or Woody might be doing at any specific moment. When she caught herself thinking of Woody eating breakfast or Rita as she turned behind the bar at Shelly's to mix another drink, Margaret tried to counter these pictures with neutral thoughts. Sometimes she recited the words to a song without running the melody through her head or she added a string of numbers together until the nines looked like fours or found that the only number she could clearly see would be the seven. One night as dusk fell Margaret started a list: 'Thoughts I Could Think About.' She numbered each line to the bottom of the page, one through twenty-five. It took a long time to come up with her first entry: Can Wind Be Predicted? It looked so silly sitting at the top of the page, not even any space for an answer if she could find one, that Margaret crossed it off, balled up the piece of paper, and lobbed it into the wastebasket.

The following Friday night was a game against Modern Auto and Machine. Margaret decided to skip the pre-game pep talk Sullivan always held in the card room at the back of the bar and simply show up on the field as close to the start of the game as possible. Sullivan was right; she was a coward. The false smiles, the vacant chit-chat, the shifting of eyes in those long moments while Sullivan laid out his usual rap seemed more than Margaret could bear. When she thought of walking through Shelly's Leg, her hands began to sweat and Margaret noticed for the first time a tiny twitch beneath her left eye.

Sullivan called half an hour before game time. Margaret assured him she would be there; she was just running a bit late, she said. She sat in her uniform and smoked a cigarette while she watched the end of a TV show.

She arrived at the field shortly after the infield warm-up began and noticed right away that Rita's car was not in the lot. Maybe Rita was the coward tonight, she thought, and for the first time tried to imagine how Rita might feel.

Margaret was pitching risers to Coker when she heard the rusted cough of Rita's Edsel. Her pitches flattened out while Rita suited up. By the time Rita waddled over, her glove caught between her knees while she buckled the straps on her chest protector, Coker was disgusted. "She's pitching so sloppy she makes me look good," Coker told Rita as they swapped positions. Rita crouched, pounded her glove, and said nothing.

MAM had a bad night; by the end of the game they had logged

eight errors to the Shelly's Leg three. Margaret's pitching didn't improve much after the flat risers. She pitched as well as Coker could have managed any night. But Margaret had not pitched for two weeks now. She hadn't practiced. By the fifth inning her arm ached, but she said nothing and concentrated on the game. In the dugout she watched her team as if they were the competition. She studied their batting and stance and rehearsed what pitch she would give each woman, the exact combination that would send each of them down swinging. She refused to let herself think about Rita.

Shelly's Leg won 10–8 and as the women walked the formal line shaking hands, Margaret's left eye began to twitch. She was going to take Adam and Allison to that teenage pizza joint they liked so much and imagined how ridiculous she would look sipping a Coke in her loud maroon uniform. She would listen to the high school chatter and the silly disco music. Margaret was surprised to realize how much her present situation was like the problems she had worried over in high school. She couldn't decide if these were problems one never outgrows, or if she had never developed any more sophistication than a sophomore.

Mechanically, Margaret stuck her hand out to each of the MAM team and wished for just a moment that she could join the others at Shelly's for a drink. But she knew she could only see herself getting to the door of Shelly's; she could not imagine going in.

Rita touched her arm as she was putting on her sweat jacket. "Don't go yet," Rita said. "I have a surprise for the kids."

I'll bet you have, Margaret thought. A surprise for their mama too. But she watched Rita hurrying off to her car, her black braids bouncing against her shoulders as she jogged over to the parking lot. Margaret lied to the women as they gathered their gear. "Yeah, see you in a minute," she said to Diane. "Got to put the kids to bed," she told Lolie, who offered a ride.

Sullivan strolled up behind her. "I know what you're going to do," he informed her. "You're going to slip out on us." He looked slowly at the corners and angles of her face.

Margaret said nothing. She could not lie staring into his eyes.

"Yep," Sullivan said as if he had been reading her thoughts. "There's nothing I can do about it except tell you I think you're making a mistake."

Margaret shrugged. Her arm ached.

"Foolishness and pride often get mixed up," Sullivan said. "You think on that for a while and we'll be waiting when you're ready." He tugged at the bill of his baseball cap in a parting salute and walked over to his pickup, his hands deep in his jacket pockets.

Rita appeared lugging a Styrofoam cooler and a wicker picnic basket. "What I got here," she said, "is a little piece of my childhood fantasies."

Adam stood at Margaret's side, shifting anxiously from foot to foot. He eyed Rita's hampers suspiciously. "What is that?" he asked.

Rita looked around the deserted diamond. It was full dusk now, a light purple playing through the air. The umpire was unanchoring the last of the bases and carting them off to the gear room behind the concession stand. "In here," Rita said, and she looked around again to make sure they were alone, "is a perfect kid's supper."

"What? Let me see." Allison reached for the wicker hamper.

"Not yet," Rita said. "Come here." She led Margaret and the children out to the pitcher's mound. "When I was a kid," Rita explained as she opened the wicker basket, "I had a perfect supper, the kind of supper I knew my mother would never let me have. At night before I went to bed I would dream about this dinner. I could taste each thing." Rita pulled 7-Eleven sacks out of the hamper. She handed one to Allison. "Part of a perfect kid's supper is the surprise."

Allison opened the sack and took out two packages of baseball bubblegum; the cards were Willie Stargell and Luis Tiant. Also in the sack were two Hershey bars and two packs of Red Hots.

Rita handed another 7-Eleven sack to Adam. He found two Coca Colas and two packages of Hostess Twinkies. "Oh boy," Adam said. "Can we eat these, Mom?"

Margaret was amazed. As Rita continued to pull food from her hamper, two hot dogs with everything from the Bijou Theater, a box of popcorn, Margaret realized it was indeed a perfect kid's dinner. All junk food. Margaret laughed, embarrassed by Rita's kindness and yet aware of the obvious bribe. She imagined Rita racing through the 7-Eleven on her way from Shelly's to the ballfield.

"This might be a little soggy," Rita said as she opened the cooler. She produced a box of plastic spoons and a quarter section of watermelon.

"I learned to spit seeds in school," Allison said proudly.

From the melting ice at the bottom of the cooler Rita took a leaking quart of strawberry ice cream. She pulled a penknife from her pocket and punched two holes in the top of a can of chocolate syrup. "When I was a kid," she said, "I used to put the popcorn on the ice cream, the chocolate syrup on top of that. Cover it all with Red Hots."

"My god," Margaret said. "They'll be sick all night."

"No they won't," Rita said. "You can't get sick on a perfect kid's supper."

Margaret watched her children's delight as they tore off the wrappers and let them drift across the field on the slight night breeze. Stars were beginning to appear in the darkening east. She could hear crickets in the tall grass, as clearly as if they were singing at her feet.

"And I didn't forget us," Rita said. She took a wet bottle of wine from the cooler. "But I couldn't manage the glasses."

Margaret watched Rita whisk her penknife around the top of the bottle to cut the seal. Maybe that's all you need to be prepared for this life, she thought. A penknife in your pocket.

Rita handed her the wine bottle. "Here's to the win," she said.

"I didn't pitch for shit," Margaret said. "My arm aches. Feels like someone's threaded a harpoon through it."

"You're out of practice."

"Is that what this is?" Margaret held the wine bottle out to Rita. "A bribe? To get me to come to practice?"

Rita took the bottle, tipped it and drank. "Come on," she said and inclined her head. "Let's take a walk."

Margaret followed her away from the mound where her children sat eating junk food. The quart of ice cream balanced on the pitcher's rubber; the watermelon juice ran in a dark stream across the dust. Over by the base line, pieces of cellophane drifted on the wind, glowing faintly silver as they rolled across the ground.

"Get down here," Rita said. She crouched behind the plate, her knees splayed as if waiting for the pitch. "Things look different from down here."

Margaret knelt next to Rita, looking out at her children on the pitcher's mound and across the still field. From this angle the field looked more rolling, not as flat as Margaret had always assumed. She saw hollows accentuated by the dusk light, rises that looked as if they would lead off into the trees.

"Sometimes I watch Miriam out in right," Rita said, handing over the wine bottle again. "Miriam plays right different than I would. Once I got out that far, with nothing to do most of the time, I'd be tempted to keep right on backing up, back clear off into the trees and be gone."

"Well," Margaret said. She sat down heavily next to the plate and crossed her legs in front of her. "That's kind of what you're doing, isn't it?"

"Sort of." Rita picked a pebble out of the dust and tried to spin it through her fingers like a quarter. The pebble was too round, too heavy, and fell back into the dirt. "It's not the way you think," Rita said. "I'm not taking Woody away from you."

"You've said that before."

Rita pulled the rubber bands out of her braids and shook out her hair. "We lived with my grandmother on the Res., my father's mother," she said. "She used to tell me I would have a hard time. She said it was important to try and live a long time, long enough to grow old. That's the only reward for a woman, getting to be old. And she told me to remember being a girl, to try to memorize my childhood. Those are the only good periods in a woman's life. For men, my brother James, it would be different. Men couldn't enjoy their childhood; they had to get ready to be a man. And when they're old they're useless. It's being in the prime of life that's so hard for a woman. You don't know whether to lead or be led."

"Is this a little course in sociology?" It was the kind of remark

Margaret would make if she were threatened, all her nerves braced for battle. Yet she felt relaxed sitting in the dirt next to Rita, not defensive. There was an odd sensation in her body, like strange tastes mixed together in her mouth. A summer melon and Brie cheese.

"It's just so hard to start," Rita said.

"Skip it," Margaret said. "Just skip it." Whatever Rita wanted to say might be better left to just this moment, the sun dying in the west, the air mixed with the odor of their sweat. Margaret could accustom herself to this situation slowly. There would be time later to embrace the whole picture.

"Well, I can't skip it," Rita said evenly. "I don't want you to get it from anyone else."

"My ass is getting cold." Margaret felt the fear rising in her again and stood, shaking out her shoulder, and began walking the base line out to first.

"We're leaving on the tour right after the finals," Rita said as she trailed behind Margaret. "First over to Washington, then Lloyd's got us gigs all the way down the coast. Woody's been talking to that scout from Warner's and we'll be spending some time in LA doing a demo."

"Doing a demo," Margaret repeated.

"Maybe not me," Rita said. "Back-up work doesn't usually include vocalists. After LA we swing over to Tucson, Taos, Austin. Then up through Denver and home by Christmas." Rita was speaking too fast.

Margaret felt her ears ringing.

"It could have been you," Rita said. "He wanted you to go. Not me."

Margaret stood by the first-base anchor, flipping the metal ring back and forth with her toe. Out behind right were the choke-cherry bushes where the rabid dog had appeared. Over to the left, in Shirley's short field, was where the dog fell. Margaret expected to hear that shot again. But she heard nothing except the crickets. Even the children were quiet. "You're going," she said.

"I got no choice," Rita said. "I don't hold with that Calvin Coolidge line about sitting on your front porch and sooner or later a Chinaman will walk by. I'm beginning to believe if you sit still nothing moves."

Margaret watched Rita's face, the shifting of her eyes as she looked back into Margaret's. The scent of wild mint was on the air.

"I got no choice," Rita said again. "I'm pushing thirty-five and I've done nothing but watch Indians die of depression and whites spend their life drunk."

"I'm supposed to pity you?"

"Don't pity me. And for God's sakes, quit pitying yourself. You have to think about your kids, give them a home and some steady money. I see why you can't go. Me, I got some broken-down pets, a garden that won't grow, and a leaky shack."

"You have Woody." It surprised Margaret she felt no pain when she said this. She expected something inside her to hurt, but there was nothing. She couldn't feel her heart beating.

"Having Woody," Rita said, "is like having a handful of air. Like Anthony. You can't keep those boys in your mind. They're still children, following dreams. That's no use to you; you need something steady."

"And what do you seem to need?"

"Listen," Rita said. "It was all I could do to get my ass out of Browning. I got down here and no further. I'll probably die in this damn town, but I want to see something happen to me before I do. Woody's not the issue at all. I've got to get out and see some of the world before I'm happy with my spot in it. It just drifts away from you in that bar. Maybe if I get out and see something I'd have a chance."

"Meaning what?"

"I wanted to go with Anthony when he left," Rita said softly. "It's been on my mind to get out of this rut for a while. But Anthony wouldn't take me. He didn't even come back." Rita tucked a strand of hair behind her ear. "I just can't get on a bus and get off wherever my ticket expires."

"So you are going to ride with Woody."

"Yes," Rita said. "I'm going to ride with Woody."

Margaret moved down the base line toward second, pausing for a moment to consider walking off into the trees, to step out like an amnesia victim into a future you couldn't imagine and a past you couldn't remember. She and Rita had spoken; that was enough. If it meant anything at all it would still mean something tomorrow. She didn't blame Rita though, because she understood some of this. If Mike hadn't brought her out here ten years ago, Margaret would still be in the East. It seemed to her that women never had anywhere to go and men surely and always did.

"This doesn't make anything right," Margaret said. "I feel my heart rusting at night."

"That's because you're such a half-ass," Rita said. "It's not enough to figure out what you need, as opposed to what you want. You need stability; you want Woody. You've got to figure out how to make all this work."

"Like you, I suppose," Margaret said.

Rita laughed. "God I hope not. Here. Sit." She grabbed Margaret's hand and pulled her down on the grass off the base line. "In a way I'm fulfilling a tradition. The Blackfeet have a story about the Deer Woman. The Deer Woman excuses all Indian whores, kind of like the patron saint of fallen women. She's very beautiful and comes to the dances on the equinoxes. She has deer feet, cloven like the Devil's."

Rita pulled a piece of grass and twiddled it in the twilight. "There's a lot of slutty Indian women," she said. "I'm just one of them. Legend tells us that we are charmed by the Deer Woman at dances. That she spirits us away to white men who use us and leave us. The Deer Woman is the reason for illegitimate children and half-breeds. But in return, we have a new vision of the world."

Rita stuck the blade of grass in her mouth and lay back, her hands folded under her head. "I can't make this break alone," she said. "On this trip I'll see some of the things I've missed. When it's over I can come back home in peace."

"Well that's mightyfine," Margaret said. "Fuck me over and call it your cultural heritage."

"You know," Rita said evenly, "I don't have to do this. I'm doing this because I'm your friend, no matter what it looks like. You're just starting to make a home here, in a town that *is* my home. We'll know each other long after Woody's made his first million or gone belly-up for the fiftieth time."

"You are like a god-damned country and western song, you know that?" Margaret narrowed her eyes in the growing darkness. "Sappy lyrics and a code of honor a twelve year old finds simple. 'Take what you need and leave the rest.' You've never grown up. You don't know what it's like to give someone a place in your heart and say: 'I trust this to you.' You don't know what it's like to plan, to believe in a future with someone. You don't know what it's like to believe you'll live happily ever after."

"Damn straight," Rita said. "That happily-ever-after shit can't lead to nothing but trouble. And besides, you didn't do any of that with Woody." Rita shifted on the grass, the sound like the sighing of silk. "You kept a cool distance that said: 'You can't touch me. Not really.' "

"You got this all figured out, don't you Pocahontas? You're real smooth. You just work all this around so it comes out your way." Margaret wondered why everyone's rationales, their view of this situation, sounded so much more valid than her own. She knew no matter what anyone said, what was happening between the three of them was cheap and low. And she also knew it was the three of them, not Woody and Rita alone.

"We all think in the past," Rita said. "Maybe at some point you believed in a happily-ever-after. Maybe once you trusted your heart to someone. But that someone wasn't Woody."

"Woody give you this rap?"

"No," Rita said. "I figured it out all by myself. Gives me something to do while I wipe slop off the bar. Me, I could never make that leap. I've had lots of men in my time and there never was a one of them I could give my heart to. When I looked into my future, suddenly the guy vanished."

Rita took a sip from the wine bottle and handed it to Margaret. "Maybe," Rita said, "maybe you gave your heart to Mike. Maybe you planned and trusted. Two kids can't be all accidental. But you hung back on Woody. Now you're like me; can't make that leap of faith."

"No," Margaret said. "Maybe you're like me. Afraid to get off your ass alone." Acknowledging this truth was as quick and painful as a slap. Illusions die the way glass explodes. Margaret remembered a little blond boy in her third grade class who told her Santa Claus didn't exist. Margaret had picked up an abandoned orange crate and threatened to break it over the blond boy's head if he didn't take back that remark. The boy stood his ground, his eyes fluttering between the upheld orange crate and Margaret's face. "Go ahead," he had taunted. "You can hit me. It doesn't change the truth."

"Wouldn't it be wonderful," Rita said, "if life were like a ballgame. Everybody gets lots of turns at bat."

"How's that supposed to make anything better?" Margaret felt it all slipping from her, unmoored from consoling beliefs. I'm thirty years old, she told herself, and still believing in fairy tales. Santa Claus. Happily-ever-after.

"Keeping alive." Rita leaned back on her elbows and spoke to the sky. "Just keeping alive."

"Is that what you're doing with Woody? Just keeping alive?"

"It's not Woody," Rita said. "I'm stuck. If something don't happen to me quick I'll be like all those others I left behind in Browning. I'll be like half the people in that bar, just killing time until they die. I'm trading what I got for a little piece of what's out there."

"Trading on your back."

"If that's the way you want to see it, yeah. The Deer Woman seduced me. I want a piece of her vision. But it's not Woody. It's not even me that has the problem. It's you. You've got to decide what you're after. Whether it's Woody or something else."

Margaret recrossed her legs; she picked clogs of dirt out of her cleats. She had lived without Santa Claus since that autumn afternoon in the third grade. Now she wondered if her life wouldn't have been better if she had lived without the silver image of the shining knight, her mother's magical man, who would someday rush in and take her life in hand. It hadn't been Mike, although she had thought so at first. It hadn't been Woody. "I don't buy your bullshit," Margaret finally said. "Adam and I read about the traders and trappers, the miners and ranchers out here. Every once in a while you'll run across a widow who became a cattle baron or a whore who became the town doctor. Back home I always thought of women in groups, by occupations like nurses or schoolteachers, or in families. I've realized that women who came out here had to invent themselves. As individuals. Like Shelly invented that bar."

"So?"

"So since Mike left me I've been in the process of inventing myself. I've been doing it a long time now, not even realizing it. You're letting Woody invent you. Rita, the country and western singer."

Rita rolled over in the grass. "So what's the fuss? I invented my way out of Browning. One morning I threw my shoes out the window, jumped into them and they brought me here. Mike invented you by giving you those kids. Same process. Different timing."

"What Mike didn't give me," Margaret said, "were some rules. I had to figure them out for myself. Maybe you're right. Maybe I'm viewing Woody with different eyes. But by now ..." Margaret stood quickly and looked at Rita sprawled across the ground as if in a bed. Her own imprint looked like a man lying next to Rita. "It doesn't matter how you get there," Margaret said. "You have to try to respect each other. Sullivan would say you don't steal another man's horse. It leaves him afoot on the prairie."

Rita rolled on her side, her fist cocked to her chin, and looked up at Margaret. "Is Woody your horse? That don't make you no different than me."

"Woody is not my horse," Margaret said. "Or some Lear jet into a fantasy future. As you say, the point is not Woody. It's you and me. You should have let things be."

Margaret began to walk across the infield, hearing for the first time the shrieks and squeals of her children, who were playing tag back among the bleachers. She tried to imagine her life without the fantasy of that perfect man her mother had promised her and felt her breath collapse inside her body, the air whistling in her lungs. But as her breath came back and her eyes steadied again on her children playing in the twilight, Margaret could see it. Without her fairy prince there would only be a series of men, each flawed in his own way, as she was flawed in hers. No one man, no one person,

could ever be perfect for more than one day. Never two days running. The other alternative was exactly what she had been doing
since Mike left, just passing the time, waiting for perfection.

She sensed, more than heard, Rita following her. "Do you
think," Rita said, her voice coming from behind Margaret's shoulders, "that everything would be straight if I didn't go with
Woody? Just jumped a bus to wherever? Would that make it right
for you?"

Margaret searched Rita's brown eyes, then felt the pressure of
Rita's hands holding her own. For a long moment she looked at
Rita, trying to imagine Rita as an old woman, the lines deepened
around the mouth, the long black hair shot with silver. Margaret
imagined herself with her own children grown and gone. It was
just possible to see that at the edge of her mind. And the picture
was clear enough that Margaret knew Woody was not part of it, as
Mike should have been part of it. She knew now what Rita meant
when she said the men in her future vanished. Woody was air, a
floater, a dreamer. He could afford that in much the same fashion
Margaret couldn't afford it. If Woody floated away from her or
back to her, he would be only as predictable as the wind. You can't
chase the air or your fortune.

Margaret smiled and squeezed Rita's hand. "You're just as afraid
as I am," she said.

"Yes. That's something Woody will never know." Rita reached
out to Margaret's face and touched one of the fading scabs on her
cheek.

They began to walk back to the mound together, their shoes
whispering in the dry grass. Together they stuffed wrappers and
bottles into Rita's picnic basket and cooler. "I think we've lost our
wine," Rita said.

Margaret looked around the dark field. Somewhere out beyond
second base Margaret knew the wine bottle was lying on the grass,
the pale green of the bottle catching no light from the waning
moon. Perhaps they had been sitting in one of those depressions
Margaret never saw from the mound, the small hollows that only
Rita could see from behind the plate.

sixteen

It was Miriam who suggested taking the kids to the Fair since her daughter, Robin, had decided Allison was her best friend in the Summer Playgroup. Miriam was firm about not letting Margaret accompany them. "You need some time to yourself," Miriam told her. "I understand how it is," she said, "when things change." Margaret accepted Miriam's offer gladly.

But after the kids left that Saturday afternoon Margaret felt uneasy. With a whole afternoon and most of the evening free, it seemed a shame to waste the time scrubbing floors or doing laundry. There was a nervousness inside her, like those moments when a good hitter took her time settling into the batter's box. By three o'clock Margaret decided to go downtown and buy some material for new kitchen curtains. But when she found herself walking past Shelly's Leg, she decided to step in.

As she came through the back door Margaret made a swift survey of the bar. Amos and Randa, Deadeye and Valgaardson, sat at the bar talking to Sullivan, who looked bored. Shirley was cleaning the Keno machine, her hair in rollers, no makeup on her face. Margaret looked around the cool, dark bar again. Birdheart, Rita and Woody were not there. But she could feel them like a scent lingering in the smoky air.

"Well," Sullivan said as he moved up the bar, away from the others and over to the corner where Margaret had taken a stool. "We've missed you in here."

"I've been busy," Margaret said.

"A rat's ass," Sullivan said. He pulled a bottle of bourbon out of the well and poured two drinks. "Here's to the end of cowardice."

"Unkind," Margaret said. "I've been busy. But I never turn down a free drink." She cocked her glass at Sullivan. "Cheers."

"Cheers indeed," Sullivan said. "I always like to know how my bar is going to sort out."

Margaret raised an eyebrow and sipped slowly.

"I mean," Sullivan said, "there were bets as to whether you'd ever show up in here again."

"Who won?" Margaret asked.

"You did."

"You know I can't stay away from here." Margaret's voice was teasing, flirting with Sullivan.

He did not rise to her tone. His voice was blunt, a voice he could use with a liquor salesman. "It's been over three weeks."

Margaret looked down the bar toward Amos and Deadeye. "Doesn't look like I've missed anything."

"It changes," Sullivan said. "People come and go."

"I don't like to think of it changing," Margaret said. "I like to think that I can come down here any time and I'll know people and we'll all be nice to each other."

"That's always true," Sullivan said. "The changes are small. It takes a while to realize what's happened. You know, when we first opened this bar, it was almost all women in here then. Except for Amos. I think Amos must have come with the place."

"Maybe you should build him a room."

"No," Sullivan said. "Too many people live in here already. Too many people and too many ghosts. Some days I come down and it's like all those women are still around. I can hear the hum of the dryers in that old laundromat and see women sitting along the bar, talking to Shelly." Sullivan pointed his finger at Margaret. "Now there was a bunch of hard-drinking piss-rollers. Lord." He shook his head as he remembered. "They could be as nasty as that Butte team. Looks like that's who we'll be up against in the finals. Unless Sweet Grass surprises them."

"Christ," Margaret said. Two years ago the Butterbutte Bandits had lost the state finals to Shelly's Leg. It had been an ugly, name-calling game and afterward some of the Butte women had tried to cut Rita's hair. Lady fights, Sullivan had said, are part of the thrill of the sport.

"Probably," Sullivan said, "if they hadn't been such rollers, Shelly would have never started the team."

"What?" Margaret was remembering the Butte team, the way the first and third basemen hazed each batter.

"Shelly started the team to sweat some of the booze off. She didn't want her ladies to turn into drunken sacks of meat. She liked watching the men who watched the women. If her women got sloppy, she was afraid the men would go somewhere else for their evening's entertainment."

"You make her sound like a social director," Margaret said.

"Oh she was. In her way." Sullivan's eyes drifted over to the picture above the jukebox. "They were like her family, like she felt responsible for each one of them."

"You do that too," Margaret said. She studied her drink for a moment and then decided to ask: "You going to miss Rita?"

"Oh yeah," Sullivan said. "But I'll miss her like I miss you when you're not here. Maybe a little more, since I've known her longer. But she'll be back. I'm getting so I can spot the ones who'll come drifting back."

"Drifting back? Who's drifted back?"

"Birdheart for one." Sullivan seemed to still be speaking to Shelly's picture. "And Coker. She joined the second year, played a year or so, then went off and got that husband. Now she's back. Different though. Calmed down a lot."

"You think Woody will be back?" Margaret found herself holding her breath.

Sullivan smiled. "That's up to you." He refilled her glass. "Rotgut booze," he said, adding a twist of lemon to it. "I have a theory about all of them." He touched up his own glass with some lemon and ice. "Or maybe it's Shelly's. It's been so long now I get her thoughts mixed up with my own. Shelly thought bars were churches. Modern churches."

"Churches?" Margaret looked around the room. "I've never seen a more godless place in my life."

"Sure. Churches. You don't think people go to church to really talk to the Lord, do you? I mean, maybe some do, but most go to be with other people. To have something happen between them. While they're there they feel safe and happy. Same thing with a bar."

"Well, I don't know," Margaret said. "I never was very religious myself."

"Well, we are. Shelly and me. Or were. Went to Catholic boarding school together. Of course, that was about forty years ago." Sullivan laughed to himself.

"I really don't think it's the same," Margaret said. She tried to imagine Adam and Allison in a Sunday School class, clustered around the pinball machine, the lights flashing.

"Think of all the stuff churches do," Sullivan said. "The Sunday picnics, church league teams. Taking care of the sick and needy. Same as a bar."

"How come none of us goes to church then? How come we spend our Sunday mornings here?"

"You just don't have a hair of a notion about what I'm saying, do you?" He laughed at her, a kindly chuckle. "You see, churches are limited. Sunday morning sermons and Wednesday night choir practice. Confession don't count because it's solitary. A bar's open any time and you can walk right in and feel at home."

"I'm sure there's a flaw in this logic here," Margaret said. But the idea intrigued her. The cool darkness of Shelly's Leg was like the cavernous stone church her parents had taken her to every Sunday as a child. There were times in this bar, she had to admit, when she felt they all might stand up and sing. "It's a nice idea," she said.

"Nice idea? It's a dandy idea," Sullivan said. "And a bar has something a church doesn't."

"Booze," Margaret said.

"Not just booze. A bar has forgiveness."

"You get forgiveness in a church," Margaret said. "You know. 'Forgive us our sins, our daily bread.' All that."

"You don't know if you're truly forgiven or not in a church. You're just talking to the air." Sullivan fanned his fingers through the space between them. "Most people don't really believe in talking to the air. In a bar you can see forgiveness. Like old Birdheart, when he punched Rita. We all realized there was something terrible going on. And we forgave him."

Margaret kept her eyes down as she remembered the weight of Birdheart's body on her own, his smell, and the feeling that his bones were deeply rooted inside him, hard and calcified to the muscles. Birdheart's body could not be separated into parts. She wondered if Sullivan thought he was offering absolution for her sins.

"Forgiveness," Margaret said and looked squarely at Sullivan. "You know, sometimes I think you sit here all day making up and practicing lectures for me. You sip your Chivas and scratch your head. Do you do that, Sullivan? Practice lectures for me?"

Sullivan laughed. "You sure are a self-important little number," he said. "It happens like this: When a fellow doesn't have much to do, he thinks a lot."

"You've got plenty to do," Margaret said.

"I've had nothing to do since Shelly died. This bar don't take no time. The softball doesn't mean anything. When you've got nothing to do you think a lot. There's a place for it. Everyone else is busy out running their lives, too busy to think much about what they're doing. I do that for them. When they need it, I've already done the work."

"Anybody know this but me? That you spend your time dreaming into other people's lives." The idea seemed repulsive. After all, she had spent the summer trying to double-think Rita and Woody. Perhaps that was what she didn't like, the fact it hadn't worked for her.

"We compare notes," Sullivan said. "Two heads are better than one."

"I don't think we've compared anything," Margaret said. "I think you're trying to convert me."

Sullivan chuckled. "Maybe," he said. "You just may be right."

Margaret turned her glass slowly on its bottom rim. "So you think I ought to believe that bars are churches."

"That's just to get you into it," Sullivan said. He reached out and took her hand away from the glass and placed it on the bar, palm down. "You need to know about forgiveness."

Margaret looked into his eyes. "You think you can talk someone into forgiveness?"

"People come down here for a lot more than the booze," Sullivan said.

"And me?"

"Nobody's killed you. Your heart ain't broke. You keep wallowing around and something that's not worth raindrops will become the center of your life."

Anger flashed in Margaret's eyes. "You think I don't feel hurt, or scared, or betrayed? Any of that normal shit a woman who's been dumped feels?"

"You got to pick up your act," Sullivan said. "Don't walk around with your hat in your hand. Besides, women who have been dumped are a whole different category from you. You threw your man out."

"Like hell," Margaret said. "I helped you box it up. You had a list."

"That changes nothing," Sullivan said. "What I want to see is you have a little pride and quit pissing and moaning your life away."

"Oh yeah? You think that's what I'm doing?"

"Yes," Sullivan said quietly. "Your life will never turn around if you don't face the right direction."

"Of course," Amos said when the laughter died down, "you've heard the one about the cowboy on *Name That Tune?*"

"Oh tell that one," Randa said. "That's a good one."

"Don't tell that," Sullivan said. "You tell terrible jokes. Let Randa tell it."

"It's his joke," Margaret said. "It was funny the last time he told it."

"Come on," Randa said, nudging Amos's elbow. "Tell the cowboy joke."

Amos said: "They thought the cowboy was dumb, too stupid to play *Name That Tune*. But there he was in all his riggin', his boots, hat, a bandana in his hip pocket. So the MC says to him, 'For one hundred dollars, Name That Tune!' And the cowboy puzzles over it for a moment and then says 'Bury Me Not on the Lone Prairie.' 'Correct!' yells the MC, and he's more than a little amazed the cowboy pulled it off." Amos took a sip of his drink.

"So the MC gives him another try. 'For one thousand dollars, Name That Tune!' The cowboy scratches his chin a moment, then says 'Yellow Rose of Texas.' 'Correct!' yells the MC and by now he's more than a little pleased with his cowboy. He thinks this cowboy has real potential. He wants the cowboy to be a star, so he signals up a real easy one. The National Anthem.

"The MC says, 'For ten thousand dollars, Name That Tune!' The cowboy's eyes light up and he's got a big smile on his face. 'Why, that's the "Bronc Riders Get Ready," ' he tells them."

Randa cackled and giggled while Sullivan merely smiled. "See?" Sullivan said. "Amos can't tell a joke."

"I thought it was funny," Margaret said. "Funnier than the Kansas bumper sticker."

"Funnier than the Kansas bumper sticker? Never," Sullivan said. "Besides, that's not even a joke. That's a true story."

" 'Bronc Riders Get Ready,' " Randa laughed.

From behind Margaret's shoulder Woody said: "What burns five gallons of gas and don't go nowhere?" Margaret turned, surprised to hear his voice, even more surprised when his hand glided onto her shoulder.

"Oh, that's Deadeye's," Randa said. "That's funny. Tell that one."

"A Buddhist monk," Woody said.

Randa began laughing again. Margaret felt the warmth of Woody's hand on her shoulder.

Amos said: "You know why they won't sell gas to Buddhist monks?"

"They never return the cans."

"Your jokes are no better than Amos's," Sullivan said.

"That's because it's not mine," Woody said. "It's Deadeye's joke."

Woody was still standing behind Margaret's stool, his hand resting lightly on her shoulder. "Could I tear you away from all this fun and excitement?" he asked her. "I know where there's a quiet little table for two."

Margaret managed to smile and say, "Sure." As she and Woody crossed to the tables, she felt Sullivan's eyes on her back. She tried to compose herself. She wanted to be candid and cool. She arranged her face into what she thought might be an open and pleasant expression, tried to settle her breathing and the racing of her heart.

"I stopped by the house," Woody said. "So you'll have a surprise when you get home."

"A surprise?"

"It even surprised me," Woody said. "I was standing there at the door like some stupid teenager on a date, ringing your bell. I felt real foolish. Then I got into it. I wanted to write you a poem. But instead I left you some flowers."

"Flowers?" Margaret laughed, delighted. "You probably picked them out of my garden."

"Oh no," Woody said. "These are real store-bought flowers. But you still weren't home when I got back."

"Flowers," Margaret said again.

"Do you know anything about flowers?" Woody asked.

"Do I know anything about flowers? I've got a whole garden full of them."

"I mean," Woody said, "what they mean."

Margaret shook her head. Her left eye twitched. The flowers seemed less delightful now, threatening in some way.

"My wife Phyllis used to know what flowers meant," Woody said. "Once, before we were married, I gave her some columbines or dahlias or something. And she got pissed."

"That's terrible," Margaret said. "How could any woman get angry over flowers?" But Margaret could imagine it. Soon after Mike left she had received a box of long-stemmed red roses, each one wilted or dead. She called the florist to complain and was told that the purchaser, Mike, had wanted them sent that way. He had ordered a box of dead roses.

"Phyllis majored in Old English or something like that in college. And she's the type of person who takes all that stuff seriously.

She said columbines or dahlias or whatever meant the equivalent of 'piss up a rope' in Old English."

"God," Margaret laughed. "You definitely have strange tastes in women."

"I bought you an orchid," Woody said. "I don't know what orchids mean in Old English, but to me they're rare and beautiful, and I wanted you to have one."

Margaret didn't know what to say. A simple 'Thank you' seemed too cold and impersonal. 'I love you' was something she just couldn't manage at this moment. She sat staring at Woody, then stretched her hand across the table and touched his arm.

"I've missed you," Woody said. "Missed the damnedest things about you."

"I've missed you too," Margaret said, hoping her hand would feel warm to him. "I miss your hands on my back." She could see a flutter cross Woody's face and it surprised her. Woody's face had never revealed anything to her before.

"Well, there's that," Woody said. "And simpler stuff too. Like, I miss your coffee."

"My coffee? I thought you hated my coffee."

"Your coffee is like fine music, classical jazz, compared to the coffee at the Hotel Palace."

Margaret bridled at the lie. "Rita doesn't live at the Hotel Palace." There was a pinching sensation near her nose and she knew her carefully constructed composure had vanished like steam.

"See?" Woody said. "Do you know what your face looks like right now? Your mouth just did this little dive into a frown." He waved his fingers like strumming a guitar. "It's not pretty. I never see that when I fantasize about you."

"I don't imagine you have much time to fantasize over at Rita's." She was at sea already, wanting to be nice to Woody, wanting to hurt him too.

"I'm not at Rita's. I'm at the Palace. Which you could have found out easily if you weren't so self-absorbed in being a bitch about all this. And at the Palace I fantasize about you a lot. I miss seeing you in the bathtub. A lot of my fantasies are about taking you in the water. It's real sexy." He smiled.

Margaret wouldn't let it go. "Rita says you're leaving right after the finals. She says she's going."

"Yeah. But let's not talk about that. I want to have a nice time with you. I've missed you, talking to you and all that. If we talk about the tour, you'll just get upset."

Margaret concentrated on keeping her voice even. "No I won't." She tried to believe this.

"Well, okay," Woody said. "Then maybe I'll get upset, so I don't want to talk about it. Let's talk about sex."

"Haven't had any."

Woody cocked an eyebrow. "You could smile when you say that and I'd melt at your feet."

"You could charm warts off a frog."

"My only natural talent." Woody smiled warmly. Margaret thought he looked like a bemused cat, a cat cornering a broken bird.

She sighed. "Don't do that to me," she said. "It's confusing. It's like there are two of you and I can say: 'Woody, I'm having this problem with Woody.' Like one of you has really done me dirt, and the other one will always be my friend and will help me out of any trouble. Even trouble with you."

"What kind of trouble are you having?"

"I'm having trouble figuring out what you want." Margaret kept her eyes down; she cradled her glass in her palms. "Figuring out what I want. There's part of me that wants to hurt you real bad. But I just end up hurting myself. And there's part of me that wants to love you too. And that hurts, maybe worse than the other way."

"I've got to do this, Maggie. It's important to me."

"Is Rita important to you?"

"It's not that simple." Woody shifted and the wooden chair groaned. "The tour's important, but I don't want to talk about that now."

"I do. I want to talk about the tour."

Woody took a deep breath. "I want to talk about the things we used to do. I want to pretend it's ten years from now. We can sit around and reminisce. You know."

"I don't want to play pretend with you, Woody. I want to talk about you and me." Margaret searched his eyes for a gleam of light.

"Remember that big storm we had last summer, the one when the power went off? And we were so damn hot, it was like standing in a blow dryer. Allison was frightened, so you got us to play this Eskimo game. It's a hundred degrees outside, lightning's flashing all around, the wind's going to blow the house down, and you had us inside pretending we're in the Arctic. You said the lightning was the Aurora Borealis, the thunder herds of caribou, and we were hunting for our dinner. Remember that?"

Margaret laughed, amazed that Woody could entertain her in the middle of all this nonsense. "That was just to calm the kids."

"I loved it," Woody said. "I believed I was cold."

"Charm the wings off birds."

"I think about stuff like that," Woody said. "Like when I'm taking a shower or sitting on the stage. It's like I drift off when I should be doing something else. The other night Lloyd cracked me one with his drumstick. Just to get my wandering attention."

Margaret laughed, pleased she could believe him. "Ah," she said. "Poor baby."

"I remember," Woody said, "there was a month last summer when I was so much in love with you the sun shone in the rain."

"Don't," Margaret said. "Don't depress me."

"This is nice," Woody said. "Beautiful to me. It was when we all went camping up on Flathead. The time we took the boat out to see the ospreys on the island. We were rolled up in the sleeping bags and I was showing you the constellations."

"You fell in love because you could teach me constellations?" There was a mean edge to her voice that Margaret wished weren't there. It's all so pitiful, she thought, to not even have control of your voice.

"No, silly. You told me when you were a little girl you never saw stars. That the lights of the city made the sky black and it never got dark at all on the New York side. You thought stars lived in planetariums like animals in a zoo."

Margaret nodded unhappily. "It might be easier," she said, "if you didn't love me at all. Least of all for my stupidities and coffee."

"See? There you go again," Woody said. "I'm supposed to love you the way you want to be loved. How would that be? For your hair? Your softball?" He reached across the table and took her hands, holding them between his own. "I thought about the way you saw stars as a kid. About living somewhere where it never got dark. You seemed incredibly beautiful and brave to me that night. To sleep on the ground under a sky full of stars."

Margaret's thumb circled one of Woody's fingernails. "Please don't," she said. "It would be easier if you hated me." She shrugged. "For breaking all your stuff."

"Stuff is stuff," Woody said. "But I've got to know."

Margaret looked up and felt all the pain of this conversation sitting in her eyes, somewhere inside where vision forms. "Know what?"

"If you ever loved me like that, in that dumb and foolish way that leaves you feeling the stars can talk."

"Oh Woody." Margaret couldn't think. The only thing that her mind could hear was the tune playing through the jukebox. *'Just tella me one thing that I can hold on to.'* Margaret didn't even know what song it was from.

Woody let go of her hands.

Margaret was afraid of her voice, as if it could scorch her throat. "You feel that way with Rita?" The question was less than a whisper.

Woody looked her dead in the eye. "No."

"Well? What then?"

Woody sighed and leaned back in his chair. "There it is again," he said. "You know, I'm a grown man. I could take it if you'd just be gutsy enough to say No. No, you didn't love me. No, you didn't care. But you've got to drag all this up again."

"Yes," Margaret said and she felt the word itself had given her strength. "Yes," she said again. "I have to drag all this up. I mean, who is conning who here?"

"She's a good singer. Adds a lot to the group. We get along."

"Get along! You god-damn fucking live together!" Margaret clapped her hand over her mouth. "Oh god," she said. "I'm sorry. This little high-wire act gets to me."

"It's okay," Woody said. "I know you're upset." But Margaret could hear the tone go out of his voice.

"Every time I open my mouth I'm saying I'm sorry," Margaret said. "It's a pitiful way to live."

Woody's hand touched her arm. "It's okay," he said. "Let me get you another drink." And then he stood and moved away from her toward the bar.

There was a calmness and a fear circling through Margaret like dark and light hawks riding a thermal. She listened to Woody's boots mixing with the music from the jukebox, each tap of his heel. This was her moment, the time when she should take control. But exactly how, what gesture, was the problem. When she met Mike ten years ago courtship had been different. Margaret understood how those patterns played out. She knew when to pause in the conversation, the subtle ways women told men they were admired and loved. She wanted Woody to take her home and stay with her for just this night. Not as her Fairy Prince, just as Woody. But in those ten years the rules had changed. She couldn't count on Woody to understand those old traditional signs, to make the expected moves. There was a whole type of sexual education she had missed, the way the other women on the team bartered and bargained for men. She had watched, but not bothered to learn. She had been safe with Mike, until he left, and Woody had come to her like a gift. She had not even wished for him and he had appeared in her life. Settling in as suddenly and quietly as a bird.

She couldn't run her life on wishes and magic. She heard Sullivan's words in her head. 'You can't turn your life around if you don't face the right direction.' And a woman's got to do what a woman's got to do.

Woody placed a drink in front of her. "Dreaming of Portugal?" he asked.

"Timbuktu," she said and smiled. The smile was hollow, she knew. It was a smile designed to hide her fear. But it was the right thing to do. "You work tonight?" Margaret looked at the clock. Miriam would have the kids back in an hour or so.

"Don't I always work on Saturdays?"

"Are you seduceable?"

"What?"

Margaret thought she saw surprise, perhaps delight, in his face. "Are you seduceable?" she said again, more slowly this time.

"You can't have me all night. My public awaits."

"How about for an hour or two?" Margaret smiled again to hide her embarrassment. Indeed, she was just about three IQ points too stupid to run her own life. She should have figured this out long ago. It was like a child's love, given and taken on a whim with the swift oscillations from devotion to hate. It was like the tremendous pleasures and pain of drinking. Like the moment to moment chance on the ballfield. We own nothing.

Now it did not matter if Woody came back or not. It mattered that she could let him go. She wanted to share her spirit with Woody, her body with him, but she wanted most of all to be separate. "I want to give you a going-away present," she said.

Woody looked at her, his eyes calm and solemn. "I want to take you to the ends of the earth."

"I'm staying at the center," Margaret said. "You can always come back."

Woody tipped his chair on its heels and reached for one of Margaret's cigarettes. He twirled it through his fingers, unlit, and looked into the planes and angles of her face. Margaret's mind had stopped again. She could hear only the jukebox and did not feel Woody's stare upon her. She was memorizing his face, a still picture in the darkening barroom, seeing for the first time, and maybe the last, the wiry red beard, the clear and calm blue eyes. She knew his teeth were hidden behind his lips.

There was a silence as the song ended, a song Margaret had not really heard, and through that space they heard Randa cackling at the bar. "Oh that's a good one!" Randa laughed. "Tell that one."

Woody brought his chair back to all fours. "Let's blow this pop-stand," he said. "My place? Or yours?"

"Neither," Margaret said as she rose from the table. "Neutral territory."

They chose a small motel outside of town, each room a tiny log cabin. Lombardy poplars shaded the cabins and a stream ran behind.

"A picnic," Woody said as they walked to the little store. They picked out imported cheeses, two bottles of champagne, salted nuts in a can. At the checkout counter they vied to pay, and settled on splitting the treat, each paying half. "Liberation," Woody laughed, "takes a lot of the fun out of being good to a woman."

"Liberation," Margaret said, "is for those who aren't free."

They undressed each other slowly in the shadowy motel room, Margaret memorizing the curves and folds of Woody's bones, and the feel of Woody's calloused fingertips on her skin. She would miss that. They kept their eyes open, defiantly. Margaret touched the soft hairs on Woody's shoulders, the coarser hairs on his chest. Her fingertip felt the pulse of his heart in a spot beneath his earlobe.

The bedspread was worn corduroy and Margaret realized that this was not some clean, anonymous place. They could carve their initials in the knotty pine paneling, spill champagne on the floor and the spots would never come out. Woody's breath was hot and sour on her neck, yet Margaret could remember, even smell, the peppermint of his breath after he brushed his teeth, the lime scent he used on the small spots of his cheeks that he shaved. His feet, as always, were cool to the touch of her toes.

Her hands cupped his waist and she felt the muscles moving beneath his skin as he rode with her. And his eyes, ever open to look at her, to look at them both lying on the bed in the fading afternoon light. It saddened Margaret to realize that these are not the moments when children were born. In the eye of her soul she knew these moments were not meant for futures.

Woody's hands fit into the hollows beneath her shoulderblades. His body warmed her against the chill of the room. Her spine was liquid silver drifting smoothly up and down the bed, a music playing somewhere between her mind and her body.

At that last moment before thought failed, Margaret noticed the sunlight slanting through the shuttered windows, a beam of light playing through Woody's red hair, casting gold across the bed and the room.

seventeen

The best times for Sullivan had been the late Sixties when he and Shelly would hop in his pickup and drive the long miles out to Lolo Hot Springs. Sullivan would tell Shelly stories. And now that he thought about it, with the dawn birds chirping in the trees outside the bar, the stories Sullivan liked best were about reversals. Shelly must have had a strange picture of this part of the country, he thought. If she believed everything I told her, this country would look backwards to her.

In the truck, sipping beers and listening to country and western pouring out of the radio speaker, Sullivan told her 'lolo' meant 'crazy' in Hawaiian. He told her about the De-file, where the dishonest Mongolian trader had been defiled, his body dismembered and scattered as miserly as his goods had been dispensed. He told her about the Chinese wife Lewis and Clark found living with a Kwakiutl chief in 1806, and the yens that hung from her pierced ears.

Entering the hot pools was the only time Shelly allowed herself to be carried. "I'd want you to carry me anyway," she said. "It's bridal. I feel like a virgin each time you walk into the water." In the steam of the thermal springs Shelly's hair fanned across her wet shoulders. Sullivan would touch her breasts as if gauging the specific weight of butterflies.

With the water warming his back, Sullivan would hold Shelly against him, rocking his body into hers. "I'd like to die this way," Shelly said. "They say if you don't panic, drowning's quite sensual."

And all those years ago Sullivan would laugh at her. "You won't die," he had told her. It was a truth he believed like others believe in God. "You lead a charmed life," he had said. "You should have died once, so now you're immune."

With the first streaks of daylight creeping through the lone window of the bar, Sullivan remembers how he had clung to that notion even after she sickened. He had obsessively wondered who she would love after he was dead. He could clearly imagine Shelly, never aging, and could only comfort himself with the knowledge he had been first, that they had been together since they were children.

"She was right," Sullivan said to the empty bar. "Drowning's quite sensual." He tipped back his second bottle of Chivas, looked at the daylight now flooding the bar and ran a hand back over his head. He touched the stubble of his beard and massaged the base of his throat.

"Today's the trickiest day of the year, my dear," he said to the dawn-brightened bar. "Just like Christmas and New Year's, your birthday and mine." He saw Shelly as a shadow near the window, her copper hair catching highlights from the sun. "Do you think," he asked the empty spaces, "this mantra will work forever? Do we win these championships because you're here?" He heard her laugh and knew that by the end of the day she would be speaking with him, clear words in his mind more perfect than conversation.

This was a balancing act Sullivan had perfected. He knew that if he did this every day, as he was often tempted to do, he could be considered crazy, lolo in Hawaiian, and some kind soul, Rita perhaps, would have him locked away. That didn't bother him; he thought it might be rather nice to talk to Shelly each day until he died. And once he was dead there was nothing. No pain, no gladness. If it weren't for the people in this bar, Sullivan might walk over that line, if indeed, he could have that choice.

It was time to move on now, to keep to the rhythm of this day. A constant pattern like the horizon to keep you straight. Out to the hot springs, his Chivas in his hand, and to the field by six for the championship game tonight. As they played the final game of the season and the lights came on in the fifth inning, Sullivan would be sitting with Shelly, talking about the women, sizing up the Butterbutte Bandits for signs of fatigue. It had been like this every year. Maybe you only fall in love once, Sullivan thought. Fall head over asshole for the first woman who was ever nice to you and made you feel special. No one else can ever live up to that first time.

He felt the sadness of the others, his family. Rita thrashing around in the quicksand of her life. Maggie asking everything and giving nothing in return. Birdheart, just waiting. Woody running away. We all learn different lessons, Sullivan decided. Somehow that didn't make him feel any easier.

He went into the bathroom to relieve himself and stood staring at a strange shape on the floor behind the toilet. He blinked his eyes and ran a hand across them. The shape was still there, something different about the contours and colors of the pipes and dingy baseboard. It must be drugs, he thought. Damn, drugs in my bar. He bent to flush and reached for the package, brown paper something enclosed in a ziplock bag. Sitting on the toilet, facing the scribbled numbers of his books, Sullivan's hands opened the baggie, carefully removed the brown paper bag. The contents of the paper bag were smooth, not sharp like a needle, or spherical like a syringe.

It was a book, a paperbound edition of *The Joy of Sex*. Sullivan thumbed through it, his eye falling on the charcoal line drawings of couples in various positions, the man generally elevated so that the entry of his cock could be clearly drawn. The women's legs were looped over the man's back, locked behind his knees, straddled around his waist. The charcoal figures stood, sat, lay upon a bed or some sparse drawings of grass. The figures had no faces.

Sullivan felt a numbness drifting down his spine like the last of a dying wave cresting on a beach. It stopped at the joint of his hips and sat in the small of his back, yet at any moment might spread throughout his groin. Sullivan thought he might be paralyzed; he knew he didn't care.

The book was Valgaardson's, no doubt. Valgaardson who had not known a woman since he had moved into the room in Shelly's Leg. Sullivan sat with Valgaardson's book in his hands and imagined Valgaardson masturbating to the faceless couples drawn in soft charcoal shadings upon the page. Without looking, Sullivan knew there would be no pictures of men or women alone in this book. And those men and women were joined, arms and legs wrapped around the other. He knew the feel of their mouths touching and wished that if he only tasted the softness of Shelly's lips he could be released from this ridiculous spot, sitting in the men's john at dawn, another man's masturbation book lying in his lap.

It wasn't just the sadness of Valgaardson jerking off to pictures of faceless couples. No airbrushed woman with red lips and parted thighs waited for Valgaardson in the men's head. Faceless couples, a new combination on every page, waited carefully wrapped in a zip-lock bag so their arms and legs, the paper they were printed on, wouldn't warp from the leaking toilet. Had Sullivan had a woman since Shelly died? Could he recall the warmth, the feel, the smell of any of them? Or was each night and each woman only a drunken fantasy where Shelly became real to him in the person of another woman's body. Sullivan wasn't sure. He tried to remember the face of the woman who lived out by Lolo Creek. He could remember the road; he could remember the house. He could remember her bed. But he couldn't remember if she was blond or dark, had clear or cloudy eyes.

Sullivan stood, surprised his body would move. But his hands, he didn't know what to do with his hands. He wanted to replace the book, wrap it back up in the brown paper bag and press the seal on the ziplock bag. He thought all the motions through once, to prac-tice, then made his hands do the work. Valgaardson should be pro-tected. Lonely men that share secrets must have their respect too.

Sullivan was breathing hard when he replaced the package be-hind the toilet pipe. He wondered if he was shaking, if there was wind in his ears. From the back bar he pulled another bottle of Chivas, but knew the magic was gone. Shelly was gone. And he himself was not really alive.

Margaret believed in will power. Warming up on the sidelines with Rita, she was determined to take the championship again this year. But more than taking the championship, Margaret wanted to shine. She wanted this game to be some sign to herself, to her world, that she had made the right decisions. She would pitch the whole game, taking no relief from Coker. She would hit well, concentrating on the arc of the ball rather than the feel of her arms, the way she usually did. Sullivan nagged her about the strikes she wasted just stretching her arms. He wouldn't tonight.

Today was the first time she had seen Woody since their afternoon in the motel. He had called and asked if he could take Allison and Adam to the game. Margaret had set her hair, a useless gesture, only good for the first few innings before the sweat on her forehead washed out the curls. But he had seen her, kissed her lightly on the mouth before he left. She would play well for him, for herself. Concentrate on nothing but softball.

When a baby is dropped on its head, the assumption is that it will be brain damaged. But there is always the possibility that something in the fall might be shaken loose into genius. Things couldn't always go downhill, starting from only a tenuous hold on the good life and always in danger of slipping away. Rita was right. The world wasn't going to stand up and applaud her morals. But they would applaud her pitching. A good game today would be a sign she could understand. A sign she had made the right decisions. No man goes to war believing he is fighting for the wrong side.

"Watch that curve," Rita called. "It's a little wide."

"How wide?"

"Walking the line."

"Good," Margaret said. "That's right where I want her." She pitched another curve to the same outside corner.

"Over," Rita called. "That's a ball." She whipped it back to Margaret. "That's *not* where you want it."

Margaret pitched a fastball, saw Rita smile. Okay, she thought. Concentrate. In the real leagues there's a superstition that no-hitters only occur in non-thought. The last pitch will drop if you think about a no-hitter. Margaret tried to believe she didn't want a no-hitter. Nothing flashy, just steady throughout the whole game. She wanted the batters to step up to the plate with sure knowledge in their hearts they would strike out.

Sullivan walked up holding his bullet-shaped bottle of Chivas. "Wet the whistle?" He stood midway between them and waited for the women to walk in. "A hit for good luck?"

Margaret shook her head, feeling her curls shaking softly beside her ears. Rita loped up to Sullivan and took a quick swallow.

"Going to play virgin?" Sullivan said to Margaret. The skin beneath his eyes was liver-colored.

"You been up all night?" Margaret asked.

"Ritual," Sullivan said. "My ritual date. Can't win without it."

"You'll be no good to us at all," Margaret said. "The condition you're in."

"You won't need me," Sullivan said. "Everybody's looking so fine tonight."

"Except you," Rita said. "You're a mess."

Sullivan smiled. "Never felt better." He drank from the bottle. "That's a lie." He lowered his voice as if to share a secret. "I feel like this a lot. Thank god for small pleasures." He left them and wandered toward Coker, who was pitching a roundhouse batting order.

"After I'm gone," Rita said to Margaret, "you look after Sullivan. He's got some problems."

Margaret felt her heart drifting in her ribcage, but she smiled. "Don't we all," she said and turned her back to Rita.

Damn you, she thought. Damn your Indian hide. She pitched a slider that nosedived and heard the clack of the ball against Rita's shin guards. Margaret looked up into the stands and saw Woody and her kids making their way to the top of the bleachers, their arms loaded with junk food. And damn you too, she thought. She pitched a fastball. Too high.

"You ain't even drunk," Rita called. "Watch yourself."

Concentrate, Margaret thought. Don't think of anything but the way the ball lands in Rita's glove. That sound, she tried to imitate it. But as she pitched a knuckleball Margaret's mind kept time with the rhythm of Rita's words. 'Af-ter I'm gone,' the *n* sound echoing as the ball slapped into Rita's glove. Floating at the edge of her thoughts were pictures of Rita and Woody driving in sunlight, singing in darkness, smiling.

Margaret caught the pitchback and held it. "That's it. I'm warm."

"My ass," Rita said. "You can't hit a church with those."

"I'm saving myself for the game." Margaret walked over to join the batting practice.

Country music drifted through her head as Margaret stood to receive one of Coker's pitches. 'Af-ter I'm go-on,' the last syllable rising. She settled her feet and swung viciously at one of Coker's pitches, missing by a wide margin. She kept seeing Woody's face, hearing his laugh. 'Af-ter I'm go-on.' She swung at three pitches.

"Go along," Coker called. "Get back to what you can do. If you ain't using Rita, send her over here. She's got a batting average to maintain."

Coker laughed and Margaret smiled as she wandered away. She watched the women on the field. The team looked good, everyone in full uniform, washed and pressed, even Irene, who probably didn't wash her uniform but once a year. Margaret watched the choreography of their movements, each part of the field moving in response to its own rhythms. Everything still, Coker wound up and pitched, Shirley swung, the ball soared left, where Lolie raced to get under it and fire it back to Coker. And then the whole thing again, only this time Shirley hit right and Miriam began to run, the dazzling spiraling whiteness of the ball caught for a moment between the blue of the sky and the green of the field. Margaret heard their chatter and laughter, saw the swing of their hair, the flash of their eyes, and the white bars of their teeth as the star pattern of the roundhouse practice broke open and reformed, the movements of the women gracefully timed to the ball.

Margaret could see herself in the center of that star pattern. She imagined the hunch of her shoulder, the cock of her leg. This was going to be a good game, she tried to tell herself. But she kept hearing the country music and Woody's laughter and wondered if there might be emptiness at the sides of her eyes.

Sullivan watched the outfield umpire hose down the base lines and relime the paths, neatening and straightening the stage for this dance. The home umpire walked to each base and kicked it several times to make sure the anchors held. For the second time he dusted the plate, checked his watch and looked impatiently into the late afternoon sun. Shadows of the Lombardy poplars stretched across the field. Around the fourth inning the light would get bad, coming from behind the pitcher facing east, making the pitching and fielding easier but the hitting harder. By the seventh inning the lights would be on and it would be full dark when the game was over.

Sullivan liked the umpire at home, a local man who sometimes stopped into Shelly's Leg. That will affect him about as much as a hair, Sullivan thought and waited for Shelly's voice to come to him in response. He heard nothing; it had been like that all day. Driving the pickup, soaking in the thermal hot pools, Sullivan had expected to hear Shelly as clearly as if she were sitting beside him. But today her voice drifted. Sometimes when he wasn't thinking about her, checking the air pressure in the pickup tires or watching the flight of a hawk, he would hear her speak. Other times, like now, when he expected her voice, she was silent.

Sullivan watched his team in the pen waiting for Butte to finish their warm-up. Rita smoked a cigarette, Maggie trimmed her nails, and farther down the line Miriam and Edithanne were discussing a new day-care center that would open next week. Diane and Lolie hung over the end of the cage talking to Birdheart, who slipped them his Tank and Tonic. Shirley had her mirror out, checking her makeup. Behind the dugout Sullivan heard the rhythmic slap of Coker's pitches landing in Irene's glove. Everyone was here but Shelly.

The home umpire strolled out between the mound and the plate and began juggling six baseballs. He did this every time he umped at home, some signal he thought meant they should start. Sullivan liked him for this. In the fog of his Chivas, Sullivan watched the balls floating so precisely through the air, the smooth movement of the umpire's hands as he fingered each ball quickly and tossed it back aloft.

The Butterbutte Bandits huddled up football style, a ragtag collection of T-shirts and cutoffs and jeans. They chanted:

"We beat them in the mountains.
We beat them in the plains.
We beat them in their own hometown,
We beat them 'cause we're named
BUTTER BUTTE BAN DITS!"*

They cheered, high voices shrill on the slight wind, and scattered out onto the field. Sullivan watched them pepper the ball around while Rita, the top of the order, stubbed her cigarette out in the dust and walked to the batter's box.

"Kick ass! Kick ass!" Amos Espinosa's voice rose above the others. Silent Sam blew a few random notes on his trumpet. Each year Sam passed Sullivan a note saying he would learn a tune for the finals. Maybe the "Garry Owen" or "Dixie." Each year he never got around to it, but could be counted on to blare away on his trumpet when the spirit moved him.

This year, in seventy-nine turns at bat, Rita had gotten on base fifty-six times. But that was against local teams. Butte was a different matter, a different kind of ball club. The Butte team were all big-bodied working women, women who bucked hay bales or ran machines in the mine. Some sported bandages and knee braces like medals. Sullivan looked them over and could not find a decent looking woman among them. The left fielder wore a red T-shirt that said HEAVY PETTING and had a white dewlapped scar across her top lip. The woman at second had woven feathers in her hair and stared with small, mean eyes like a pig.

Terrible Terry, her eyes hidden behind opaque sunglasses, was pitching for the Bandits, and she deserved the name. Local pitchers might walk a good hitter like Rita; Terrible was likely to injure them. Sullivan watched the Butte team go wide and knew Rita would get a pitch. Terrible had a fastball that didn't give the batter time to get out of the way. If Terrible pitched that fastball directly into the hip, Rita might not be quick enough to jump back. That would cripple Rita up good, and that was exactly the kind of strategy Terrible liked best.

—It's too early for that, Sullivan heard Shelly say. He smiled.

Yacky Yvonne came down the base line from first while Lumpfrey strolled in from third with her rolling gait like a sailor's or cowboy's. Yvonne and Lumpfrey were the hazers on the Butte team. They had perfected their razz to the point that Sullivan wondered if they would play if either woman got laryngitis. Most of his women had learned to ignore them, all but the weak players. Irene for sure would spook. Sullivan wondered about the new woman, Diane.

Yacky Yvonne started it. "Just watch her," she called over her shoulder to her teammates out in the field. "She's going to bite into one of them Terrible pitches and pull every muscle in her arm. That good catching arm. Watch it go, girls." Yvonne was crouched nearly halfway to home, her farm woman's body like a big blond bull shuffling from foot to foot just outside the base line. "Take a big swing, Honey." Her voice was mockingly seductive. "I want to hear those muscles pop."

Lumpfrey joined in from left. "See that Indian wiggle her ass. You still got that rat's nest of hair, those horseapples hanging on your ears."

Yvonne cooed: "Look that puppy over." Terrible had pitched two balls so far. Sullivan wondered if Terrible was deaf or perhaps had gone deaf from playing with such talky women.

Rita got a piece of the third pitch and raced to first before Yvonne could make the tag. "Lucky swing," Yvonne said and turned her attention to Lolie, who fingered her gold earrings before moving out of the on-deck.

"Kick ass! Don't let them see no light!" Sullivan heard the shufflings and cheers of his crowd. Valgaardson made a speech. "You should've punched that bitch in the mouth!"

Lolie sacrificed the first strike so Rita could steal second, running with her elbows tucked, her toes like a bird taking off over water. "Bride of Mercury," Birdheart hooted. "Fly on home!" Lolie's next hit was a little can of corn right to Lumpfrey, keeping Rita on second. Coker struck out. Edithanne pop-flied to the pig-eyed second baseman with the feathers in her hair.

"That's the last man I want left on base," Sullivan said as his women jogged out to their positions. "And none of them balls better hit the ground. No grass stains!"

—Don't flatter yourself, Shelly said to him. They can't hear you. Sullivan turned around, tried to focus his eyes on some specific spot in the air.

With the Shelly's Leg team on the field, the hazing started again, only this time it came from the stands. Maggie and Rita were working well, putting the first batter down 1-2-3. The second batter was Lumpfrey, and Valgaardson and Deadeye kept up a steady stream of insults. "Eat that pitch! Use it for dentures!" Lumpfrey popped out to Irene at second. The third batter struck out. Silent Sam hooted on his trumpet.

The next two innings were static, kept in hand by the pitchers. Sullivan watched the stances of the women at bat, the ones who moved from low in the hips like dancers and whores, and the ones whose swing seemed to come from the shoulders and the napes of their necks. Yvonne and Lumpfrey were booed repeatedly as their verbal onslaught became more and more vicious. When fat Miriam with her glasses got up to bat, Yvonne came almost down to the plate. "Just so you can see me," Yvonne said. "All blind people should play baseball." Miriam popped out on the first pitch.

Maggie and Rita looked good, working together steadily, using the sliders more than Sullivan would have liked, but mixing them up with the other pitches so the sliders always looked surprising. Sullivan took a hit on his Chivas and found Shelly next to him with the specific presence of a child's imaginary friend.

—We could have used her a few years ago, Shelly said. Damn good pitcher.

"Looks real good," Sullivan said as Maggie struck out another Butte woman.

—Remember Caroline? Pitched '70 and '71. Ever see Caroline again?

Sullivan shook his head.

—She got pregnant, Shelly said. I lent her money for an abortion and she never came back.

Same thing, Sullivan thought, with that fellow who wanted to do that billboard of Maggie. Of course, it wasn't all that much money, but he took off too. Never saw him again. Sullivan watched Maggie whirl around to check the runner from stealing second.

"Got eyes in the back of my head," Maggie called and the Butte woman smiled and dropped into a sprinter's crouch. Damn good picture of Maggie, Sullivan told Shelly. Maggie toyed with the straps of her bra before winding up for the next pitch.

By the fifth inning Maggie had held the Butte team to no runs and Shelly's Leg had two, a nice run of Shirley's after stealing second without sliding, and a straight drill of Miriam's that should have been a homer but Miriam was too slow to get past third before Butte had fielded the ball. Miriam had literally fallen across third base.

—She could run all day in a hat, Shelly said.

Maggie sacrificed to bring Miriam home.

Edithanne stood at the plate, the light of the setting sun in her eyes coming over Terrible Terry's shoulder. Yacky Yvonne and Lumpfrey were almost on top of her, and Sullivan could see Edithanne tense, flexing her ringed fingers nervously against the bat.

That's two, he told Shelly. They've spooked Irene so bad she'll never get a hit. Now Edithanne. Damn. She's been doing so well. Four homers this season, a beauty in the first game.

Edithanne was batting left and Lumpfrey was only about six feet off the plate. "You're so skinny, I wouldn't be surprised if Terrible don't even see you. Might throw that ball clean through you."

"Stick your chest out so she knows where to chuck that ball," Yvonne said. "Let old Terrible see those toggle switches."

Terrible pitched a fastball. Edithanne clutched at the bat as though striking a snake with a stick, angling to get the bat between herself and the speeding ball. Sullivan heard the ring of the bat as it connected with the ball and then the torn sound of screaming as the ball smashed into Terrible's legs.

Sullivan was on his feet, running woozily out to the mound where Terrible lay, her teammates gathering around her. Out of the corner of his eye Sullivan could see Edithanne's white face, the bat still in her hands. He waved her on to first.

"Get a doctor," Sullivan said. But the doctor was already there with the home umpire and the Butte coach. Gently the doctor touched Terrible's legs. She screamed again when he placed his hand on her knee.

The Butte coach was swearing. "You're supposed to catch the fucking thing! Catch it, my god! Catch it!"

In the haze of his Chivas, Sullivan stood on the edge of the group at the mound and watched Terrible and the doctor kneeling over her. The hit had surprised Terrible, perhaps it had broken her knee. Sullivan always believed a broken knee or elbow was the most painful of injuries. A cowboy on his father's ranch had shattered a knee breaking horses. He was called Gimp after that because he couldn't walk right, a limping, stiff-kneed gait that was painful to watch.

They had the lights on by the time the ambulance arrived to take Terrible in to the hospital on a stretcher. Lumpfrey came in to pitch for Butte. A boxy-looking, knock-kneed woman with a 69 on her jersey came in for Lumpfrey at third.

Yvonne would not chatter on her own. Lumpfrey struck out Shirley and Miriam in silence.

Sullivan took a hit on his Chivas. They're spooked, he told Shelly, but she had disappeared from him, vanished from his mind once again. He watched his team straggle out onto the field and they seemed to dissolve into shadings of charcoal gray, their backs moving away from him. He thought he heard music, the slow, mournful sounds of a funeral march. The dirge they had played at Shelly's funeral. He remembered the feel of the heavy wine-colored velvet drapes he had clutched in his hands to keep his balance that afternoon. He saw Birdheart dressed in a three piece gray suit. He saw Shelly's eyes closed, the thin blue light of her stare forever gone, caked over with makeup so that she didn't look real.

Sullivan shook his head to try to clear it of pictures of Shelly lying dead in her casket. Instead he saw her lying on the bed in the apartment above the bar and felt the weightlessness of her papery dry hand as he held it. It seemed he had spent half his life sitting in that room, holding her hand and watching the faint rise and fall of her breasts as she breathed. He wondered what her last words were, her last thoughts as her eyes glazed closed. He had wanted her to say 'I love you.'

There was a shout from the Butte team, high, joyous shrieking. Sullivan looked up and saw the Butte team flocking to the third-

base line to slap hands with the pig-eyed woman who trotted leisurely along the line slapping hands, the feathers in her hair bobbing. "For Terrible!" they yelled each time their hands touched.
"For Terrible!" Out in the field Sullivan saw Lolie hopping over the
fence to find and relay the ball back to Maggie. A fat woman with
absurdly small and dainty feet jogged down the base line from
second to third. She ran lightly on her toes toward home. "For
Terrible!"

Sullivan rose and felt the weight of all his bones as he tried to
walk over to the scorekeeper. The woman flashed him a grin. "I
think your girls are spooked," she said. Over her shoulder Sullivan
could make out the blacked-in diamonds for the two Butte runs in
the bottom of the fifth. The score was tied 2-2.

Sullivan signaled time and moved out to the mound, waving his
hand at Rita to join him. He started off with a smile, but neither
woman returned it. They looked at his face, then down at the
ground. "You spooked?" he asked them.

"A fluke," Rita said. "Never happen again in an elephant's age."

Sullivan looked at Maggie. "You want me to send in Coker?"

"No." Her eyes were bright, a hardness settling into her features.
"I'll take her all the way."

Sullivan patted her shoulder. "That didn't spook you. Good girl.
Now let me tell you something." He leaned toward her, swaying
slightly, remembering his boozy breath and keeping his mouth
down. "Go kick some ass. That's it. Just beat the piss out of those
cracks." He straightened and smiled. It seemed a perfect speech.

Maggie dropped two of the pitchbacks and walked the next hitter on balls.

—Better let Coker pitch, Sullivan heard Shelly say. He smiled
and sighed, relieved he had not lost her totally. —She's rattled,
Shelly said. She's seeing balls bounce off her body at a hundred
miles an hour. She's listening to her bones crack.

Sullivan shook his head, hoping Maggie would straighten out.
Just a few pitches to get warm again and she would be okay. The
count was 3 and 2 when the next batter popped out to Diane at
short. Only one down and two runs in already. The runner at first
did a little tapdance on the base, her hands on her hips.

Yvonne was up next and swung down hard on the first pitch. She tipped it. Rita raced along the foul line, but couldn't field it. The runner at first stole second and took a long, skipping lead.

Maggie pitched a curve that didn't break as it should have, and Yvonne connected with a heart-dropping wallop. Sullivan watched Shirley and Lolie racing for the fence, but knew the ball would drop well behind the Lombardy poplars. Four runs in this inning and only one out.

—Better let Coker pitch, Shelly said again.

Maggie struck the next batter out and Sullivan hoped she was regaining her control. The next batter popped up to Shirley at center. The inning was over and Sullivan would have to speak to Maggie.

"You want me to put Coker in?" he asked her when she sat down.

"Nope," Margaret said. "I want to go the whole game."

"You're losing it out there. This *is* the championship, you know. No more chances after this."

"I want to go the whole way."

"You going to pretend those runs didn't come in?"

Margaret picked up the bat, twirling it through her hands like a baton, and moved out of the dugout into the on-deck circle. "I'll fix one of them myself," she said, taking a few practice swings. She popped out on the second pitch. When she returned to the bench, she saw Coker throwing to Lolie.

"I'll do it," Margaret said to Sullivan. "I can win this. Tell Coker to go sit down."

"Who's in charge here?" Sullivan said, Margaret's face floating slightly in front of his eyes. "Here, want a drink?" He waved the nearly empty Chivas bottle under her nose. "I am in charge here and I say you are to let Coker pitch. You're too spooked. Have a drink."

Irene simply stood at the plate and didn't swing at any of Lumpfrey's pitches. Diane swung at them all and struck out too. Margaret picked up her glove and headed for the mound. Rita and Coker trailed behind her and Sullivan waited to see how it would all sort out. Coker moved to first. Maggie toed up against the pitcher's rubber.

First foul-up, Sullivan said to Shelly, and she'll work first for the rest of the game. She's not the only one out there.

But Shelly had left him again; there was no soft reply in his ear.

Maggie held the Butte team through the sixth, not so much on her pitching but because she was facing the bottom of the order. She relied on the curve, pitching some of them wide, and the slider. Coker wouldn't do much better, Sullivan decided. Coker didn't have the slider and pitched only competent ball at best. Sullivan watched them lope in at the bottom of the sixth, herding together in twos and threes for comfort like horses before a storm.

"We need some hits," he told the women when they returned to the dugout. "You," Sullivan said, grabbing Rita by the shirt before she stepped into the on-deck. "You are going to get on base. Wave at me from first. Whistle when you get to second." Rita popped out.

"God damn it!" Sullivan shouted. "Don't none of you want to win this game?" He felt the wind shift, coming in more from the south, and thought he smelled rain on it. Dandy, he said to Shelly. Just dandy. We'll finish this shipwreck in the dark and the rain. He looked up into the lights, the prismed halos blinding him.

—Can't see rain in a light anyhow, Shelly said.

Lolie, with her dancer's hips and gold earrings, struck out. Coker kept wiggling her foot on the plate, unable to decide to swing. His women were afraid of the ball.

Knock-kneed number 69, who was playing Lumpfrey's third, bunted on Maggie's first pitch. It angled up the field for the mound and was perfectly positioned for Maggie to reach out her glove and snag it. But Maggie folded, clutched the glove to her chest and dropped down on the mound, her knees splayed under her. The ball dribbled out to Diane at short, but by the time she relayed it to Coker, number 69 was safe on first base.

Sullivan called time and walked out to the mound, signaling Coker and Rita in with him. "Okay, ladies," he said. "Let's finish this game and go have a drink."

"I'll finish," Margaret said. "She'll never get off first."

"That should have been yours." Sullivan tried to make his voice stern. "You didn't field it."

"A mistake. I'll watch it."

"Too late," Sullivan said and was tempted to reach out and touch her arm. "Don't you think every woman on that team saw that very same mistake? Every ball for the rest of the game is going to be coming right at you. And you're afraid to field them. So out. Coker can take it in."

"I'll pitch." There was that same hardness in her face.

"Out."

"No." Margaret shook out her arm and turned her back to Sullivan.

"Come on," Rita said. "Cut the hero stuff. You played a good game."

"No."

"Christ," Coker said. "Let's get this pussy over with."

Sullivan took Margaret by the arm. "I don't want to have to drag you off."

Rita said: "Let go, Sullivan. No rough stuff."

"You shut up." Sullivan pulled on Margaret's arm. The stands began to boo, to cheer. Silent Sam blew some notes on his trumpet that sounded like a wounded elk.

"I'll pitch," Margaret said. She pried his hand off her arm with her fingernails. "No drunk's going to get me off the mound."

"Forget it," Coker said, moving back toward first. "We'll lose her anyway. All this fighting."

"Get back here," Sullivan shouted. Coker stuffed her glove into the pants of her uniform and began cartwheeling across the field. The crowd cheered, even the Butte fans. Coker balanced up and walked across the base line on her hands, the glove flopping against her ass.

"Come on," Rita said, taking Sullivan's arm. "Let's finish up. Go sit down." She led him back with her toward the plate.

"Play Ball!" the umpire yelled.

Back in the pen, Sullivan watched Margaret strike out the next batter on three sliders. She ignored Rita's signals for the change-up and curve. What the hell, Sullivan thought. We can't keep winning these games forever. Number 69 was still on first when Butte's short fielder swung at Margaret's next slider, a low, loping cut of the bat that connected and tossed the ball over left. It caught Edithanne by surprise and she dropped it before getting the throw off. The runners tagged up at first and second.

—Remember Candlestick Park? Shelly said softly in Sullivan's ear.

"Damn!" Sullivan pitched his empty Chivas bottle out into the parking lot and waited to hear the smash of the glass. Paul knew all along, from that first trip to San Francisco when Sullivan was fresh out of the Navy. Paul had hired a detective to spy on his wife. And Shelly had known Paul knew. Only Sullivan had been left ignorant, his dreams intact then.

Sullivan saw the funeral again and waited as breathlessly as he had four years ago for Paul to walk through the door. But Paul did not walk through the door any time during that long afternoon. He had known. The afternoon Shelly died Sullivan had sent him a telegram, carefully spelling out the arrangements that had been planned months in advance when Shelly knew the cancer in her right leg was terminal. The day after the funeral Sullivan received a telegram in reply. 'I'm sorry. Paul Newhouse.'

Sullivan heard cheering and looked back to the field. Rita had her mask off and was waiting for Miriam's return to reach her. Number 69 scooted past Rita's back. The throw slapped neatly into Rita's glove and she turned, almost slowly, seconds behind the next runner, who was safe. Butte 6, Shelly's Leg 2.

—We always pull it out in the last inning, Shelly said in Sullivan's ear. Sullivan wanted to shake her, see the shower of her copper hair swirling around her shoulders, feel the softness of her skin beneath his fingers.

In the top of the eighth, Lumpfrey's first pitch to Rita was an inside fastball. Rita jumped, but wasn't quick enough. It grazed her hip and left her sprawling in the dust under the floodlights. "For Terrible!" Lumpfrey yelled as Rita picked herself up and limped off toward first.

"Rotten ball!" Rita yelled, shaking her fist at Lumpfrey. "Rotten miner's crack!"

Lolie popped out. Coker struck out. Edithanne took a step back from the plate each time Lumpfrey released the pitch and swung at the empty air. The game was over 6–2 and Shelly's Leg Women's Fastpitch Softball Team had lost their first state championship after six years at the top.

eighteen

Margaret stood at attention as the president of the Woman's Softball Association, a woman with a pointed nose like the beak of a hawk or eagle, handed the silver trophy to the Butter-butte Bandits. Yvonne, as their captain, dusted her hands off on the thighs of her sweat pants and donned a black cowboy hat before accepting the statuette. In unison the Butte women yelled "For Terrible!" and Yvonne threw her hat in the air with a cowboy yip.

Then Rita limped forward to accept the smaller second place silver trophy. Margaret knew Sullivan would never display it in the bar; it would find a place in his office or a storage room, not set out prominently and polished and dusted like the six first place trophies he was so proud of and kept lined up behind the cash register. And Margaret had to wonder if things might have been different if Coker had pitched after that fifth inning.

As Margaret wandered back toward the dugout she tried to determine if she was really superstitious enough to believe the loss of the game, the loss of the state championship, could in any way truly represent the losses she had suffered all summer. It was just a game, she knew, but she had played this game for all the stakes, just like she did with anything else. And they had lost. Could Coker have pulled it out? Would Margaret have felt any better if the loss was attributed to Coker and not to herself? Sullivan would surely kick her ass for this one.

Coker and Lolie and Edithanne were just behind Margaret and

they surrounded her and clamped their arms across each other's shoulders. Coker began to sing and Lolie and Edithanne threw in a couple of chorus girl kicks.

> *"For she's a jolly good fellow,*
> *For she's a jolly good fellow,*
> *For she's a jolly good fellow,*
> *That nobody can deny."*

Margaret didn't feel like such a jolly good fellow, but she appreciated their kindness. They were in front of the dugout now, high-stepping and kicking, a chorus line of softball players.

> *"For we are jolly good fellows,*
> *For we are jolly good fellows . . ."*

Shirley joined them, breaking into the middle of the line, kicking to the left and entangling her leg with Lolie, who was kicking to the right. They all went down on the base line, laughing and singing, hooting and tossing their caps.

> *"That nobody can deny!"*

They laughed and lay on the ground, the lights of the field shining down upon them. "This is terrific," Coker said. "Let Butte carry the damn trophy for a while. Me, I'm tired of all the publicity."

"Yeah," Edithanne said. "It was getting outright ridiculous. I don't want to be playing softball when I'm eighty, just to uphold a tradition."

"We had to lose this one," Lolie said. "Sullivan doesn't have any more room for another trophy."

"He's still out on the field talking to himself," Shirley said. "Has anyone told him the game's over?"

"I feel I let you down." Margaret's voice was small.

"Hell no," Coker said. "This was the most exciting game we've had in years."

"You damn betcha," Shirley said. "It's more interesting when you don't know if you're going to win or lose."

Woody came up to where they were sprawled across the ground, Adam and Allison trailing behind him. "I'll tell you," he said, "those fat asses from Butte might have beat you, but they didn't outshine you." He angled his hands in front of his face like a box and walked around them, swiveling his head and shoulders from side to side. "Click!" he said. "I'm a photographer from *Playboy*. Click!" He snapped an imaginary picture as he zeroed in on Shirley. "Click! Sexiest Center Fielder in North America." He turned to Coker. "I took these when you were walking on your hands. Click! Click!" He sat down in front of Margaret. "I love to watch you throw them balls. Makes me horny," he said. "But I won't take your picture until you smile."

"Youbetcha," Lolie said. "All us *Playboy* bunnies smile."

Edithanne bared her teeth. "See?" she said. "When you grin at the ball nothing bad can happen."

"I think I'm going to go grin at a drink," Coker said.

"We deserve this one," Shirley said. "We worked for this hangover."

Lolie groaned as she got to her feet. "I'm not running one inch until next spring."

Sullivan stood above them, swaying slightly, his hands stuffed in the pockets of his jeans. "I don't serve nobody sitting on the floor," he said slowly. "And there's no point being this drunk alone."

Before Margaret was quite aware of how it happened, she saw Lolie and Coker and Shirley and Edithanne moving off the field, their arms looped over each other's shoulders, their voices raised in what might have been Christmas carols. The line of women in their maroon striped uniforms jogged irregularly up and down as one of them would throw in a skip or a chorus kick. But their backs were to Margaret; they were moving away from her. Margaret wanted to apologize, to face her responsibility for this loss squarely. Instead, the women were gone and Margaret found herself standing with Woody. And Sullivan and Rita. Adam and Allison looked at her with large, sad eyes.

"I'm sorry," Margaret said. She stared at Rita.

"Don't trouble about it," Rita said. "I shouldn't have signaled a curve for that first bitch. Should have been able to tell by her ass. She settles in just like Miriam."

"I'm truly sorry," Margaret said again, this time looking at Sullivan. She felt tears standing in the corners of her eyes. Sullivan would be the one most hurt by this loss.

"There ain't nothing to feel sorry about in softball," Sullivan said. "Tragedies don't traffic in games."

Woody put his arm around Margaret's shoulder. "Coker couldn't have pulled it out," he said. "They just had a rally after Terrible went down. You think the great umpire in the sky gives a shit?"

"Next year," Adam said softly, "we'll win, won't we, Mom?" His eyes looked puzzled as he stared at Margaret.

"Next year I'll play," Allison said. "Me and Phyllis Schlafly. We'll get to kick ass too."

Margaret wanted to apologize once again but realized no one would hear it but herself. She could be as sorry as she wanted to, be as sorry as Sullivan, and it wouldn't make any difference. The game was over, the season was over. Some phase of her life was over. She wondered if she would even play softball next year.

"Come on," Rita said to Margaret. "I'll give you a ride. I think what we all need is a drink."

"And you," Woody said, poking Sullivan in the arm. Sullivan looked back at him blankly. "You," Woody said again to get Sullivan's attention. "I'm giving you a ride." Margaret watched them walk slowly off the field.

Rita limped over to the rusted Edsel and cranked over the motor until it coughed and caught. The kids sat silently in the back seat and Margaret knew they were waiting to hear whatever it was Rita and Margaret would say.

At the first stoplight Rita broke the silence. "I've been meaning to ask you," she said, "if you'd do me a favor."

"A favor?"

"You can look at it any way you want," Rita said. "But I sort of think of it as a favor."

"What do you want?" Margaret said and heard the coldness creep into her voice. What more do you want from me, she thought.

"Well, there's Bruegel and the fish. I thought the kids might like to take care of them while I'm gone."

Margaret sensed Adam and Allison rustling in the back seat and knew how delighted they would be to take care of Rita's pets. And she knew that in some way Rita meant this as a gesture of faith, a reconciliation. But Margaret kept up the game as she knew she should. "I'll have to ask the kids," she said. "They're the ones that'll have to do the work."

"I'll let Bruegel sleep with my dolls," Allison said. "Gloria Steinem gets lonely at night."

"Fish are as good as a dog," Adam said. "Almost."

Rita smiled. "Good," she said. "That's settled." She reached over and patted Margaret on the knee.

Country music poured out of Shelly's Leg and Margaret was surprised to see how happy everyone looked. After all, they had lost the state championship. And they had lost it because of Margaret's stubbornness. But as she looked around her no one seemed to be troubled by that notion. Amos Espinosa was dancing with Randa, her small bird body lost against Amos's fluffy, fat belly. They carried their drink glasses angled in a stylized tango. Birdheart had a softball in one hand, his other hand around one of Diane's breasts, as if gauging how the two related. Valgaardson and Deadeye were arguing about money. The bar was flooded with the maroon striped uniforms of the Shelly's Leg team and the tap of their cleats against the floor was lost in the music. Many of them were behind the bar, clustered around the trophies.

Sullivan had a new bottle of Chivas and sat at a table near the door, idly twirling a rose through his fingers. Margaret joined him and took a sip from his bottle. She had given up any notion of apologizing and wanted to sit in Sullivan's silence and watch as the night unfolded. She had been seated only a moment and said nothing to Sullivan when Woody came up. He straddled the back of a chair and took one of her hands between his own.

"This is my last night in town for a while," Woody said. "I feel like I'm going off to war. I'm going to drink till I'm drunk, dance till my feet fall off. I'm going to start this adventure with the grandest god-damned hangover you've ever seen. But before I get so drunk I don't know what I'm doing, I want to dance with you, Lady. I want to hold you in my arms."

Margaret silently followed him out onto the dance floor and placed her arms around his neck like so many other times in the past. She felt his arms encircling her ribcage, his body moving rhythmically in time to her own. His smell was so familiar, the silky brush of his hair against her face, that Margaret knew these things would always be part of her. When the dance was over, when Woody and Rita were gone, Margaret would have this moment to carry with her like a picture.

At the end of the third song Woody pulled back from her a bit and looked into her eyes. "I don't want to make this hard," he said. "Not any harder than it's going to be. But I've got to ask. Will you come with me?"

Margaret watched his eyes, the snowy blue of his stare. She could feel his breath on her face and the nervous movements of his hands tracing small patterns against her spine. Her hands rested on his neck and she felt the brush of his beard against her fingers. She looked at his broad nose, the flush of his cheeks. She watched his eyes moving over her face.

She raised her hands to cup his chin and balanced up on her toes. She kissed him full on the mouth, his lips soft against her own. She felt her nose resting against his and felt the flutter of his eyelashes against her forehead. Her breasts rested against his chest and Margaret thought she could hear the clocking of their hearts against the purr of the music. They swayed together in this long embrace until Margaret felt she might faint. Releasing his face, she put her arms around his neck, holding on tightly. She pinched her eyes together as her fingers found their way under his collar and she remembered something Sullivan had said: 'Men move on. Women mourn.'

"Oh Woody," she said. "No."

It was as if it took him several moments to understand, as if he had to think through every possible meaning in her tone and that single word. Then, he released her, his hands holding her shoulders and his face trying to smile. "Well," he said as if that word might have been a laugh. He said it again. "Well," and looked thoroughly across her face again. "Just don't let your fancy ass fall in love," he said. His tone was light and joking. "I might just come back and sweep you off your feet."

He led her back to the table where Sullivan sat brooding over his Chivas and the rose, lying carelessly next to the ashtray. He seated her and saluted her with his hand and turned back to the dance floor. Linda Ronstadt sang "Desperado" as Margaret watched Woody walk over to Rita and take her in his arms. She watched as Rita, limping slightly, followed him slowly around the dance floor, her dark hair nestled against Woody's shoulder, his reddish gold hair catching the dim bar light. Margaret felt Sullivan reach out and take her hand.